A remote island in the south pacific pla strangers. One of them is a murderer.

An advertisement in a newspaper brings a disparate group of people to a tropical paradise. They will live together for a year, work and build a community, and film everything that happens for a documentary that will only see the light of day at the end of the trip.

Almost at once, things begin to go wrong.

They are meant to be strangers, but some of them have met before. They are meant to receive regular visits by the company funding the documentary, but nobody ever comes.

And their only link with the outside world - a small portable radio transmitter - is incapable of transmitting anything...

MURDER IN PARADISE

by
Greg Wilson

Chapter One

It would have been impossible without the matches. Whoever thought up the rules had no idea how difficult this was going to be. The kindling refused to catch light. 'Oh, for God's Sake!' Sue Durrant exclaimed. That was the third match wasted. Her legs were aching now. She had been squatting for nearly five minutes and her feet were beginning to go numb. It would be pins and needles next. She pulled herself up and stretched out each leg in turn; then she started scratching her thigh. Another blotch had appeared. *Bloody insects,* she thought. She looked down at the fire and scowled.

The stupid thing was, Sue had volunteered to do this. The others had gone off picking fruit or gathering wood and she had stayed behind to get some water on the boil. Somebody had to do it. They were not allowed purification tablets.

She struck another match and cupped the flame in her hand, moving it slowly towards the edge of the kindling. To her relief, one of the palm fronds started to catch light. *Thank Christ for that.* She blew on the wood and the flames began to spread. Given time, they might even begin to generate some heat. She crouched lower and blew a second time.

'Hey, Sue!' a voice called out from somewhere behind. It was Steve, one of the others.

'I'm over here,' she responded, irritably. 'I've got the fire going.'

Steve Bramagh came into view. 'Oh, good on you.' He had a thick Australian brogue. 'Did you hear the boat?'

She glanced up. *What boat?* 'No. Not since this morning, anyway.'

'Just coming back when I heard it. I reckon it must be the new guys.'

Sue tried hard not to grimace. The thought of more people arriving on the island did not fill her with joy.

'Come on,' Steve said. 'Let's go take a look.'

'I've only just got the fire going. It'll go out if I leave it.'

Steve grinned. 'Don't worry about that. I can sort it out later.' He jerked his head down towards the beach and she rose reluctantly to follow him.

It was mid afternoon, but the sun was still high in the sky. Sue had not made up her mind whether to cover up and hold off the inevitable sunburn or to strip down and make the most of it. Not that she cared for the sun much, but she figured she had probably better get used to it.

Steve had stopped halfway across the beach and started rummaging in his rucksack for the video camera. It was a small, lightweight digital model. He found the Record button and pulled the eye-piece to his face.

The boat was just coming around a curve. It was a small motorised dinghy. The main vessel was circling somewhere a few miles out to sea; at least, it had been when they had left it that morning. There were three figures in the dinghy. Sue recognised Clive Monroe, even at this distance – his balding pate glinted in the hazy sunlight – but she could not make out the other two figures. She scowled. That was another thing: all this secrecy. Why couldn't they have met up beforehand; got to know each other? Then they would have found out if everyone was going to get on.

So far, five people had been brought out to the island. Aside from herself, there were two Australians, a Canadian and a British photographer called Jeremy. None of them had much going for them, she thought, except perhaps Steve, who was quite bright but was a bit too smug for his own good. Perhaps these new people would prove more interesting.

'Why don't you take the camera for a minute?' Steve suggested.

Sue gave the Australian a withering glare. She hated cameras. It was one of the things she had been forced to lie about at the interview. But she took the device from him all the same. Sliding her hand into the grip, she brought the camera up to eye level.

'I'll just say a few words,' Steve said, clearing his throat.

Sue adjusted the frame so that the Australian was on the left of the picture. The man was of medium height, thirtysomething, with black curly hair and a not unattractive face – what she could see of it behind his bulky sunglasses.

The speedboat was on the right of the picture, cruising inwards now towards the beach.

'Yeah, well, here we are on the first afternoon,' Steve said. 'I've just been out collecting some fruit and some sweet potatoes and having a general look round. I was heading back down here when I heard the sound of a boat heading by and came down to the beach to investigate.'

That's right, just pretend I'm not here, Sue thought. She zoomed in past Steve and focused on the dinghy. A man and a woman were sitting either side of Clive Monroe. One of them, the man, had his own video camera raised. She could not make out his face. The woman, though, was young and had long brown hair. She was probably in her mid twenties.

'Well, as you can see, the boat's just about to land,' Steve was intoning pointlessly. 'It looks like two new recruits, a guy and a girl…'

Oh for God's Sake, shut up! Sue had only met Steve the previous evening but already he was becoming insufferable.

The boat had indeed pulled to and Clive and the others were scampering over the side into the shallow blue water some fifty metres down the beach.

'Well, I'm just going to run over now and give them a proper welcome,' Steve said, glancing confidently at the camera and racing across the sand.

Sue was less enthusiastic, but she had no choice but to follow him, camcorder in hand. The beach was scorching under her feet and she cursed it silently.

The Australian had already arrived at the boat and was proffering a hand to one of the new arrivals. 'Hi, I'm Steve Bramagh,' he said. 'Welcome to paradise.'

Another man was filming them both; a tall fellow, strong and broad-shouldered.

Sue panned across to the woman as Clive made the introductions. 'Okay, well, Steve, this is Isabel Grant. Isabel, Steve Bramagh.' The woman nodded perfunctorily but she barely glanced at the beaming Australian.

Sue panned back to the other man. There was something oddly familiar about him.

'And this fine man here is Duncan Roberts.'

The man Duncan dropped the video camera and moved forward to shake Steve by the hand. He had a bland, inoffensive face and a diffident manner.

It was a face Sue recognised at once. She let out an involuntary cry. Duncan caught sight of her and his jaw dropped open. It was difficult to tell who was the more surprised. Sue dropped the video camera and it hit the ground with a dull thud.

Andrew Baker had not ridden in a helicopter before. He hadn't anticipated the sheer noise of it. There was something odd about the furious volume of the rotating blades, set against the tranquillity of the ocean below.

If only me mam could see me now, he thought. She had been dead set against him going – reckless and foolhardy, she'd said – but what was there to lose? It wasn't much fun back home right now, not without a proper job.

The journey from Manchester had been a long one. Andrew had stopped for the night in a posh hotel in London – all expenses paid – before flying on to St. Moreau. He had barely had time to acclimatise there before being bundled into a helicopter and flown out to the middle of the Pacific.

He hadn't even spoken to the other passengers yet. They would be spending the next year of their lives together, but such was the noise of the whirring blades that all they could do was grin at each other and mouth 'hello's. Now he was starting to feel giddy. The entire front section of the helicopter was see-through and Andrew had never been much of a one for heights. But it wasn't just the long drop that was making him nervous, it was the whole situation; the thought of where he was going and what he was about to do.

I could be making the biggest mistake of my life.

He scratched his nose. His skin was already bright red. He did not react well to the sun. That was another thing. He was going to be outside most of the time. With his complexion, that could be disastrous. Andrew had pale, lightly freckled skin and a crop of short ginger hair. Very short. It was asking for trouble.

The pilot raised a hand and pointed down to a white speck in the distance. The yacht cut an impressive trail through the water, a sizeable presence even set against the emptiness of the Pacific.

Another, more immediate concern crossed Andrew's mind. *I hope there's going to be enough room to land on that thing.* Would it even be able to take the weight? He stopped himself. Of course it would. They had whole aeroplanes landing on aircraft carriers, didn't they? And now they were getting closer, he saw there was a long stretch of flat, sturdy deck. There was even a grid laid out, with a circular marker. He could see a man down there in the middle of it, waving back at them.

The pilot moved the throttle control and the helicopter tilted downwards towards the ship.

Andrew glanced across at the other passengers. One of them, an older woman, looked absolutely terrified. He tried to smile at her. She just gripped onto the sides of her chair.

It was good to know he was not the only one who was nervous.

Sue Durrant had stood immobile for a moment, her body shuddering; then she had turned and ran across the beach into the undergrowth.

Steve Bramagh turned back to the director.

Clive Monroe seemed every bit as surprised as the rest of the group. 'I didn't realise they even *knew* each other,' he confessed. Clive had overseen the selection process but each of the potential islanders had been interviewed separately. 'If I'd known there was any history between them, I'd never have let them come.'

Steve felt inclined to believe him. If anything, the balding director looked more shocked than Duncan Roberts.

The man himself refused to comment on the nature of his relationship with Sue Durrant. 'It's personal,' he grunted.

'I can't apologise enough,' Clive told him. 'I just hope… I hope this isn't going to cause any problems…'

'Not for me,' Duncan responded firmly. His voice was deep and powerful, but he hesitated now. 'She…may not feel the same way.'

'I am dreadfully sorry,' the director repeated.

'I did think it was a little unwise not to let us all meet up beforehand,' Steve commented. 'But there's no point crying about it now. You know, I think someone ought to go and see if Sue is all right.'

Clive nodded. 'Yes. Yes, of course. I really must apologise to her as well. I had no idea…'

'It's all right. I'll go.' Steve smiled.

The director was happy to surrender the task. 'Well, if you're sure…'

'I expect Isabel here would like to meet some of the other islanders,' Steve suggested helpfully.

Clive gave a start. He had all but forgotten about the other new arrival. 'Yes, of course. You must forgive me.' He turned to her now. 'I do hope this hasn't been too trying for you…'

Isabel raised an eyebrow. 'Interesting, certainly. I prefer Bella,' she added, glancing at Steve.

'Bella.' The Australian nodded. 'Good to meet you.' He bent down and picked up the video camera. It was lying neglected in the sand where Sue had dropped it. The lens was scuffed and covered in grit, but it was still recording. Steve put it in his rucksack and turned to leave.

The edge of the beach gave way to muddled foliage and Steve Bramagh followed the flattened path around the edge of the island to the entrance of a large cave.

Sue Durrant was sitting in the mouth of the cave, her knees pulled up against her chest. She was a pale-faced woman in her late twenties with straight black hair and a slender figure. It was obvious she had been crying. When she heard the Australian approach, she quickly rubbed the tears from her face.

Steve waved at her from a distance, giving the woman time to regain her composure.

'What do you want?' she snapped, with little spirit.

Steve move towards her. 'I just thought you might need a friend.' He watched his feet carefully as he arrived at the entrance to the cave. The ground here was pebbled and uneven.

Sue laughed. 'Yeah, right. And *you* are?' The two of them had only met the day before.

'It's none of my business, I know.'

The Englishwoman grunted her agreement.

'So what's the story? Who is he?'

'I don't want to talk about it.'

Steve shrugged. 'Fair enough.' He found a convenient rock and planted himself down next to Sue. For a moment, there was silence; then he said: 'The other girl seems all right, anyway.'

Sue was not in the least bit interested. 'Really?'

'Isabel. Well, actually, she prefers to be called Bella. I think you'll like her.'

The woman snorted. 'Oh yes. And you're an expert on my likes and dislikes, are you?'

'Sue, I'm just trying to help.'

She glanced across at him then. 'What are you, some kind of psychiatrist?' she sneered.

The Australian smiled with mock humility. 'Well, actually, I majored in psychology.'

Sue scoffed. 'You told me last night you worked in a car factory.'

'That too. I've done a lot of things in my time.'

'Oh, sure. Look, if you really want to help, why don't you just piss off and leave me alone?'

Steve let out a sigh. There was no mistaking the anger in her voice. 'Well, if that's what you want...' He rose slowly to his feet.

Sue closed her eyes and took a deep breath. 'Look, I'm sorry, all right? I'm not angry with you. It's just...I've tried so hard to put all this crap behind me.'

'Put what behind you?'

'I…I *really* don't want to talk about it.'

'You know, Sue, we're going to be living together for a whole year. I think we're going to have to be honest with each other at some point.'

'Not about this.'

Steve spread his hands. 'Eventually. Look, if there's a problem, it's got to be sorted out. And sooner rather than later. You know, I don't think Clive's going to be staying long and then it's you and this Duncan guy marooned together.'

Sue hesitated. 'He's not…?'

'From what I could gather, Duncan has every intention of staying on.'

'He can't.' She shook her head vehemently. 'I won't let him. He's not going to ruin my life a second time.'

Steve shrugged again. 'Well, you know, Sue, he is a part of the group. He's gone through a lot to get here. Probably not as much as I did, but that's another story. He has every right to stay.'

Sue was shaking now. 'If you knew what he'd done to me…'

'Well, tell me.'

She let out an anguished cry. 'I can't.'

'Well, perhaps if you talk to *him*…'

'He's not coming anywhere near me!'

Steve sat down again. He was not prepared to mince words. 'You know, Sue, sooner or later this is going to have to be sorted. You can't not talk to a person for a whole year. Not in a place like this.'

'I told you. He's not staying.'

'I hate to say it, Sue, but the way things are looking he probably will be. Unless you give Clive a very good reason for getting rid of him.'

'I shouldn't have to…'

'Or unless you're prepared to leave the island yourself.'

Sue looked at him sharply. 'No. I'm not leaving. Not because of him. I'm not doing anything because of him. Not ever.'

The Australian raised his hands. 'Fair enough. But then ask yourself: what *are* you going to do?'

Clive Monroe was continuing the introductions.

Chris Hudson, a young Canadian, was sitting at the bottom of a coconut tree a little way from the beach, eating quietly. He was blond, nervous and in his early twenties. He pulled himself up when the new people arrived.

The director waved a greeting and introduced the others. Duncan Roberts had his video camera raised and was filming the introductions for posterity. Isabel Grant stood back and smiled quietly.

'Where are the others?' Clive asked the Canadian. The dinghy had delivered five people to the island that morning, but so far he had only seen three of them.

Chris Hudson shrugged. 'I think they're off, like, gathering some wood.'

The director glanced at his watch. 'Not to worry. Look, I just wanted to wish everyone good luck for the first night. I hope it all goes well.'

'We'll get by,' said Duncan, from behind the camera.

'I just wish I knew what to do about...' Clive stopped himself. This business with Duncan and Sue had flustered him.

'She'll come round,' Duncan said, though his voice lacked conviction.

'I suppose I really should go and speak to her myself.'

'Speak to who?' asked Chris. The young Canadian had no idea what the two of them were talking about.

'Er...Duncan and Sue have met before,' the director explained, sheepishly.

'Oh. Cool.'

Duncan grimaced.

Isabel Grant, the other new arrival, cut in quickly to save them from further embarrassment. Isabel was a striking young woman, darkly handsome with large brown eyes and long, silky hair. Her accent was cut-glass English. 'So did you climb that tree?' she asked Chris, 'or did the coconuts just fall down?' There were two or three broken shells lying amid the foliage.

'Well, I was going to,' the Canadian responded, awkwardly, 'but it looked kind of difficult so I just thought, like, maybe if I shook it, kind of thing…'

Isabel nodded.

'Good idea,' the director agreed. 'Conserving energy. Splendid. So you've obviously had a good first day?'

Chris shrugged. 'I guess.' He was trying very hard not to stare at Isabel. She really was a very attractive woman.

'Well, anyway, look,' said Clive, 'I really am sorry, but I'm going to have to love you all and leave you. I did promise I'd be back at the boat before sunset…'

'That's all right,' said Duncan.

Isabel caught the director's eye. 'I'll come and see you off.' Clive nodded and the two of them moved away together.

'Catch you later!' Chris shouted, watching them go. He took out his penknife and returned to the coconuts.

Duncan Roberts stood immobile, lost in thought.

Steve Bramagh was already walking back to the beach. As he stepped out onto the sand, he saw Clive and Isabel making their way towards the motorised dinghy. He called out to them and they stopped to wait as he moved across to join them.

'How's your friend?' Isabel asked when the Australian drew near.

'Well, you know, I think I've managed to calm her down a bit.'

Clive was relieved. 'Oh good. Thank you for that. I…but did she say what the matter was?'

'Well, no. Not exactly,' Steve admitted. 'But I have a pretty shrewd idea.'

'So…what do you – ?'

'I don't think it would be fair of me to say.'

'But you do think…?' The director hesitated. 'You do think she's going to rejoin the group? At some point? This could be rather awkward otherwise.'

'Well, you know, Clive, if I'm honest, I'm not really sure. I think she'll stay where she is for tonight. But if I can't get something sorted by tomorrow, then you might have to take her back on the boat with you.'

Clive shuddered, glancing across at Isabel. 'I do hope it doesn't come to that.'

'I think she'll be all right this evening, anyway.'

'That's a blessing. I can't tell you how much of a surprise all this has been. If only I'd known…'

Steve shrugged. 'Well, you know, life can be like that. You just have to learn to ride the blows.'

The director muttered his farewells and wished the two of them well for the night ahead. The dinghy had already been prepared for the return voyage. He scrambled onto the boat and yanked a cord to start the outboard motor.

Andrew Baker had been trying to decide whether to unpack his rucksack or to leave everything where it was. When he heard a sudden buzz from outside, he rushed to the port-hole and caught sight of a large dinghy churning its way across the water towards them.

He went up on deck. The two women he had flown out with were already there. Andrew looked over the railings and saw the familiar figure of Clive Monroe steering the motorboat through the water. It was the first face he recognised since leaving Manchester.

The dinghy pulled in to the side of the larger craft and Clive attached the guide ropes to secure its position.

There was a metal ladder descending to sea level. The director grabbed the lowest rung and quickly began to pull himself aboard. Andrew stepped forward and gave him a hand at the top.

'I'm so glad you got here safely,' Clive said, when he had found his feet on deck. 'All of you. I hope the journey wasn't too stressful.'

'No, it were great,' said Andrew. The two women nodded their agreement. 'I've never been in a helicopter before.'

11

'I must confess, neither had I before I got this job.' Clive grinned and looked back out across the ocean. 'And such a lovely day. You couldn't have arrived at a better time. Have you been allocated rooms?'

They all nodded. The girls were sharing a bunk for the night, but Andrew had a cabin to himself.

'Excellent. Jolly good. We've got a meal arranged for you all this evening. The food here's absolutely fantastic.'

'It'll be our last proper grub,' Andrew reflected.

'Well, quite,' said Clive, 'so only the best, of course. Say, eight o'clock?' The others agreed. 'Well, if you'll excuse me, then…' The director glanced down at his clothes and grimaced. There was a lot of spray out at sea, even on a quiet afternoon like this, and his shirt was wet-through. 'I really must get changed.' He took his leave and strode away across the deck.

Andrew Baker caught the eye of one of the women. 'Nice bloke, isn't he?'

The girl smiled back at him.

The first priority was setting up the mosquito nets. Even during the day there were a lot of insects buzzing around and it would only get worse after dark. Luckily, netting was one thing they had been allowed to bring with them.

The two islanders who had disappeared in search of wood had returned to the beach before sunset, laden down with branches. One of them, the group was astonished to discover, was an old school friend of Duncan Roberts. This was the second coincidence in as many hours.

There was much work to do, however, and little time in which to do it. Steve Bramagh began busily coordinating the action, with the help of a brash Australian woman who had been one of the first to arrive on the island. Logs were quickly tied together with vines to set up some basic A-frames. The branches were propped against each other and bound firmly at the top. A second tripod was set up a few feet away and the two frames were joined together by a single cross-beam to support the mosquito net. A further set of beams would be needed to complete the beds, but that would have to wait for another day. A skeleton could hold the nets up well enough for one night. Blankets would have to be put down on the sand, though, to prevent insects from crawling in under the edges.

'You know, I'm not so sure of the wisdom of setting these up on the beach,' Steve reflected. There were likely to be an awful lot of insects. 'I think everyone should cover up pretty thoroughly tonight.' He wiped the sweat from his forehead.

A fire had been started nearby, using the small wooden pyramid Sue Durrant had constructed earlier on. A tin pot was hanging down from the top of it. Chris Hudson, the young Canadian, was watching over some broth. He was also on video duties for the evening and was already zooming in on the slowly heating food.

'How's it looking?' Steve asked, coming over.

Chris was non-committal. 'Okay, I guess.' He zoomed in closer on the brown liquid, which was bubbling away nicely in the large metal tin.

'I want to take some over to Sue,' Steve said. 'I think I should go see how she's getting on.' The sun had set a few minutes before and the sky was darkening rapidly. He dipped a shell into the tin and scooped out some of the broth, sipping it gently. It was hot and lumpy, with no real taste to it. 'You know, that's not bad,' he lied. 'But it could do with a little more garlic.'

Chris nodded, missing the joke. There was unlikely to be any garlic on the island. 'I guess,' he said.

Steve smiled back at him.

Sue's rucksack was lying neglected not far away. Her mosquito net would be packed inside it and her blanket too. She would be bitten to death without them. Steve would have to take it to her along with the broth.

Over by the shore, Duncan Roberts was chuckling along with his old friend.

The sand flies were everywhere. Steve was wearing his long pants and a long-sleeved shirt, but still the insects managed to bite him. His arms and legs were covered in blotches. It took an effort of will not to scratch the wounds.

The cave was a silhouette in the distance. It was dark now. The stars were twinkling brightly but as yet there was no moon.

Steve took each step along the path with great care. There was little light to see by and the terrain was somewhat uneven.

No light radiated out from the cave. Sue had obviously not bothered to make a fire. She could not have eaten either, though there was a small basin inside the cave which seemed to collect a fair amount of rainwater. The sky was clear tonight, and the air seemed reasonably warm.

Steve stumbled momentarily on an unseen stump of grass, but he managed to recover without spilling any of the broth. The soup would almost certainly be cold by now, but it would do Sue good to eat something. Besides, it was the thought that counted.

As he neared the cave, he called out to her gently but there was no response. Perhaps she had already gone to sleep. He moved closer, bringing himself to the mouth of the cave. 'Sue!' he called again. 'Susan! It's all right. It's only me.' Still there was no answer.

He moved inside, but he could make out nothing of the cave's rocky interior. All he could hear was the sound of dripping water, faint against the roar of the ocean outside.

Steve gave one last call, but there was no reply.

Sue Durrant was not here.

'To be honest,' said Clive Monroe, 'it wasn't my idea at all.' He took a mouthful of beef and swallowed it quickly.

Andrew was sitting opposite him at the small plastic table. There were windows in every direction and he could see the dark ocean surrounding them and the starry sky beyond. It was a beautiful night, calm and peaceful.

Inside the boat, the conversation was flowing well.

'You didn't decide what we could take?' one of the women was asking the director, while the others tucked in to their food.

'Not at all, I'm afraid. I came quite late to the project. I'm a freelance, you see.'

'So it weren't your idea?' Andrew said, somewhat surprised.

'This? Oh, no. It was all set up by the production company. They got the commission and then they hired me.'

'But you *did* choose us lot,' Andrew pointed out. Clive had been the one who had interviewed him, at least the second time around. His friend Mark had nominated him for the adventure. Andrew had been furious when he'd found out. Mark had seen the advert in the local paper and put him up for it. But it was the director who had finally put him at his ease.

'Oh, yes, I was in on the selection,' Clive admitted, putting down a fork and picking up his wine glass. 'But the company had ultimate say. It's their money, after all. I'm just here to work through their ideas.'

Andrew understood. 'But I'm going to get *so* sunburnt without suntan cream.'

Clive smiled sympathetically. 'I know. I'm so sorry.' He took a sip of the wine. It was a rather good Burgundy. 'I did argue the point. But I think the producers wanted to go for authenticity.'

'It's not exactly consistent though, is it?' said the girl to Andrew's right. She was the one who had spoken before. 'Mosquito nets but no sun block. Cooking pots but no matches. Knives and no forks…'

'I did try and slip some things through,' the director asserted. 'But not as much as I would have liked.' He took another sip of wine. 'I did suggest it might be a good idea to pay for some survival training, but…well, they were adamant nobody should meet before we came out here.' He shrugged. 'Silly, really. I think they just wanted to throw everyone in at the deep end.' He glanced apologetically around the table.

Andrew swallowed a mouthful of beer from his glass. 'Makes it more fun, I suppose.'

'And more interesting for the viewer as well.' Clive nodded. 'Although I'm beginning to think…' He stopped himself. He was frowning slightly. 'Well, anyway, I'm sure everything will work out splendidly. It always does in the end, doesn't it?' He changed tack. 'So, Andrew, are you looking forward to tomorrow?'

The Mancunian nodded eagerly. 'Aye. I can't wait to get started now.' The more he thought about it, the more excited he was becoming. Especially now he had met the other two. It was good to know he wasn't the only one nervous about the days ahead.

'That's the spirit!' Clive beamed. 'Just think of it as one long holiday.'

Andrew drained his glass and returned it to the table. That was it: a year long holiday. He glanced at the empty container. But without booze, without football and without any telly. Just lots of hard work instead.

He grinned. It'd be bloody marvellous!

Chapter Two

Nobody said a word when Sue Durrant came and sat around the fire with the rest of the group. She did not care what they thought, in any case. They were all strangers to her. Why should she care? The wood was burning brightly and the flames were giving off far too much heat. It was unnecessary on such a warm night. Someone was just showing off. Her own fire that afternoon had been far less wasteful. But at least the flames provided them with some light to see by. Torches were yet another item on the prohibited list.

Sue had realised pretty quickly that she could not spend a whole night in that cave. It wasn't just the darkness and the damp. Even the insects she could put up with, if she absolutely had to. It was more the thought of being all on her own. She didn't feel safe there; it was as simple as that. She needed to be with other people. There was security in numbers, even with such unpromising strangers as these.

Sue had not looked at Duncan Roberts when she had sat down by the fire, but she could sense his presence, scarcely more than a few feet away. He was sitting cross legged, talking quietly to some bearded guy. He made no attempt to come near her or even to glance in her direction. For that at least she was grateful.

She was less happy to discover her rucksack had been moved. She had left it near the cooking pot. Steve Bramagh had probably picked it up and taken it to the cave. *Interfering idiot.* She hoped he would come back soon. She badly needed a change of clothes. Her arms and legs were exposed to the elements and the sand flies were dancing hungrily around her. Some of the bites were already starting to itch and when she scratched them they only got worse. The smoke from the fire did seem to deter the insects a little, but the fumes made her cough, which was just as bad.

Beyond the flames, visible in the flickering light, she could just make out the A-frames that had been erected across the beach. They were crude, ugly things; clumsy wooden constructions, all in a row. Eyesores, really. *Typical,* Sue thought. *One day here and we've already ruined a perfectly good beach.* The group would be better off sleeping inland. Perhaps they should clear a space somewhere. *I wonder if anyone's set up a bed for me.* It didn't seem likely. Why on earth would they bother?

She looked up from the flames. The islanders were sat in a rough circle around the fire. Chris Hudson was moving among them, dishing out some kind of broth. He was a lanky, awkward creature. Not good-looking by any stretch of the imagination, but passable, she supposed, if you preferred boys to men. He wasn't happy having to play mum with the soup, though. He lifted a ladle-full of broth and proffered it to her. Sue didn't have a bowl and he hesitated, not wanting to give away his makeshift ladle.

'There are some coconut shells over there.' He pointed.

Sue shot the Canadian a withering glare and was about to get up when Isabel Grant, who was sitting next to her, passed her a bowl instead. She nodded her thanks. 'So who nominated you cook?' she asked Chris, as the boy ladled some broth into the bowl.

'I sort of volunteered, type thing. I figured it was the easy option…' From his manner, it was obvious he was having second thoughts.

'Didn't think you'd have to serve it as well.'

Chris shrugged. 'I don't mind.'

She stifled a laugh. The kid had obviously never done a day's work in his life. Some rich bastard of a father, by all accounts. It would do him good to get his hands dirty. She stared at the broth. 'So what's in it?'

'Just fruits and stuff. A bit of rice and some sweet potatoes. Sort of anything they could find, I guess.'

Well, that's reassuring. She took a sip. The broth was warm and tasted salty. *Too much sand in there.* Chris had moved on before she could berate him. She took another mouthful and swallowed a couple of solid lumps. At least the vegetables seemed vaguely edible.

Steve Bramagh came up behind her. 'You know, I thought you must be here,' he said, in his typically breezy manner. 'And there was I going off on an errand of mercy.'

Sue put down her bowl and looked round at him. 'And who gave you permission to walk off with my rucksack? I'm being bitten to death here.'

'Well, you know, I was just trying to help.'

'Look, Steve, if I need help I'll ask for it.' She reached out a hand and grabbed her pack. 'If you've touched anything in there…'

Steve stared at her for a moment. He gave a theatrical sigh but refrained from comment.

Sue rummaged inside her bag and produced a thick, long sleeved top, which she slipped on hurriedly. *Try biting through that, you bastards.* She grabbed a pair of jeans as well; the only ones she'd been allowed to bring with her. One pair of trousers each, they had been told. And she'd have to take her shorts off to get into them. She was not about to strip off in front of anyone, however, so she pulled herself up and moved away from the fire. No-one paid her any attention as she stepped out of the light, but as she disappeared into the gloom she heard laughter coming from behind. The man next to Duncan was guffawing loudly. Another English bloke, apparently. A bearded photographer. Sue looked back and for a moment she could have sworn he was staring directly at her. Then he looked away.

Sue shivered and dressed herself quickly.

The metal box was heavier than it looked.

Stephanie McMahon shifted her arms to get a proper grip on the large container. Sea water was splashing at her legs. The bronzed Australian took a moment to steady herself and then moved off.

'You want a hand there, love?' asked Jeremy Fielding. He was the man with the beard, a tall, over-friendly Englishman.

Stephanie shook her head. 'I can manage.' She sloshed through the water and back onto dry land.

The box was not the only item that needed unloading. Clive had arrived earlier than expected with the last of the new recruits, but the dinghy had also been used to bring over the emergency supplies from the yacht.

Some of the islanders were still in bed – it wasn't much past seven thirty – but Stephanie had risen early, as was her habit. In truth, she had not slept well. The insects and the roar of the ocean were distraction enough, but she had also made the mistake of settling down a few yards from Jeremy Fielding. The bearded Englishman had snored the whole night through.

Stephanie thumped the metal container onto the sand and opened the lid. Inside was a sturdy plastic radio and the pieces of an antennae. She looked up at Steve Bramagh, her fellow Australian, who was putting his own box down nearby. The man's forehead was glistening with sweat. He was another one who had got up early. He had gone for a run, apparently, shortly before dawn. 'We were going to put this in the cave, weren't we?' she asked him.

Steve nodded. That was likely to prove the driest place on the island, at least until they had constructed some kind of communal hut.

Now that the heavier items had been removed from the dinghy, Clive Monroe was manoeuvring the boat onto the beach, with the help of Andrew Baker. Andrew was one of the new people. Another Brit. He looked to be in his early twenties, quite tall, but lanky and rather boyish. Stephanie had barely said hello to him yet. There was too much else to be getting on with.

Once the dinghy was secured, the director waded out of the water and came over to view the equipment. 'Well, that's the last of it, you'll be happy to know.' Alongside the radio, there was a medical box, some blankets, several dozen batteries for the video cameras, four large torches – for emergency use only – and the inevitable blank cassettes.

'We'll take these across to the cave,' Stephanie suggested.

Clive Monroe lifted his hands. 'You're in charge. It's your island now.'

'You know,' said Steve, 'We should start finding names for all these places. I think it might help the new people settle in.'

Stephanie replaced the lid on the smaller box and picked up the medical supplies. She would let Steve carry the heavier radio transmitter.

'It's all right, I'll take that,' Jeremy Fielding cut in. The Englishman bent over and lifted the large container with exaggerated ease. 'Where is this cave, anyway?'

Stephanie bit her lip. 'Over there,' she said, gesturing reluctantly. She had spent far too much time in Jeremy's company already, though the bronzed Australian was too polite to say so. She would just have to play along with him for now.

'Nothing like a bit of exercise first thing in the morning, is there?' the man beamed cheerily. He was tall and heavily bearded, with large blue eyes and a prominent brow. Everything about him exuded confidence but he was altogether too cocky for her liking.

Stephanie looked away. She had spent much of the previous afternoon with him, collecting wood for the bed-frames, and she was fast becoming bored with his jovial manner. At first, she had admired the good-looks and friendly banter, but it had soon become rather wearing. Jeremy was trying far too hard to attract her attention. He was so transparent. She would have to keep him at arm's length from now on.

There were more promising possibilities.

The two of them strode quickly through the undergrowth. A rough path led off from the beach. The cave was about five hundred yards further on. Reaching the entrance, Stephanie surveyed the interior.

'What do you reckon?' Jeremy asked, in his broad off-London accent. 'Bung it down here?'

Stephanie shook her head. 'It'll get wet there. We'll need to put it further inside.' She placed the medical kit down and scrambled carefully across the rocks. 'Here. Pass it to me.' She gestured for the radio.

Jeremy leant forward and handed her the silver box. Stephanie twisted around and searched for a suitable flat area. There was a large surface off to the right. She ran a hand over it to check for dampness but the rock was completely dry. She reached back for the medical kit and the other supplies. Jeremy handed them across to her.

'Nice little cave this, init?' he said, looking around. The place was not so little. In parts, it was even possible to stand upright, though Stephanie was tall enough that she might still bang her head.

'Steve thinks it might be useful when it rains. At least until we can build a proper shelter.'

'Doesn't look very comfortable,' Jeremy thought, dubiously. 'Still, we could snuggle up together, couldn't we?'

Stephanie raised an eyebrow. *Dickhead.* 'I don't think so,' she said. 'Give me a hand, will you?'

The Englishman leant across and guided her back onto more even terrain. His arms lingered around her waist longer than was strictly necessary.

'Are you always this obvious?'

'No point being backwards, is there?' A predictable glint had entered his eye.

Stephanie grimaced. 'I'm afraid you're wasting your time with me. Anyway, we've got work to do.' The Australian woman had no intention of spending another night on the beach.

Sue Durrant was glad to be rid of Clive Monroe. The director had come over to her as she was crawling out from underneath her mosquito net. It had been a god-awful night. She had not slept a wink. The sand felt rock solid underneath the blanket. And then some bastard had started snoring. Now she felt exhausted. There was sand in her hair and her skin was red with bites. She was probably sunburnt too. Her clothes were filthy, her breath stank and there was no coffee to be had in two hundred miles. None of this was likely to put her in the right frame of mind for a serious chat. But the conversation needed to be had.

Sue had made up her mind. She had lain awake all night considering the matter and now she had decided: she was going to stay on the island, no matter what. Duncan Roberts could go to hell.

'That's the spirit!' Clive exclaimed when she told him of her decision. The director was still in the dark over the nature of their relationship – and Sue had no intention of confiding in him – but he was more than happy to accept her change of heart. 'If you do have second thoughts,' he said, 'I'll be back in a week so we can discuss it then.'

'I appreciate that.' Sue was holding her tongue with some difficulty. She desperately wanted to lash out at him – Clive did bear some responsibility for her predicament, after all – but she knew if she said anything it would only create more problems. *For God's Sake, just go!* she pleaded silently.

The director was mercifully quick to comply.

'Well, everybody, best of luck!' he called out. 'I'm afraid I'm going to have to love you and leave you! But I do hope everything goes well.' He made his way towards the dinghy.

Sue grudgingly supposed he was being sincere. Not that it made much difference.

'You know, I think we'll all get along just fine,' Steve Bramagh declared confidently. He moved forward to help Clive push the motorboat back into the water.

Isabel Grant was filming the two of them.

'We've got a great team,' Steve added, to camera.

Sue watched as the little dinghy pulled away. *Don't hurry back,* she thought.

Andrew Baker was rather impressed by the team spirit the islanders were displaying. The small group had already made a start attaching the cross beams to their bed-frames and they appeared to have the rest of the day worked out too, activity wise.

Steve Bramagh and Stephanie McMahon had more or less taken charge and they seemed to know what they were doing. Judging by their accents, they were both Australian, though Steve said they hadn't met before.

Stephanie was very attractive, Andrew thought, especially for someone in her late thirties. She had short blonde hair and a prominent bust. Her skin was brightly tanned and she spoke in a precise, educated manner.

Steve seemed like a nice bloke, too.

Andrew volunteered to help clear a patch of long grass away from the beach. Steve had suggested they level a decent area so they could build some kind of hut. Everyone wanted to get away from the sand flies on the beach.

By mid-morning, the project was already well underway. 'What do you want us to do?' he asked Stephanie.

The Australian pulled herself up and considered for a moment. 'Erm…' She stared blankly at him. 'Sorry, what was your name again?'

'Andrew. Andy.' He grinned nervously.

'Okay. Right, well basically what the others are doing. Pulling out as much of the vegetation as you can and throwing it out of the way over there. Try and level the ground as much as you can while you go. The idea is to get everywhere as flat as possible.'

Andrew nodded. That seemed straight forward enough.

'Perhaps if you concentrate on that area over there.' Stephanie gestured to a clump of foliage, near where some of the others were already working. 'You might need to do a bit of digging.'

Andrew did not mind that at all.

'There's nothing like being thrown in at the deep end, is there?' Francesca Stevens straightened her back and paused to catch her breath. The work was exhausting. She had only arrived on the island a few hours before and already she was in the thick of things. It was midday and probably thirty-five degrees in the shade. That kind of temperature didn't exist in the UK. She wiped the perspiration from her eyes and glanced at Isabel Grant. 'What time's lunch?' she asked.

The other woman wasn't sure. 'I think we're just waiting for the rest of them to come back.' Isabel lifted a clump of bramble and moved to dispose of it at the edge of the clearing.

Francesca watched her go. It was strange seeing her friend here, in this environment. Bella was a little older than Frankie, though both women were in their twenties. They had known each other for some years. Isabel had met Frankie at an evening class back in Cambridge. It was Francesca who had seen the advertisement in the local paper but the two girls had nominated each other as castaways. Neither of them had expected to be selected. When they were both chosen, they could scarcely believe it. A year on a desert island, together. It had sounded too good to be true. Frankie was worried Clive Monroe might find out that they knew each other and stop them from going, but as luck would have it the two women had been kept apart until their arrival on the island.

Isabel grinned, returning to her friend's side and proudly surveying their morning's work. Together, they had flattened a sizeable patch of ground. Five people had been working hard to clear the area and the effort was beginning to bear fruit.

'I need something to drink,' Francesca said.

Isabel bent over her pack and pulled out a flask of water. 'It's fresh,' she said. 'I filled it up this morning from the cave.'

Frankie regarded the flask dubiously. 'Is it okay to drink?'

'It's rain water. It should be all right.'

She took a quick sip. The liquid was cool and refreshing. Francesca took another gulp and then wiped her mouth. 'That's good,' she admitted. It was strange how something as simple as rainwater could feel so invigorating. She never drank it at home, even from the tap. As she made to refasten the bottle, a nervous voice cut in from behind.

'Could I possibly have a sip of that?'

Frankie looked round.

Jane Ruddock was standing on the edge of the glade. Jane was one of the last people to come ashore that morning. Francesca had met her the previous day with Andrew Baker, when the three of them had boarded the helicopter in St. Moreau. Frankie and Jane had shared a cabin for the night and now they had spent the best part of the morning working together. Jane was a short, nervous woman, in her early forties. She had a

25

pretty, girlish complexion and an air of sisterly warmth which was immediately endearing. Now, however, she looked exhausted. Her face had turned puce and her clothes were dripping with sweat.

Francesca handed the water bottle across and Jane took a large gulp. 'I haven't done anything like this in years,' the woman admitted, once she had drunk her fill. She returned the flask to Isabel, with thanks, and wiped the dregs from her mouth.

For a time, the three women stood in silence, admiring their handiwork. A little way away, Andrew Baker was still pulling ferociously at a clump of bramble. Beyond him stood the lithe, statuesque figure of Stephanie McMahon.

'It's such a lovely place this,' Jane remarked, observing the dense forest surrounding the work site. A brightly feathered bird chirruped from one of the treetops. 'I'm so glad to be a part of it.'

Isabel nodded, following her gaze. 'There's certainly an interesting variety of flora and fauna.'

'And people,' Frankie added.

Andrew had won his battle with the bramble, but had fallen over backwards for his trouble.

Francesca scratched her head philosophically. It still hadn't really sunk in that she had arrived. It seemed like only a few days ago she had responded to the advertisement and now here she was, in the middle of the Pacific, with Isabel, Jane and all these others. They would have to work hard to support themselves over the coming year. At times it would be difficult, but they would persevere, and in the end, she was sure, the community would prosper.

She could hardly imagine a more pleasant contrast to the life she had left behind.

Steve Bramagh was helping Jeremy Fielding to fit crossbeams to the A-frames on the beach. It was a time consuming process. The work had started shortly after breakfast, but now – in the early afternoon – they were running out of cord. More wood would be needed, too, if they were to finish the task before nightfall. There were ten sets of frames to complete.

'Looks like we're here for the day, don't it?' Jeremy boomed cheerfully. The bearded Englishman had thrown himself into the work with some vigour.

Steve nodded. 'But, you know, I think it'll be worth it if we get it all done.' He pressed down hard onto the newly laid branches to see if they would support his weight.

'I think some of the girls want to move the beds away from the beach.' Jeremy pushed against the edge of the A-frame to check its balance. The construction seemed sturdy enough.

'Well, you know, that was certainly the impression I got. And I don't think it's a bad idea.' The two men moved over to the next frame and Steve unwound some more cord from the roll. 'But we can sort that out when we've finished the cross-beams.'

Jeremy leaned over to pick up another piece of wood. 'You wouldn't think something as simple as this would take so long, would you?' They had been working steadily together for some hours, without even a toilet break.

'Well, you know, in my experience, it always takes a while to get into the swing of these things. But I think by the time we get to the last one we'll have speeded up quite a bit.'

'Yeah, course we will. Doing it with our eyes closed.' Jeremy held the branch across the gap and compared the length. He marked a notch on the wood with his knife and laid the piece down next to the others. 'I reckon these ones are more or less the right length,' he said, looking down at them.

Steve agreed. 'You know, I think you and Stephanie did a good job collecting all those branches yesterday afternoon.'

The other man shrugged. 'There was a lot of stuff just lying around.' He marked the two longer branches and started to cut the ends with his knife. 'Nice girl, that Stephie, don't you think?'

'She's certainly got a lot going for her.' Steve smiled to himself. 'I must say, I did think something might be going on when the two of you went off together like that.' Stephanie and he had been gone the whole of the previous afternoon.

The Englishman grinned. 'No point wasting time, is there? And it's not as if there's much competition. Oh, no offence.'

'None taken. But, you know, you're not the only one here who might be interested. What about your friend Duncan?'

Jeremy snorted. 'Him? Nah. He don't like older women. I reckon he'd be better off with – what's her name? – Bella. She's more his type. Real fit bird, too.'

'She is attractive,' Steve agreed.

'Bit snooty, mind. Stuck up. Not that Duncan'll care. He's usually a bit slow on the uptake anyway, if you know what I mean. Oh. Don't tell him I said that.'

Jeremy finished working on the branches. He lifted one up and held it against the frame while Steve began to tie it into place.

'Have you known him long?' the Australian asked.

'What, Duncan? Yeah, since we were kids. Haven't seen him in years, mind. We had a bit of a falling out over some bird.'

Steve pulled the cord taut and secured it firmly. 'Not young Sue?' he asked, with a hint of amusement.

'Oh, blimey, no!' Jeremy chuckled. 'No, this was years ago. Some other girl. Can't remember her name. It was just after we left school.'

'But you've made up now?'

'Yeah, course. Water under the bridge, init?'

The two men moved across to the other side of the frame.

'You know,' said Steve, 'I have to admit I'm curious about all this business between him and Sue. Has he said anything to you about it?'

Jeremy shook his head. 'He's always a bit cagey about the birds. He gets a bit mouthy with them sometimes. Especially when he's had a drink or two. But he's a nice bloke really.'

Steve nodded. 'He doesn't seem very talkative, though.'

'Oh, that's just him. He's all right with his mates. Blimey, some of the things we used to get up to!' Jeremy paused briefly, remembering. 'Anyhow, he's got plenty of time to get to know people. He'll be a right laugh once we've all settled down. You'll see.'

28

Steve began to tie the other end of the branch.
I hope you're right, he thought.

Andrew could not keep the surprise from his voice. 'So you two have met as well?' Francesca Stevens nodded. The girl had come clean about her prior friendship with Isabel Grant, and it transpired that they were not the only ones here who had met before.

Andrew's mind boggled.

The islanders were gathering on the beach in the early afternoon. It was the first time they had come together as a group and there were a couple of belated introductions. The strangers sat themselves in a rough circle, as lunch was dished out between them. Most of the group had already worked up a fair appetite. Luckily, Duncan Roberts and Chris Hudson had been out on a short foraging expedition and had brought back some bananas, some berries and some coconuts. These would supplement the small amount of imported food the islanders had been allowed to bring with them. Duncan had also procured several handfuls of lime. The juice would provide a pleasing alternative to coconut milk. Nobody minded that the food was cold. It wasn't worth lighting a fire just for lunch. Besides, in these temperatures cooked food wasn't necessarily the best option.

Andrew was munching away on a banana and trying to memorise the names of all the people on the beach. Jane and Frankie were no trouble, of course. He had dined with them on the yacht the previous evening. But the others would take a little longer to bed in.

'This is ridiculous,' one of the women declared. Andrew racked his brains, trying to find a name to fit the face. *Sue something?* 'Nobody was meant to know anybody else. That was the whole point. That was what it said in the contract we signed. What does that son of a bitch think he's playing at?'

'In fairness, Clive didn't know about Frankie and me,' Isabel pointed out. She was a young, dark-haired Englishwoman. Francesca's friend, as it now turned out. She had large brown eyes and a calm, practical manner. 'We kept it to ourselves right from the start.'

'But what about Jeremy?' Sue Durrant asked. *Durrant. That was her surname.* 'And…and me and…'

'You know,' Steve Bramagh cut in. 'It does seem an odd coincidence. But I think Clive was genuinely surprised when he found out you and Duncan had met before.'

'You can't be certain of that,' the woman snorted.

'Well, you know, I'm a pretty good judge of character. If this was all arranged, then I'm pretty sure Clive doesn't know anything about it.'

Stephanie McMahon, the other Australian, evidently agreed. 'He didn't seem to have much of an idea about anything.'

'But, you know, coincidences like this can happen,' Steve insisted. 'It may seem far-fetched, but in my experience the odds against this sort of thing are often not as high as people think.'

'Oh, you're an expert on probability now, are you?'

'Well, not an expert, Sue, but, you know, I have read a bit about the subject.'

'These things *do* happen,' Jane Ruddock agreed. It was the first time the Englishwoman had spoken. She froze for a second, finding herself suddenly the centre of attention. 'But as long as we all get along,' she added, nervously, 'then it probably won't matter.' Jane was trying to sound optimistic but it wasn't quite coming off. Her nerves were getting the better of her.

Andrew felt rather sorry for the woman. She was older than most of the others in the group but she lacked any real confidence. She had been terrified on the helicopter flight out, he recalled, and had barely said a word during dinner on the yacht. But for all that she seemed a very nice lady. She reminded Andrew a bit of his mother.

Sue was staring at the woman with barely disguised contempt. 'It matters to me!' she insisted.

'I'm sorry….I didn't mean to…' Jane looked away in embarrassment.

'It doesn't matter,' Sue breathed.

'I think the little lady has a point,' Jeremy Fielding declared. He was the Londoner with the beard. Andrew had not spoken to him yet.

'She does have a name,' Sue spat.

'Sorry, love. Er…Jane, is it? But you're right. It doesn't really matter if half of us have already met. Just makes it more interesting, don't it?'

Stephanie pursed her lips. 'Maybe,' she said. 'But only so long as there are no more surprises.' Her eyes swept the haphazard circle, challenging the group.

Andrew's jaw dropped. 'Nobody else knows anybody, do they?' That would be really bizarre.

There was another awkward silence.

'Anyone?' Steve prompted. He glanced from face to face.

Andrew had not met any of these people before, but he could not speak for the others. There had been so many coincidences already. Jeremy and Duncan. Duncan and Sue.

Francesca was shaking her head along with the rest of the group. She glanced at Stephanie. 'Not unless your surname's McMahon,' she joked.

Stephanie's mouth fell open. She did not need to reply. It was obvious that Frankie had guessed correctly.

Andrew gaped at the two of them. That was *really* strange. *How could them two possibly know each other?* The two women were from opposite ends of the planet.

'This is ridiculous,' Sue Durrant exclaimed.

Isabel turned to Francesca. 'You know her from somewhere?'

Frankie nodded. 'That's the Australian woman. The friend of my aunt.'

Isabel blinked in astonishment.

Stephanie was also frowning. 'You're Francesca Stevens? Marion's girl?'

Frankie nodded, her face suddenly cold and unfriendly.

'Now this is getting beyond a joke,' Stephanie said.

Francesca could only agree. 'This can't be a coincidence.'

'But how could anyone know?' Andrew asked incredulously. The whole thing defied belief.

'Okay,' said Jeremy Fielding, 'anybody who's not connected to anyone else please put up their hands.'

Andrew raised his arm at once and glanced around the circle. There were ten people sitting out here on the beach, in the early afternoon sun, but aside from him, only two other people had their hands raised: Steve Bramagh and the Canadian Chris Hudson.

Jane Ruddock sat staring at her lap. Andrew saw Steve shoot the middle-aged woman an enquiring look. 'It's just, I'm sort of related to the director,' she admitted sheepishly.

'To Clive Monroe?'

Jane nodded. 'His brother is married to my sister Mary. That's…that's how I got selected. It was a sort of favour, really.'

Sue was horrified. 'God, isn't that typical!' she sneered.

'I know it's not fair. It was really kind of him to put me forward…' Jane fell silent. Her embarrassment was palpable.

Steve had turned his attention back to the rest of the group. 'You know, I'm beginning to get a little worried about all this,' he said.

'A little!' exclaimed Sue.

'Seven out of ten people. I don't think that can possibly be a coincidence.'

Andrew could only agree.

'Are we sure there are no other connections between us?' Isabel Grant wondered. She glanced from Steve to Andrew, and then at Chris Hudson. These were the only members of the group who did not appear to be linked.

Steve Bramagh frowned. 'I don't think there's anything that connects the three of us directly.'

Andrew nodded emphatically. 'I never saw none of you before yesterday.'

'And you haven't got any relatives in Australia?' Steve asked him. 'Someone the two of us might have in common?'

'Or in Canada?' Isabel prompted.

Andrew was certain. 'None at all. Me mam comes from Wolverhampton. Me dad's from Wigan.'

Steve shrugged. 'But even so, you know, I don't think there can be any doubt that we've been set up here by someone.' He frowned. 'The question is: who and why?'

'I told you,' snapped Sue. 'It's that bloody director.'

'I don't think it's anything to do with Clive,' Steve said.

'He's not clever enough to organise anything like this,' Stephanie McMahon agreed.

Andrew disliked the Australian's implied criticism of the director. 'He got us all out to the island. He's a nice bloke.'

'But I'm pretty sure he didn't set this up,' Steve said.

A memory flickered up in Andrew's mind. 'He said he weren't in complete control, like. Just doing what he were told.'

'That's right,' Frankie confirmed. She too had been at the dinner table the previous evening.

'But not knowingly, I don't think,' Steve insisted. 'You know, I'm beginning to suspect somebody must have arranged all this behind his back.' He fell silent for a moment, deep in thought.

Sue was shaking her head. She turned to Francesca. 'So what's your problem with *her*?' she asked, gesturing to the Australian woman.

Frankie sighed. 'We were in a dispute over a will. She won.'

Stephanie confirmed this cautiously, without making eye contact.

'Of course, there is one simple way we can get all this sorted,' Jeremy Fielding volunteered. Everyone stared at him. It was obvious nobody had much confidence in the bearded Englishman. 'Why don't we just call him up on the radio? If he don't know what's going on, at least he can fax the production company.'

'You know,' admitted Steve, with some surprise, 'I don't think that's actually a bad idea.'

'They don't call me Mr Brainy for nothing, you know.'

Andrew doubted anyone ever called Jeremy 'brainy', but he kept that thought to himself.

'He'll still be on the boat at the moment,' Steve said. 'I don't think they're back at St. Moreau until the day after tomorrow.'

Jeremy shrugged. 'Well, that's all right. They must have a wireless or something, mustn't they?' He stood up to stretch his legs and gave a sigh of satisfaction. Obviously, as far as he was concerned, he had just solved all their problems.

'I don't have any better ideas,' Francesca admitted.

Jeremy caught sight of Chris Hudson. The young Canadian was pointing a video camera at him. 'Hey, you've not been taping all this, have you?'

Chris nodded. 'I figured somebody should. That's sort of like what we signed up for.' He hesitated. 'Isn't it?'

'None of us signed up for this,' Sue Durrant stated flatly.

Stephanie had been meditating for a few moments. 'Do you think the company might have planned all this from the beginning?'

'Well, you know,' said Steve, raising an eyebrow. 'I think that's a real possibility.'

For once, even Sue was in agreement. 'Wouldn't surprise me at all,' she muttered. 'Screw the morality, go for the ratings.'

Steve got to his feet. 'Well, I think we should try and get to the bottom of this anyway. I'll go and set up the radio.'

'I'll give you a hand,' Stephanie volunteered.

Frankie eyed her new-found relative suspiciously. 'Don't you think we should all go?'

'Who elected you leader anyway?' Sue demanded.

'Well, you know, it was just a suggestion. I'm only trying to help out. We don't need more than two people. But we can bring the radio back here if you like.'

'Steve's not trying to take charge,' Stephanie insisted. 'He just wants to get things done.' She rose up briskly to accompany the man.

'They've got their heads screwed on, them two,' Andrew commented when the Australians had departed.

'They've got one disciple then,' Sue sneered. 'Bloody Australians.'

Andrew ignored her. 'Any more of them berries? I'm famished.'

Sue pulled herself up and stretched out her legs. 'I'm going for a swim,' she declared. 'I can't believe how filthy I am. This sand gets everywhere.'

'Actually, I think the rest of us should get back to work,' Isabel Grant suggested. 'There's a lot to do before sunset.'

Sue took no notice. She pounded across the beach and plunged into the warm blue water.

'No rest for the wicked, is there?' Jeremy laughed.

'That girl is such a dickhead,' Stephanie McMahon hissed.

'Well, you know, I think she's a bit stressed out at the moment,' Steve observed. 'I think she's probably had quite a difficult life.'

'We've *all* had difficult lives,' Stephanie snapped. 'You grow up and get over it.' It was *pathetic*. They had been on the island for two days and Sue Durrant had done nothing but whinge and complain the whole time. She was certainly living up to the traditional Australian stereotype of the Whingeing Pom. The woman had not been helpful in the least.

And then there was the matter of Francesca Stevens.

'So what's the story?' Steve asked, as they made their way along the path towards the cave.

Stephanie frowned. 'We *are* relatives. Distant ones, anyway. My Aunt Agatha was her great aunt, on my uncle's side. Her original will was written out in favour of Francesca's mother. Not that I ever met the woman. But I nursed my aunt when she was dying and she altered the will in my favour.'

Steve could understand that. 'So I don't expect Frankie feels very happy about you being here.'

'I'm not exactly over the moon myself.'

'This is the first time you've met?'

Stephanie nodded. 'It was all arranged through our lawyers. She contested the will and the court found in my favour.'

'An Australian court?'

35

'Yes. My aunt lived in Melbourne.'

'So how much did she leave you?' Steve had a habit of asking impertinent questions, but Stephanie did not mind.

'About a million, Australian.' The price of a decent house. 'That was four years ago. Francesca tried to make out I was some kind of money-grabbing interloper. I suppose I can sympathise a little. She received a small pay out, but that would have been eaten up by the legal costs. And her mother died before the final settlement, which didn't help.'

'Well, you know, it's good that you can take it all in your stride like this.'

'A million dollars certainly cushions the blow. It won't be so easy for her.' Stephanie sighed. 'I suppose I'll have to do the right thing and try to be nice about it. Always assuming she'll let me. Unlike some people, I don't bear grudges.'

Steve grinned. 'I'm glad to hear it.' They had arrived now at the cave. He moved forward to survey the interior. 'Where did you put the radio?'

'Just over there.'

Steve grabbed onto the rocks and hauled himself inside. The silver box was easy to find, even in the dank gloom.

'I'll pass it back to you,' he said.

Stephanie braced herself and reached forward. Steve manoeuvred the container across and Stephanie took careful hold. She pressed it against her chest and swung the box carefully around; then she found a place outside the cave and lowered it to the ground. 'Do you need a hand?' she called, as Steve scrambled back.

'I think I can manage.'

The woman returned her attention to the container. She unfastened the catch and pulled open the lid.

'You know, if you've inherited all that money, why did you want to come out here? I'd have thought someone like you would have quit their job and become a lady of leisure.'

Stephanie smiled. 'I did. For four years. But the money doesn't last forever. I travelled the world. I went everywhere I ever wanted to go. And I don't regret a single minute of it.'

'Good on you. You know, I think that's the right attitude to take.'

'And this is just another adventure.' Stephanie pulled the radio out of its box and positioned it on top of a large rock. 'Probably my last. I suppose I shall have to confront reality again at some point.' She smiled at Steve, dazzlingly, for a moment. Then she took out the metal rods and quickly assembled the aerial.

Steve crouched down next to her. 'You know, I never really understood what reality was.' He flicked a switch on the radio and an internal light illuminated a frequency display.

'At least it works,' Stephanie observed.

A burst of static scratched unpleasantly from a speaker on the right hand side. Steve twiddled the dial and the static faded in and out.

'What about you? What are you running away from?'

Steve sighed. 'Well, you know, not really running. I've just been caught up in the rat race for so long. I wanted a bit of time to myself. And I've always liked to experience new things.'

Stephanie found a place to slot the aerial lead. 'Well, this is certainly new. I've never been marooned on a desert island before.'

Steve was scratching his neck, staring at the radio. Something was clearly bothering him.

'What's the matter?'

'Well, you know, Steph, I don't want to be the one to state the obvious, but there doesn't seem to be anything here to *transmit* with.'

Stephanie regarded him blankly. 'It's got an aerial.'

'I know. But what do we talk into?'

She pointed to the grill. 'That, surely.'

Steve shook his head. 'That's just a speaker.' He twisted the dial on the front of the radio. Now that the aerial was connected, the static gave way to music and jabbering foreign voices. 'This is just a receiver. An ordinary radio.'

Stephanie stared at him. 'It can't be.' She looked back at the device. But Steve was right. There was nothing there, except the power switch and the tuning dial. It could receive perfectly

37

well but it was incapable of broadcasting anything. 'That's absurd.'

'You know,' Steve said carefully, 'I think somebody must have wanted to make sure we couldn't communicate with the outside world.'

Stephanie shuddered. She didn't want to consider the implications of that. But there was at least someone she could blame. 'The little bastard…'

Steve frowned again. 'You mean Clive Monroe?'

She nodded. 'He *must* have known about this. Even he couldn't be that stupid.'

'Well, you know, Steph, *we* didn't realise. Not until now. No, I'm pretty sure Clive thought the same as we did. Took one look at the thing and packed it away.'

'Then who…?'

Steve shrugged. 'Who knows? Maybe one of the producers back in England.' He sighed. 'Well, I don't suppose it matters now. This is no good to us.' He collapsed the antennae. 'You know, Stephanie, I had a bad feeling about this right from the start. It didn't make sense to me, the way we were brought together like this.'

'But…'

'Now I can't help thinking there's a reason for it. Not just a cheap cable documentary. Something else.'

Stephanie shuddered.

'I just wish I knew what…'

Chapter Three

Frankie had a better sense of direction than Andrew Baker and he was happy to let her lead the way. The island of Malpaís was rich in woodland, though there were several rocky outcrops and the odd patch of long grass. It had two significant beaches, one on the northern coastline and the other a couple of miles to the south. It took a good three quarters of an hour to cross between the two – that was what Andrew had been told, anyway – and as yet there was no path to follow.

A foraging rota had been organised, to collect fruit and veg for the group, and the two Brits had found themselves at the top of the list. Andrew had emptied out his rucksack at the beach camp, as had Francesca. Between them, they would need to gather a lot of food, if they were to provide dinner for the whole group that evening.

There was more to their journey than picking fruit, however. Steve Bramagh had given them a second task, which he thought particularly urgent: finding a new source of fresh water. The cave where the supplies had been left had a decent sized natural pool but it was dependant on rain to sustain it. There was no guarantee it would provide everything the group needed in the coming weeks. Andrew agreed to keep his eyes peeled for an alternative supply.

Francesca led the way as the two of them strode through the undergrowth. Andrew had already taken a shine to the young British woman. Unlike Stephanie, she was not in the least bit intimidating. The girl seemed cheerful and easy-going. It helped that they were of a similar age. She was intelligent, too, and quite pretty, Andrew thought. She had an elfin face and large blue eyes. Her figure was pleasantly slim.

She had told him all about her legal battles with Stephanie McMahon, as the two of them were gathering food that morning. It sounded rather complicated but Frankie didn't seem to bear the Australian any malice. Andrew, in his turn, told her all about his home, his mother, his job and the reasons he had come to the island.

A heavy canopy protected the two of them from the worst of the sunlight. Andrew was grateful for the respite. He was already quite badly burnt. His freckled skin was red and sore and he had spent an uncomfortable night on the beach. Now he felt like he had some kind of fever. It was almost like he was being roasted alive. Well, perhaps that was an exaggeration, but it was certainly unpleasant. His head had started throbbing a bit too. He didn't want to get sunstroke, so he made sure he was drinking plenty of water.

'I don't think it's far now,' Francesca said, peering ahead through the branches. 'Oh, there are some limes over there.' She reached up on tiptoes to gather the fruits. 'Perhaps you should get a shot of this.'

'I think the battery's getting a bit low.' Andrew's video camera was in his rucksack, in the top section, away from the foodstuff. 'I've taken quite a lot already,' he said. He was getting adept at filming now.

Frankie tossed a few limes into her backpack. 'I think I prefer this to all that digging.' Even now, some of the others were working to lay the foundations of a communal hut, in the space they had cleared near the beach the day before.

Andrew agreed. 'Piece of cake, this.'

There had been long discussions over dinner the previous evening. The group was understandably angry about the radio. It was bad enough being set up in the first place but then to find your only lifeline to the outside world was a portable radio which could not actually transmit anything, that was unforgivable. What if somebody had an accident or got really sick? For once, Andrew felt just as vehemently about this as Sue Durrant. Someone, somewhere had treated them very badly indeed and at some point there would have to be a reckoning. He did not envy Clive Monroe's reception when the director returned to the island in seven day's time.

Until then, however, the group had no choice but to make the best of things. As Steve had pointed out, there were certain jobs that needed to be done regardless and they might as well grit their teeth and get on with it. There would be plenty of time later for recriminations. Even Sue had grudgingly seen the logic in that.

And so here they were, the two Brits, out collecting food for their evening meal as if nothing had happened. The forest was at least proving a bountiful resource. Fruits and nuts were plentiful, and there was enough variety across the island to support the entire group, if they foraged carefully.

Ahead of them, a small clearing loomed. 'I think this is the way Stephanie came,' Frankie said.

A pair of black birds fluttered noisily above them.

Andrew nodded. He remembered the description she had given them. A few more trees, the Australian had said, and then they would arrive at Cocoa Beach.

The islanders had invented lots of names in the past twenty-four hours. "Cocoa Beach"; "Candy Beach". And the cave would henceforward be referred to as "the Grotto". It all helped to make the place seem a little more homely. They had even come up with an alternative name for the island itself: "Paradise". No-one was quite sure how to pronounce the real name.

Andrew spotted a glimmer of blue between the adjacent tree trunks. 'Aye, that's it!' he exclaimed. 'I'll race you!'

Francesca shook her head, but when Andrew started to run she followed anyway, grinning. He dashed through the branches and out onto the hot sand. Cocoa Beach was a lot narrower than the northern coastline. Andrew did not stop running. He dropped his rucksack and plunged headlong into the glorious blue water.

Frankie pulled herself up, laughing. 'You idiot!' she cried.

'Come on!' he shouted. 'It's great!'

She shook her head again, making a show of reluctance, but Andrew was laughingly insistent. Francesca slipped off her sandals and her t-shirt and followed him in. 'We're supposed to be working.' She smiled, despite herself.

Andrew was treading water, trying not to swallow. The sea was cool and refreshing. 'What's the point of being on a desert island if you can't go for a swim?'

41

Afterwards, they dried themselves on the beach. Andrew lay out in the sun, his head propped up against his rucksack. He closed his eyes for a moment and felt the warm glow on his face.

Francesca scanned his body with some concern. 'You really are quite badly burnt.'

'I know.' But there was nothing he could do about it, except to cover up as much as possible.

'Have you got another t-shirt?'

Andrew's top was soaked through. 'Not with me,' he said.

'You'd better take mine.' Frankie had her swimming costume on underneath.

'It's all right. It'll dry out soon enough.' He reached a hand back into his rucksack and dug out his water bottle. He sat up, unscrewed the lid and took several large gulps.

'Go easy on that. We'll be a couple of hours yet.' Francesca rummaged through her bag to retrieve her own water.

For a short while, they sat in silence.

The plan was to work their way around the edge of the island in an easterly direction. Jeremy Fielding had seen some large rocks a little way off from Cocoa Beach and it was possible they might be able to find some freshwater there. The two of them could afford to spend a couple of hours exploring. They had already collected enough food for the evening meal.

'I suppose we'd better be going,' Andrew said, pulling himself up reluctantly.

Frankie saw him wince. 'Are you sure you're all right?'

'Aye, I'm fine.' He picked up his rucksack. 'I hope we do find some proper water, though. I'm dying to wash off some of this sand.' The grains stung at his skin, exacerbating the sunburn. There was some discomfort down below, as well.

Francesca laughed. 'You think you've got problems.' She ran her fingers through a tangle of long brown hair. 'I'm covered in the stuff.' She scratched her scalp irritably.

Andrew extended a hand and helped the girl to her feet. Frankie dusted off the sand and with a smile they set off across the beach.

Jeremy, it turned out, was right about the rocks. Some of them were huge. The boulders jutted out to sea from the eastern-most point of Cocoa Beach. It was going to be difficult, scrabbling over them all, but they would have to if they wanted to continue on round the island. Andrew's trainers were at least a little more practical here than they had been on the sand, even if they were wet through from the sea. Francesca had a pair of flip-flops on.

The youngsters pulled themselves up onto the rocks and squeezed their way between two large boulders.

'You should take those off,' Frankie suggested. 'It's not good for you, wearing wet trainers.'

Andrew nodded, looking down at his feet. 'Aye.' He would have to go barefoot. He had left his sandals back at base camp, on the other side of the island. 'I don't suppose there'll be much glass lying around.' He pulled off the trainers and tied the laces together so he could carry them both in one hand.

Francesca moved ahead, pulling herself up onto one of the larger rocks. She stood there for a moment, looking out to sea. A good half a mile away, an even bigger collection of boulders swelled up from the water. Andrew had seen them from the beach earlier on. He lifted himself up next to the girl. It might be a good laugh swimming out there, he thought, when they had the time. 'What shall we call them?' he asked. They had come up with names for everything else, after all.

' "The Rocks"?' Frankie suggested. Andrew looked at her and she blushed slightly. 'I'm not very good at naming things.'

Another forty minutes passed before they found what they were looking for. It was pure luck they stumbled across it at all. Andrew had been scrabbling off in a different direction, but Francesca had asked him to hang on and at that moment he'd glanced off to the right.

The rock pool was small but deep and the water was beautifully clear. The source of it, however, was not immediately apparent. Andrew stared down at it from above, grinning broadly.

'It might not be fresh water,' Frankie warned.

He winked at her. 'There's only one way to find out.'

She knew at once what he was going to do. 'It might be...' she said, but it was already too late.

Andrew hurled himself off the rock and plunged into the crystal blue water. Francesca shook her head. His clothes were only just dry from the last time. She reached into his backpack and pulled out the video camera.

Andrew popped his head up above the water and started swimming.

'Is it salty?' she shouted down to him. She had brought the video up to her face and was already recording.

'I don't know.'

'Well taste it, silly!'

Andrew took a mouthful of water. He swallowed it awkwardly. 'I'm not sure.'

Frankie laughed. 'What do you mean, you're not sure?!?'

He took another gulp. 'It is! It's fresh water! Tastes bloody marvellous!' Andrew splashed the water over his head. 'Wait till the others hear about this!'

Francesca smiled, switching off the camera. 'If we ever manage to find our way back to them...'

Sue Durrant was surrounded by trees and they all looked exactly the same. The group was completely lost. It was typical. Why couldn't a desert island just be desert and not like some overgrown picnic spot for kids? She wouldn't have minded, but for the company she was keeping. Jane Ruddock was little more than a mouse and as for the Canadian...

'Hey, look, I don't think this is such a great idea.' Chris Hudson had climbed a little further up the tree and was balancing precariously between the sides of a huge forked trunk.

Sue peered up at him. 'Have you got a better suggestion?' They could scarcely hack off one of the branches with a Swiss Army knife and it was too high up to play tug of war.

The Canadian reached out carefully and placed his hand on a narrow branch jutting out from the tree.

'That does look a little dangerous,' Jane Ruddock thought. She was trying to operate the zoom function on her video camera, but with little success.

'Oh for Christ's Sake!' Sue exclaimed. It was not in the slightest bit dangerous. '*I'll* do it, if you haven't got the guts...' She ground her teeth impatiently.

Chris placed his other hand on the branch. 'I've got it,' he said.

'Good. Now swing out and hold onto it.'

The young man took a deep breath. 'Okay. Here goes.' He pushed off from the main stump and swung out underneath, his hands gripping the branch tightly.

'Hang on!' Jane called out.

'I'm hanging!' he shouted back. His legs were dangling in mid air. For a moment, nothing happened; then, slowly, the young Canadian's weight began to pull at the wood, tearing it away from the trunk. 'Hey look, is somebody going to catch me here?' An understandable note of urgency had entered his voice.

'It's not that high,' Sue responded scornfully.

The branch tore further, then snapped and twisted towards the ground. Chris Hudson plummeted, landing on his feet but then falling backwards heavily onto his spine. He swore loudly.

Jane ran towards him, concerned. 'Are you all right?'

He opened his eyes and gave out a sigh. 'I guess.' The branch was at an angle now, though a thin slither was still connected to the mother tree. 'There must be, like, an easier way to do this,' he said. He pulled himself forward and rose unsteadily to his feet. Quickly, he dusted himself down.

'Like what?' Sue asked. 'Do you have any better ideas?' It was easy enough to snap off the thin branches, but without a hacksaw there was only brute force and gravity to get at the thicker ones. 'No, I didn't think you would have.' She gave a sharp tug and pulled the branch free of its moorings. The dead wood slumped heavily to the ground.

'Well, hey, then how about you climb the next one?' A flash of anger lighted in the Canadian's eyes.

Sue shrugged. 'Fine. It's not exactly difficult.' She gestured to the pile of branches they had already collected. 'Why don't you drag that lot back to the camp site? I'm sure Jane and I can manage well enough without you.'

Chris stared at her for a moment but his anger was visibly subsiding. 'Okay, sure.' He moved over to the ramshackle pile. It would be hard work carrying that lot back and Sue could see the prospect did not fill him with pleasure. 'So which way's home?' he asked, glancing around the forest uncertainly.

Sue had no idea. 'Over there somewhere.' She gestured vaguely. It was his problem, not hers.

The Canadian gathered up the thin branches first, then pulled at the broader one they had just detached from the tree. This snagged on some foliage, but he gave it a sharp tug and it soon came free. The branch was too big to carry, however. He would have to drag it the whole way back to camp.

Sue watched him go and smiled slightly. Chris Hudson had all the awkward mannerisms of a frustrated adolescent. He was thin and pale looking. Some of those branches were bigger than he was. *Serves him right. Do him good to put his back into it for a change.* She had had to brow-beat the boy at every stage in order to get any work out of him. At least Jane Ruddock pulled her weight, even if she did have the personality of a particularly uncharismatic dung beetle.

I wonder if that is *the right direction.* Sue didn't know. *So much for my leadership skills.* It was she who had got them lost in the first place. They should never have wandered so far from the beach. *Oh well.* It was too late to worry about it now. All that mattered was more wood. And this time Sue would do the climbing.

Mud bricks would have been preferable, Steve Bramagh thought. He had seen a man construct a mud hut in Malawi and he had a fair idea how to go about it. There was plenty of soil on the island and lots of water to mix it with. The bricks would need to be baked, of course, but with a little ingenuity Steve was sure the group could knock up a small oven. The time factor, however, was prohibitive.

There were too many other priorities, not least of all finding an alternative source of protein. The bags of rice they had been allowed to bring with them would not last long. There were a few small mammals scurrying across the island, but Steve was not convinced they would provide a steady supply of meat. Actually, he was not even convinced anyone would be able to catch them. The only other option, if they were not to become vegetarians, was to try their hand at fishing. But that was an idea for another day.

A decent sized building, Steve reckoned, would take at least a week to construct. Wood was the only viable material, but given the lack of tools the end result would probably be a bit of a mess. It would also require a lot of timber. Some of the group had already gone off in search of raw materials. A more difficult problem was how to make the cord to bind the wood together. The rope they had used on the A-frames was now exhausted. An alternative could be woven out of vines and long grass, but it would be a laborious process. Some kind of rudimentary thatch was also needed for the roof. No, constructing a hut of this kind was not going to be easy, but it *was* necessary. Steve was convinced of that. They couldn't leave everything open to the elements. And not everyone would want to sleep in the Grotto when the heavens opened during the night.

Isabel Grant interrupted his thoughts. 'Is this far enough apart?'

Steve glanced up. The young Englishwoman was standing a few yards away, holding a thick branch upright in one hand. 'Another half metre, I reckon.' Isabel stepped back as directed. 'That should do it.' She pressed the wood firmly into the ground. Steve looked between the two poles. He had positioned the first one himself. *About six metres.* That would be the length of the front. Now they had to mark out the depth of the building. Two other pieces of timber were laid out ready on the ground. When all four were in place, they would have a proper sense of the scale they were working to. Then, once the foundations of the hut were completed, the real construction could begin.

Isabel picked up one of the other branches. It was considerably taller than she was, and she was by no means short. She looked up at it in amusement as Steve grabbed the fourth piece. 'We'll have to try to get these two level,' he said.

The woman nodded and moved away. She was not the most talkative of people. In truth, Steve had some difficulty reading her. She was obviously intelligent and always scrupulously polite, but she never seemed to engage with him on a personal level. Even with her friend Francesca, Isabel rarely seemed to laugh or smile. But it was early days and the girl more than pulled her weight.

'Why don't we run some cord between the posts?' she suggested. 'That'll give us a better idea of the shape.'

'Well, you know, I did think of that, Bella. But we've used up most of the rope on the A-frames.' He gestured to the edge of the clearing, where some of the new beds were now in residence. Not all of the islanders wanted to spend another night on the beach. Half the group had already dragged their frames across to the clearing. In fact, it had almost become a boy/girl split.

Isabel nodded. 'Just a thought.'

Steve lined up his branch with its opposite number, then quickly assessed the divide.

'That's about right,' Isabel said, securing her own pole in the hard earth. 'I suppose we could cannibalise some clothing, just to wind around it. I've got an old jumper we could use.'

The Australian was not sure. 'That might do the trick.'

Isabel moved to the edge of the glade to retrieve her rucksack. Just as she reached it, Chris Hudson appeared between the trees and almost collided with her. The blond Canadian flinched momentarily. 'Go on,' Isabel gestured. She moved her pack out of the way.

Chris pulled at the branches trailing behind him and staggered out into the open air. He dropped the main load on top of some wood which had already been gathered. Then he dragged the big branch over to join them. The young man looked exhausted.

'Where's Sue and Jane?' Steve asked.

'Still looking, I guess. I think they, like, kind of wanted to keep going. So we can make a proper start tomorrow.'

Steve looked down at the pile of unprocessed timber. It was not a bad haul, all things considered. The branches were by no means straight or thick, but they were long and that was more important. The sides of the hut needed to be at least a couple of metres high. 'You know, I think you did well to carry all this.'

'I must have, like, dropped a couple of pieces along the way. It's kind of difficult, sort of dragging it. It gets all, like, tangled up.' Chris looked across at the wooden poles Steve and Isabel had positioned in the ground. They formed a large rectangle in the centre of the clearing. 'It's going to be big, huh?'

Steve nodded. 'I think there should be at least two separate rooms.'

Isabel was crouched over her pack in the far corner, pulling at the woollen jumper she had just retrieved. Chris wondered what she was doing.

The Australian smiled. 'Improvising a bit of rope.'

Chris watched the girl for a moment but she did not look up.

'You know, you should go get something to drink,' Steve suggested.

'I'm okay.'

The other man shook his head. 'At these temperatures, you often need more than you think you do.'

Chris did not contradict him. He was still staring at Isabel.

Francesca grasped the cooking pot firmly with two hands.

It was late afternoon and she was making her way down to the Grotto to collect some water. It had been decided to restrict the supply in the cave to drinking and cooking only. The new rock pool she and Andrew had discovered on the other side of the island could be used for washing and cleaning dirty clothes. Nobody really wanted to mix the two anyway and getting clean seemed less important now. Frankie had already given up combing the tangles out of her hair and, though she was sure her body must reek, somehow it didn't seem to matter anymore.

And I've only been here two days. It was odd how quickly the trappings of modern life fell away. There was no tooth-paste, no toilet roll, no make-up and no shampoo. If they wanted to clean their teeth, they had to do it with twigs or bits of vine. The men had no razor blades or deodorant. Some of them already wore dark stubbles on their chins. The women couldn't shave their legs or their arm-pits. In a few weeks, they would all look like cave monsters. And the men would sport beards just like Jeremy Fielding. It was not an attractive prospect.

Francesca could not imagine Andrew with a beard. She grinned at the thought of it. She had really started to warm to the young Mancunian. He was friendly and good natured; and she could tell that he really liked her. But these were early days. She did not want to rush into anything just yet. They could be friends for the time being.

As the interior of the cave came into view, Frankie hesitated. Stephanie McMahon was sitting inside. Her arms were crossed and she had a cigarette burning in her left hand. A silver box was lying on the ground and the woman had placed the large plastic radio receiver on the rock beside her. The aerial was extended.

They had taken the radio down to the hut site earlier on – just for the hell of it – and spent the best part of the day working to the beat of some bizarre Polynesian rhythms. It made a nice change. The radio had no other practical use and there were not many alternative forms of entertainment on the island. But the batteries would not last forever.

Stephanie was listening to some kind of news broadcast.

Francesca locked eyes with the Australian and smiled weakly. She had promised herself she would be friendly, but it was proving harder than expected. She could not help but associate Stephanie with her mother's death. *Now I know how Bella felt*, she thought.

Frankie was not the only one to have lost somebody close to her. Isabel had lost a sister in a road accident, a few years before. The two women had helped each other through the grief, but wounds like that rarely healed completely. And at least Francesca's mum had died in her sleep.

Stephanie switched off the radio as Frankie arrived, then took a puff of her cigarette.

Francesca placed the cooking pot on the ground and nodded at the other woman briefly.

'I was just taking a short break,' Stephanie explained. She had brought the radio back with her when they had called it a day at the work site. Frankie should have realised she would be here. She glanced at the burning cigarette.

'How many of those did you bring?' Each member of the group had been allowed one luxury item. Francesca had brought a copy of her favourite book.

'Just the one packet.' Stephanie grimaced. 'I've been rationing myself to a cigarette a day.'

'You brought a lighter too.' That might come in useful, Frankie thought. At the moment, they were using Sue Durrant's contraband matches to light the cooking fire, but those would not last a whole year.

For a moment, the two women were silent. Francesca could not bring herself to broach the subject that was on both their minds. She bent over and picked up the cooking pot, bringing it over to the pool and filling it with water.

'I suppose you've heard about Andrew and Steve?'

Frankie looked round, puzzled.

'There is a connection, apparently. They both worked for the same company, Automotive Enterprises.'

'Steve did?'

The Australian nodded. 'Apparently.'

'I know Andrew worked in one of their factories. It closed down at the end of last year. I thought Steve was in management.'

'He is. Or was. For the same company.' Stephanie took a last puff of her cigarette and stubbed it out on the side of the rock. 'Actually, he was made redundant. The company have pulled out of Australia altogether.'

Francesca lifted the pot back onto the ground. 'Small world.'

'That's not the least of it. It turns out Chris Hudson's father is on the board of the company that took them over. CNL.'

Frankie considered this for a moment. It didn't make much difference. It was hardly the worst connection they had discovered. 'That won't make Chris very popular.'

Stephanie raised an eyebrow. 'He's not exactly popular anyway.'

Francesca had already heard several snide remarks about the Canadian's lack of team spirit. 'I think he's just a bit shy.' It was often the way with young men. They would isolate themselves not because they were selfish but because they didn't understand what was expected of them.

'Adolescents we can do without.'

Stephanie was being rather judgemental, Frankie thought. In truth, the Australian was not much different from the mental image Francesca had formed of her during their legal wranglings. She was brash and cold, even when she was not being deliberately unfriendly. But perhaps that was just another way of hiding insecurities. Frankie resolved again to be as pleasant as possible, but she knew it would not be easy.

Stephanie rose to her feet and manoeuvred the radio to a safe position within the cave.

Francesca was just preparing to leave.

'I'll come back with you,' the older woman said. She did not offer to carry the pot but she was at least making some effort to bury the hatchet. 'I'm sorry about your mother,' she ventured awkwardly as they left the cave.

Frankie could not bring herself to meet the woman's eye.

'I know you probably don't want to hear that from me.'

'It wasn't your fault,' she said.

The sky was beginning to cloud over.

It was afternoon on the fifth day. Work continued apace on the log cabin, but Sue Durrant had other concerns. It was her turn to forage for the group and Steve Bramagh was her nominated companion. In some ways, she was glad it was him. Not that she liked the man much, but anything was preferable to Canadians or divorcees. And anyway, Steve probably had a better sense of direction than she did.

'Are you sure you know where we are?' she demanded.

'Well, you know, so long as we have the rough time of day and I can see the sun, it's not a problem working it out.'

Arrogant sod. 'But you've not actually been here before?'

'No.' He glanced up at the canopy. 'But I don't think we're far off the beaten track. Nobody's foraged this part of the island yet. That's why I chose it.'

Sue understood the logic. It would be stupid to pick too much food from one area. Nonetheless, she found herself irritated by the man's smugness. 'So are you ever wrong about anything?' she asked, sarcastically.

Steve smiled. 'Well, Sue, I try not to be. But, you know, I'm only human. We all of us make mistakes.'

'Tell me about it.' She scratched her head and looked up at the sky. 'You don't think it's going to rain, do you?'

'I hope so. It's certainly in the air.'

'You *want* it to rain?'

'Well, you know, we're going to have to cope with it at some point. I think better sooner rather than later. Although I had hoped we'd finish the hut before the first real downpour.'

'I'm surprised you didn't send somebody else out foraging. I wouldn't have thought you could bear to leave your pet project behind.'

'Well, Sue, you know, we all have to make sacrifices. And besides, I look forward to our little chats.'

The woman made a face. 'Yeah, right!' Try as she might, however, she could not detect any sarcasm in the Australian's voice.

'There's a clearing just up ahead,' he observed.

They moved towards it. The light was no brighter here. The sun was obscured by a heavy cloud cover.

What a bloody awful day, she thought. It probably *would* rain. It would be just her luck. Especially as they were at least a couple of kilometres from the shelter of the Grotto.

'Now, I have been *here* before,' Steve said. 'This is a short cut to the Swimming Pool. I found it on the way back the other day.'

Sue had not visited this new water source as yet, though Francesca had told her all about it. Suddenly, the thought of a proper bath and a scrub down seemed rather appealing. Frankie had said the water was actually quite warm. 'Let's go there,' she suggested.

Steve was reluctant. 'You know, I think we should be heading back. I think we've got enough supplies already. And I'd like to see how things are progressing back at the camp.'

His beloved hut. *Typical.* But Sue would not be deterred. 'I want to go,' she insisted. 'Just show me the way. It can't take that long. You can leave me there, if you like.'

The Australian sighed. 'Well, okay, if that's what you want. It's about ten minutes from here.' He put down his pack, abandoning it temporarily in the clearing, and strode off.

Sue had no choice but to follow him. 'Hang on!' she yelled. 'I'm not in that much of a hurry!'

It was only after he had left that it occurred to Sue that she was now completely on her own. It was ridiculous really, but she had been so intent on visiting the "Swimming Pool" once the idea had struck her that she had not bothered to think it through. Now Steve Bramagh had departed and she was all alone, for the first time since that afternoon in the Grotto.

She tried hard to put that out of her mind. The others would all be working on the hut, on the other side of the island. There was no reason for any of them to venture out here. Only the foraging people ever came this far, unless someone got up especially early in the morning. No, she was perfectly safe. There wasn't going to be anybody else about.

She stripped off her trousers and her t-shirt. Like the other women, Sue had taken to wearing her swimsuit more or less permanently underneath her other clothes. This was only awkward when she needed to go to the loo. She had still not got used to squatting down in the bushes. It felt so degrading. And she was torn between the need to go far enough away from people not to be observed and being so far away that she did not feel safe. That was an idea to suggest to Steve. Building a proper latrine.

She frowned, irritated at herself. Why did she need to suggest it to Steve? He wasn't in charge, no matter how much he thought he was. And if he was really so bloody clever, he would have thought of the idea already.

She glanced down at the cool blue water. It was tempting just to strip off completely. She could give her costume a wash later on. And her t-shirt. They could both do with a clean. Her clothes were covered in sand. She would have to leave the trousers, though. They would never get dry by nightfall, not with the sun behind the clouds as it was now.

Her swimsuit was a modest pale green. Sue looked around, making sure nobody could see her, and then quickly slipped out of it. She glanced down, examining herself critically. She did not have a bad body, all things considered. Her breasts were too small and she didn't think much of her hips, but her stomach was flat and at least she had a decent pair of legs. Sue had expected everything to fall apart when she'd hit twenty-five but so far it all seemed to be holding together.

It felt odd, standing naked out in the open air. She sat herself down and slid gently into the water. She had no intention of jumping in. It might be cold – but no, she found it warm and pleasant, just as Francesca had said.

She pulled her head back and submerged it in the water. Her straight black hair slicked against the scalp as she came up for air. The hair was still a bit tangled, but at least the sand was out of it now. Perhaps she would be able to stop scratching for a while.

It felt good to be in the water. The pool was rather deep, though and she was having to tread water. Her breasts bobbed at the surface. She extended her toes, trying to touch bottom, but she couldn't reach it without going under again. It didn't matter. She felt relaxed. The water soothed her skin and some of the tension in her muscles began to fade away. But only some of it. The water was not *that* soothing.

Sue pulled herself to the edge of the pool and tarried for a moment. The water had a slight green tinge close up and it gave off an unpleasant odour. It was not wholly offensive, but the longer she stayed in the water the more noticeable it became.

She grabbed onto the rocks and began to pull herself out. It was difficult, as her skin was wet and the rocks were slippery. She swung her legs around and sat on the edge, looking back down at the pool. The water dripped from her toes and formed ripples in the water.

She pulled herself onto her knees and gathered together her discarded clothing. She had no soap powder but with a bit of effort she might be able to get rid of some of the less ingrained dirt. *I can't believe I'm doing this,* she thought. *Stark naked, washing my clothes in a rock pool in the middle of the Pacific.* Thank God there were no cameras around.

Once she had scrubbed the clothes, she squeezed the water out of the wet garments and placed them to one side. Then she lent across to her pack and retrieved the rest of her clothes. Her skin was almost dry now – the sun had come out briefly – and she pulled on a pair of knickers and a white t-shirt. Zipping up her jeans over the top of them, she took one last look at the pool. Then she picked up her washing and the backpack and made to leave.

She stopped almost at once.

Duncan Roberts was standing five metres away, watching her closely.

She let out a short cry.

'Hello Sue,' he said.

'How…how long have you been there?'

'Not long. A couple of minutes.'

'You didn't…?'

He shook his head. But he was lying. She knew he was lying.

'You bastard.'

Duncan looked at her, his face blank. 'Is that what you wanted to say to me?'

'Say? I never wanted to speak to you again as long as I lived.'

'Is that a fact? Then why all the cloak and dagger stuff?'

Sue did not understand. 'What are you talking about?'

Duncan was beginning to rile. 'Don't play the innocent with me. You asked me here. I came. So say what you wanted to say.'

'I didn't...'

Duncan took a step towards her.

'You stay where you are! Don't you come near me!'

'I'm sick of your games,' Duncan sneered. 'I lost my job because of you...'

'You should have...' Sue could not finish the thought. She could barely even draw in a breath. There was no way to get away from him. There were rocks either side and only the pool behind her. And she recognised the slur in Duncan's voice.

'Nobody ever treats you the same afterwards,' he said. 'I lost everything. Because of *you*, you lying little bitch...' He was upon her now and she saw the anger in his eyes. The hatred. He had been drinking, somehow. She knew it instinctively.

Duncan grabbed her wrists and Sue could not break free.

It was happening again.

Chapter Four

Sue was not at dinner that evening, though it was some time before her absence was noticed.

Steve was busily preparing the food the two of them had gathered that afternoon. Jeremy Fielding had volunteered to lend a hand. The bearded Englishman had prepared a small fire on the near side of Candy Beach and the food was now well and truly stewed. The call for dinner had gone out several minutes before, but so far only Chris Hudson and Jane Ruddock had turned up. Once they had been served, there was nobody else in line. 'Was it something I said?' Jeremy laughed. He exchanged glances with Steve. 'Still, you can't exactly blame them, can you?' He lifted up a ladle-full of stew and peered at the mixture dubiously. 'Same old slop. They're probably all fed up with it by now.'

'Well, you know, there's only so much we can make with the raw materials we've got.' The group would have to get used to their new diet. It would be a long time before they ate a proper western-style meal again.

Francesca Stevens appeared from behind the two men and grabbed a bowl from a small pile next to the fire. Jeremy poured some mixture into the bowl and handed it back. 'There you go, love.' He winked.

'Thanks, Jem. It looks nice.' She started to move away, but then remembered something. 'Oh, Stephanie says she'll be five minutes. She's still trying to get that top piece on the door frame. I think Bella's giving her a hand.'

Jeremy raised an eyebrow. 'I'm surprised they can still see.' The sun had set about twenty minutes ago and the sky was blackening fast. The islanders generally gathered here at around this time and remained on the beach until bed. It was dangerous walking about after dark without a torch.

A queue was finally starting to form in front of the cooking pot. Andrew Baker had arrived behind Francesca. He watched as the girl moved away and went to sit cross-legged on the sand next to Jane Ruddock. Then he grabbed a bowl and handed it to the cook.

'Make the most of this,' Jeremy told him. 'Last of the rice.'

Andrew looked down at the steaming liquid. 'I'm famished!'

'Exhausted more like. Working like a maniac he was today,' Jeremy confided to his fellow cook.

'I know. I surprised myself,' Andrew agreed. 'I never worked this hard back home. And I was getting paid for it then.'

Steve Bramagh smiled. 'Well, you know, you certainly *would* have done if *I'd* been your manager.' The two men had worked for the same company, after all, albeit on different continents. 'You wouldn't think it, but I was a pretty tough boss. I always liked to reward hard work, but if they didn't get results, they were out.'

Jeremy poured some stew into the bowl.

'Blimey! I'm glad we didn't have you at our place!' Andrew laughed, taking the food from the other man.

'No meat today, I'm afraid,' Jeremy told him.

Andrew grinned. This was becoming a standard joke. There was *never* any meat.

'Here, Chris said you used to do a bit of fishing or something. Is that true?'

Andrew nodded. 'Aye, down by the canal, when I were a lad. Why do you ask?'

There was a twinkle in Jeremy's eye. 'Oh, I was just thinking. Maybe we should have a crack at that some time.'

'What, fishing?'

'Why not? Might liven up the old diet a bit.' He gestured to the unpromising mixture in Andrew's bowl.

'You know, that thought had occurred to me too,' Steve cut in. 'There are certainly a lot of fish about, even in the shallows.'

Andrew had noticed that as well. 'They're quite colourful, aren't they? Do you know anything about fishing, then?' he asked Jeremy.

The other man nodded. 'I used to go down the same canal you did. Years ago. And down the coast in the summer.'

Andrew's jaw dropped. 'The *same* canal?'

Jeremy nodded again.

'I didn't know you ever lived in Manchester.'

'Yeah, for a bit. As a teenager. Didn't think much of it, mind. Oh, no offence.'

Andrew was more confused than offended. 'But that makes three of us, don't it?'

'Three what?'

'Coming from Manchester. Everyone seems to come from there. Or Cambridge.'

'Well, you know, that's not strictly true,' Steve said. 'I've only been to the UK once. And that was five years ago. I don't think I went anywhere other than London or Stratford. But I take your point.'

'And he's not the only one,' Jeremy added. 'What about Steph? And Chris. He's Canadian, isn't he?'

'Yeah, but I were talking to him earlier on,' Andrew said. 'Apparently, he went to University in Cambridge. Graduated a couple of years back. He said it were one of his mates what nominated him to come here. And Frankie and Bella live in Cambridge. And Stephanie's related to Frankie. And Jane lives down the road. And then there's you and me from Manchester, and Duncan as well.'

Jeremy acknowledged the truth of this. 'But *I'm* not from Manchester. Londoner born and bred, ain't I? I was only up there for a couple of years. Doing my GCEs.'

'Did you pass?'

The bearded man nodded. 'Yeah, I got a couple.'

'But actually, you know,' said Steve, 'there's quite a simple reason why so many people have connections with Cambridge.'

'Why's that?' Andrew asked.

'Well, because the production company is based there. I was talking to young Frankie about it. The company ran a series of adverts in the Cambridge Gazette. Actually, I think that's the one *I* saw. A friend of mine in England heard I was out of a job and faxed it through to me as a joke.'

Andrew laughed. 'The one my mate Mark saw was in the Manchester Evening News.'

'Well, there you go,' said the Australian. 'That's why the rest of the group are from Manchester.'

Jeremy plopped his ladle back into the pot. 'Come to think of it, it was an old school friend of mine who nominated me. Small world, init?'

Steve smiled. 'You know, you'd think they'd have a wider advertising base than that.'

'And why Manchester if they're all in Cambridge?' Andrew wondered.

The Australian did not reply. It was just one more peculiarity to add to all the others.

'I *would* quite like to have a go at fishing,' Andrew said, suddenly. 'Maybe swim out to that rock.' He glanced at Steve. 'If you don't mind, like.'

Steve smiled. 'Well, you know, I think it's quite a good idea. Why not do it tomorrow? I don't think anyone will object.'

'We can pick up the vegetables and stuff on the way.'

'Why not?' Jeremy grinned. 'It'll make a change from working on that hut of yours. The bloody thing's driving me up the wall. No offence.'

Stephanie McMahon had joined the queue behind Isabel Grant. Andrew moved aside and went over to sit with Frankie and Jane.

'Just in time,' Jeremy breathed. 'We were going to shut up shop.'

Isabel grabbed a bowl. She was wearing a tight blue swimsuit and the Englishman stared lecherously at her breasts as she handed it to him. She pretended not to notice. Steve nodded a greeting to her. 'Where's Duncan?' she asked.

'Probably sleeping off a hangover,' Jeremy said, ladling stew into the bowl.

From behind, Stephanie narrowed her eyes.

'Brought a bottle of booze with him, didn't he?' Jeremy chuckled. 'Whisky. Trust old Duncan. It was good stuff, as well. I saw him having a go at it earlier on. Probably got smashed. I reckon he'll have crashed out somewhere. It wouldn't be the first time.'

'I can't pretend I'm surprised,' Stephanie said.

61

Jeremy shrugged. 'No harm in it, is there? You've got your fags, he's got his booze. Anyway, he's only got the one bottle. Wouldn't have minded a swig of it myself. For medicinal purposes.'

Steve listened to this exchange with some concern. Duncan was entitled to a drink, of course – that was his chosen luxury – but the fact that Sue was absent from the group at the same time was a little worrying. 'Has anyone seen Susan this evening?' he asked. Now that he thought about it, he had not seen her himself for at least a couple of hours.

'I thought she was with you,' Stephanie said.

'Did anyone see her arrive back from the Swimming Pool?'

'I haven't seen her since this afternoon,' Isabel confessed. 'When the two of you went off foraging.'

Steve shouted across to the other diners. Chris and Jane were sitting cross-legged on the sand with Andrew and Francesca. But it appeared that none of them had seen Sue either, not since mid-afternoon. Steve had been the last, when he had left her behind at the Swimming Pool.

'Perhaps she's gone to bed,' Jane Ruddock suggested, trying to be helpful. 'She might have been tired after all that walking.'

Stephanie knew better. 'We've just come from the clearing. She wasn't in her bunk.' Isabel confirmed this with a nod.

'And, you know, Duncan's not here either,' Steve pointed out quietly.

A shudder flickered across the faces of the two women. Everyone had felt the tension between Duncan and Sue. It was not something that was easily ignored. The two Brits had done their best to keep apart but the hostility between them was deep-rooted. Everybody knew there would be a flair up at some point.

Steve had special reason to be concerned. He remembered the fear in Sue's eyes that afternoon in the Grotto. The animosity between Duncan and Sue was more than just bitterness at a failed relationship. The woman had been absolutely terrified. Ever since then, Steve had been keeping a close eye on Duncan Roberts, ready to step in if it ever proved necessary. But Sue had seemed a lot calmer the last day or so. He had taken her decision to go swimming on her own as a sign of growing confidence. Whatever her fears had been, they were becoming less acute with time. Even so, the Australian would not have left her alone had he not been certain that Duncan was working on the other side of the island. Now it transpired he had left the hut site before sun down. Steve had not seen him when he'd arrived back at the clearing. And the man had also been drinking. Perhaps in this state he had wandered aimlessly south and maybe crossed paths with Sue on her way back from the Swimming Pool. It was a realistic possibility. Words might have been exchanged; or perhaps more than just words. Steve grimaced at the thought. This was precisely the kind of situation he had hoped to avoid.

Stephanie shared his concern. 'I suppose we should go and look for her.'

Jeremy was not keen. 'It's getting too dark now. She's probably just got a bit lost.'

'And Duncan?'

The Englishman shrugged. 'He's probably just crashed out somewhere. Sleeping it off.'

'Well, you know, we can at least go and check the clearing again,' Steve suggested. 'One of them might have come back by now.'

Isabel thought that unlikely.

'You never know,' Jeremy said, 'they might have had a reconciliation. Perhaps they won't want to be disturbed.' Stephanie shot him an angry look. The man shrugged. 'Just a thought.'

'We'd better go *now*,' she said, 'before it gets too dark to see anything.'

Steve nodded. Dinner would have to wait.

Francesca Stevens did not sleep well that night. A sense of unease pervaded the camp. How could anyone sleep when the matter of Duncan and Sue was unresolved? Perhaps there had

63

been an accident. One of them might even have been hurt. In this sort of environment, anything could happen. A proper search had not been possible during the night. There were emergency torches in the Grotto but the terrain inland was treacherous. Only a handful of people knew the way to the Swimming Pool and as yet nobody had attempted a night journey. It would be safer, Steve said, to wait until morning. After all, there was some hope that either Duncan or Sue might return to the camp under their own steam.

Now morning had arrived. The sun was glittering gently through the trees as Francesca flicked her eyes open.

Someone else was already up and about.

Stephanie had swung her legs over the side of her bed. That was the noise that had woken her. Stephanie was always one of the first to rise. Frankie watched as the woman got to her feet and padded off into the woods. She was sporting a long green t-shirt and a pair of sunglasses. Her legs were exposed but she didn't appear to be wearing any underwear. Not that it mattered, out in the wild like this.

Francesca rubbed her eyes and sat up. Jane Ruddock was still asleep in a far corner. Isabel Grant was yawning and stretching herself out. Frankie smiled, observing her friend. Isabel had a peculiarly feline quality, a lack of tension in the muscles that belied her character. The girl was no more an early riser than she was.

She remembered the first time they had met. It was four years ago now. They had both been studying French at evening classes. Isabel was working as a stenographer for a legal company. She had just moved to the area. Francesca was a PA in a pharmaceutical firm. This was shortly after her mother had died. Isabel gave up her job and they had both dropped out of French classes in the second year; but they had stayed in touch and now they were good friends.

Isabel raised a hand and stifled a yawn.

Stephanie returned to the glade, carrying an armful of fruit. The Australian had developed a custom of gathering breakfast for the girls first thing in the morning. There was no need for her to do this. Sue thought she was trying to curry favour, but Frankie saw it for the simple kindness that it was. In fact, it was exactly the sort of thing she herself might have done, if she hadn't had such an aversion to getting up early.

Francesca pulled back the netting on her bed-frame and said good morning. Stephanie returned the greeting and offered her an apple and a banana. Frankie took them gratefully. 'Did you sleep well?' she asked, sliding her legs off the platform.

'Actually, no,' Stephanie said.

'Me neither. Is there any sign of them yet?'

The Australian shook her head. 'We'll have to organise a proper search, just as soon as everyone's up.' She waved a hand at Isabel and then looked up suddenly at the sky. 'Oh, perfect!'

Francesca followed her gaze, momentarily perplexed; then she felt a splash of water on her face. 'It's not…?'

Stephanie nodded. 'Steve will be pleased.'

Frankie felt a second splash, then a third. Within half a minute, the rain was falling steadily.

Jane let out a cry from the adjacent bed-frame.

Isabel pulled herself out from underneath her mosquito net.

Stephanie returned to her own bed, where she quickly gathered together her things and pulled on a pair of light grey shorts.

Isabel was already picking up her rucksack. The downpour was becoming heavier by the second. 'We'd better get everything down to the Grotto,' the woman suggested, calling over. 'Before it all gets soaked through.'

Stephanie nodded. 'This is all we need,' she muttered.

The islanders were sprinting for cover.

Steve Bramagh had already stripped down to his swimming trunks. He had risen at first light, intending to go for an early morning run. He had thought about crossing the island, to see if he could locate Sue before the others got up, but a quick look at the sky told him a serious storm was imminent. As soon as he felt the first splash of rain, he packed everything away in his rucksack and brought the lot over to the Grotto for safe keeping.

I ought to gather some firewood as well, he thought. Anything left outside the cave would be soaked through and useless for burning. But the downpour was too intense now. *Everything will be saturated already.*

The rest of the islanders were slow to join him. Some had been asleep when the rain had started and there was a mad scramble to gather things up. But within fifteen minutes most of the group had arrived at the Grotto.

A clap of thunder ricocheted above their heads.

Water was dripping down from the roof of the cave in several areas and small pools were forming on the ground. It was not an ideal place for a gathering. There were few flat surfaces and scarcely anywhere to sit, let alone to stand. The cave was quite large, however, and although the ground was uneven there was plenty of room to store packs.

Several of the group followed Steve's lead and stripped down to their underwear. Stephanie needed to put some on, and Chris Hudson averted his gaze as the attractive blonde pulled off her t-shirt. Only Jane Ruddock allowed modesty to get the better of her. She was far too embarrassed to undress in front of the men and sat shivering in her wet clothes.

Steve lingered at the mouth of the cave, staring out now through a wall of rain at the angry sea and the harsh waves battering the coastline. The sky above was black and deadly. This was the worst kind of tropical storm, he thought, aggressive and unrelenting. There was little prospect of it blowing itself out in a couple of hours.

Isabel was the last of the group to arrive. She had run back to the beach to retrieve Duncan's rucksack, which had been left out in the clearing the previous night. Of the man himself there was still no sign.

Andrew was worried. 'There must have been an accident,' he said. 'There's no way they'd stay out in this.' He had to raise his voice to be heard above the clatter of the rain.

Steve shared his concern. 'You know, rain or no rain, I think we're going to have to go and look for them.'

A flash of lightning illuminated the interior of the cave. It was followed a few seconds later by a low boom.

'You can't go out in this,' Jeremy Fielding said. 'You won't get ten yards.'

'What do you suggest we do?' Stephanie asked.

The man shrugged. 'Just leave them be. They can take care of themselves.'

'Not if they're injured,' Francesca said.

Andrew nodded. 'There's no way they'd have stayed out all night. Not on their own. Something must have happened.' He gazed at the savage torrent of water blocking the mouth of the Grotto. 'I don't mind going and having a look. Little bit of rain never hurt no-one.'

'Good on you,' said Steve. 'You and me then.'

There was another flash of lightning.

'You're nuts,' Jeremy scoffed.

Jane Ruddock flinched as a second boom reverberated.

'He's your friend, not mine,' Andrew pointed out.

'Course he is. But he's always had a bit of a screw loose. Especially when he gets pissed. I'm telling you. He'll have crashed out somewhere last night. He'll just be sleeping it off.'

'In this rain?' Isabel asked, incredulously.

'Not with thunder and lightning as well,' Francesca added.

'And what about Sue?' Stephanie demanded.

Jeremy winked. 'Probably with him.'

The Australian woman could barely conceal her anger. It was such a ridiculous suggestion. 'I hardly think so,' she replied, through gritted teeth.

Jeremy grinned and scratched his beard.

'Well, you know, Andrew,' Steve said, 'there's no time like the present…'

Andrew Baker pulled himself up.

'Be careful,' Frankie warned. 'It'll be quite slippery out there.'

'I'll be all right.' He grinned. But the rainfall was heavier than he had anticipated. 'Oh, bloody hell!' he exclaimed, after he'd stepped outside. It felt like someone had just tipped a bucket of water over his head. Francesca laughed.

Steve followed him out of the cave, crossing his arms over his head to protect himself from the deluge. It did him no good, however. They might as well have been standing underneath a waterfall. Steve removed his sunglasses, but even then his vision was severely impaired. He tried to clear some of the water from his eyes but the raindrops gathered on his eyebrows and gushed down. It was all he could do to blink the water away.

Andrew waved goodbye to the others. 'Won't be long,' he shouted, as the two men moved off together. Almost at once, he lost his footing, but Steve came forward and gave an arm to support him. The track to Candy Beach was fast becoming a quagmire.

'I think we should hit the camp site first and then follow the trail to the Swimming Pool,' Steve suggested. He had to raise his voice to be heard above the noise of the storm. 'We can take a look at the hut along the way.'

These last words were accompanied by another clap of thunder. A gale was blowing in from the sea. The storm was almost directly overhead.

'I hope them walls are all right,' Andrew yelled back. It was possible the wind might batter them down, if the rain hadn't already washed away the foundations. The building had four walls, but as yet there was no roof to keep the weather out. Steve had intended to start work on that today. 'In this weather, anything might happen.'

The Australian tried to be philosophical. 'Well, you know, if it falls down, it falls down. We just start again. I don't think there's much point worrying about it.' They came to the beach, and forked left along the second trail. 'We've got more important things to worry about,' he added.

A few minutes later, they reached the glade. It was now little more than a muddy, water-logged ditch. To Steve's relief, however, the walls of the cabin remained in place.

'I think I'll just take a look inside,' he said, stepping through the open doorway. The interior of the hut was as much of a swamp as everywhere else, but the walls seemed to be holding up and afforded some protection from the biting wind. Steve pushed against the near wall. It felt sturdy under the pressure. 'It looks like it's holding its own,' he called out, squelching clumsily back outside.

'You what?' Andrew yelled. The sound of the rain was now masking out almost everything else. A further clap of thunder added to the roar.

Steve gave a thumbs up sign and gestured to the far side of the cabin. That was the way to Cocoa Beach and the Swimming Pool.

Andrew nodded and followed the Australian around the perimeter of the hut. Rain was lashing hard against them, the droplets stinging at their faces. Steve's swimming trunks were soaked through and Andrew's boxer shorts were more or less invisible against his skin. They might as well have been under water. And then there was the slopping mud, which was six inches deep in some places. Steve was already up to his ankles and whenever he tried to pull a foot out he struggled not to lose one of his trainers.

Best get this over with quickly, he thought.

There was an abrupt cry from behind. Steve looked round. Andrew was standing by the near wall of the log cabin, staring down to his right. There, sitting on the ground, propped up by the wall and with her knees pushed up to her chin, was the shivering, mud-splattered form of Sue Durrant.

They peeled off her wet clothes and wrapped her in a blanket.

'Has she said anything?' Francesca asked, anxiously.

Andrew shook his head. 'She were just like this when we found her.'

Sue was sitting with her back to the rock, staring straight ahead. Stephanie had forced her to drink some water but otherwise the woman had been unresponsive.

Andrew and Steve had had to carry the girl back to the Grotto. As yet, they had no idea what had happened to her. She had not spoken a word. There was no privacy in the cave and the

69

group had all gathered around her, understandably concerned. Sue, however, was staring straight ahead, acknowledging none of them.

The noise of the rain outside was all but omnipresent.

'What did Duncan do to you?' Stephanie asked.

'Hang about!' Jeremy Fielding protested. 'Let's not jump to conclusions.'

'I don't think she's been touched,' Steve observed quietly. 'There was no blood or bruising that I could see.' He had helped Stephanie to remove Sue's clothing.

'You think that's what happened?' Jeremy asked, angrily. 'What, that Duncan tried it on or something? Forced her? What sort of a man do you think he is?'

Stephanie had already made up her mind about that. 'A man who, by your own account, was very, very drunk last night.'

'Drunk's one thing...'

'You know, nobody's making any accusations at the moment,' Steve pointed out calmly. 'As I said, I don't think she's been hurt. At least, not physically.'

'That's something to be thankful for,' Jane Ruddock put in, from over by the rock pool.

'Well, *something's* certainly happened to her,' Francesca said. She knelt down in front of the girl and held her hand gently. 'Sue? You're all right now. Everything's going to be all right.'

Sue moved her head slightly and met Francesca's gaze. Then she let out a cry and buried her head in the woman's arms. Frankie held the girl tightly and began to stroke her still-wet hair.

'I should never have left her on her own,' Steve berated himself.

'You shouldn't blame yourself,' Stephanie told him.

Jeremy was insistent. 'She got lost in the rain. Tripped up or something. I don't know why you're making such a big deal out of this.'

'Shut up, Jeremy!' Francesca snapped.

The man looked away. 'This is nothing to do with Duncan,' he muttered. 'He's not like that. I know him better than any of you do.'

'Better than *her*? Stephanie asked.

Andrew was struggling to follow the flow of inferences flying about. 'Do you think this is what happened before?' he asked Steve, in a whisper. 'Between the two of them. That he forced her or something. Before they came here?'

The Australian was non-committal. 'Well, you know, it's certainly possible. But we can't know anything for sure. It was just the impression I got from talking to Sue earlier on.'

'You should have told us,' Isabel said, reproachfully. 'If Clive Monroe had had the slightest inkling of that sort of thing, Duncan would never have been allowed to stay on the island.'

'I don't believe I'm hearing this.' Jeremy looked away in disgust.

Steve let out a sigh. 'Well, as I say, there isn't actually any proof. I couldn't accuse him without evidence. I only wish Sue had had the confidence to confide in me. That way I could have helped.'

Stephanie came across and put her hand on Steve's shoulder. 'You did everything you could.'

'Blimey! Talk about innocent until proven guilty!' Jeremy snarled. 'He could be out there now, bleeding to death for all you care. I notice you're not sending out a search party for *him*.'

'We've only just got back,' Andrew pointed out.

'And you said he was probably just lying drunk somewhere,' Stephanie said. 'I thought you were happy to leave him be.'

'That was before this. If you're going to start making accusations, then he should be here to defend himself.'

Steve wiped his face with his hands. 'Don't worry, Jeremy. I haven't forgotten about your friend. I think we *should* go and look for him.' He turned to Sue, crouching down in front of her, beside Francesca. 'Sue. Have you got any idea where Duncan might be?' The woman flinched at the sound of his name.

'What more evidence do you need?' Stephanie asked.

'I'm coming with you,' Jeremy said.

The worst of the storm had passed but it was not over yet. The two men moved through the clearing and into the tangle of trees that led to Cocoa Beach. Once they had got past the quagmire of the log cabin, they were able to quicken their pace. Jeremy was sure-footed even in the mud, and he did not protest when Steve broke into a slow jog. Neither man wanted to stay out in the rain for longer than was strictly necessary. The terrain inland was not quite as muddy as the glade and despite the continuing downpour, the islanders made good time. In less than half an hour, they had reached the beach on the other side of the island.

'The Swimming Pool's over that way.' Jeremy gesticulated. But Steve did not need to be told.

The two men headed along the beach and up into the rocks. 'Careful!' the Australian warned. Even when the sun was shining, the surfaces of the boulders were slippery. Now, they were nothing short of lethal. 'I think it's just round here.' Steve wiped the water from his eyes and placed his hand carefully on another rock. Slowly, he hauled himself across.

The Swimming Pool was a little way ahead, out of sight beyond the heavy boulders. Steve squeezed through a narrow gap and came out onto a short plateau. He glanced to his left and stopped abruptly.

A figure lay flat on the rock. His eyes were closed and his head was propped up against a boulder. A pair of shorts and a long-sleeved t-shirt were wet through in the rain. The man's scalp was stained with blood.

It was Duncan Roberts, of course. He was quite dead.

Chapter Five

Only a blanket separated her body from the cold stone floor. Stephanie McMahon was lying uncomfortably on hard rock. The Grotto faced eastward and the light began to illuminate the interior as soon as the sun had fizzled above the horizon. Stephanie could feel the warmth of it on her skin. She opened her eyes and began to stretch out her legs. The horizon was a clear blue now. After a day and a night of unparalleled fury, the storm had finally blown itself out. A strange tranquillity had descended upon the island. The only sounds to be heard were the sea birds in the distance, the gentle lapping of the ocean waves and the slow drip-drip of water from the roof of the cave.

Stephanie sat up and gazed at the sleeping figures around her, in the cramped confines of the Grotto. Andrew was lying with his head on Francesca's shoulder. Jane Ruddock was curled up awkwardly in a corner. Sue Durrant was lying on her front near the entrance. Chris Hudson was bundled up towards the back of the cave and Jeremy Fielding was snoring quietly. Only Steve Bramagh was absent. And Duncan, of course.

Stephanie pulled herself up and stretched her arms above her head. She rubbed her eyes, yawned briefly and took a step towards the mouth of the cave. The early morning sun was powerful and uncompromising. She shielded her eyes and stepped back to grab a pair of sun glasses from her pack. Then she picked her way around the sleeping figures and moved out into the light. She stood for a moment, just outside the Grotto, filling her lungs with the rich, heavily salted air.

Steve Bramagh was standing silently, contemplating the sea. He was a few yards in front of her, a little way along the still muddy pathway that led back to Candy Beach. How long he had been standing there, Stephanie didn't know. She walked over to him and the two Australians greeted each other silently. He was bare-chested, in a pair of red swimming trunks. She was in her bra and knickers from the day before. They stood together for a moment, watching the horizon.

'You know, I sometimes think people miss out, sleeping through the early hours,' Steve reflected. 'I've always thought this was the best part of the day. It's such a peaceful time. Especially in the aftermath of a storm.' He breathed the air deeply. 'I don't think people always appreciate just how good it is to be alive.'

Stephanie said nothing. There was nothing to say. The events of the previous day had exhausted them all; and Steve Bramagh had been at the heart of it. He and Jeremy had single-handedly carried the body back across the island and laid it to rest on Candy Beach. The two men had then returned to the Grotto, in the penetrating rain, to break the news of his death to the rest of the company.

The islanders followed them back to the beach and saw for themselves the battered, lifeless figure of Duncan Roberts.

It was a distressing sight.

Francesca found a blanket and covered him with it, but it was a purely symbolic gesture. It couldn't protect him from the storm or the insects that were bound to infest the body as soon as the rains departed. But it was either that or carrying him back through the mud to the Grotto; and the thought of sharing the cave with a dead man was too much for anyone to bear.

For some minutes, nobody spoke. They were all in a state of shock. Even Steve was visibly upset. Jane broke down and cried. Stephanie just felt numb. She didn't know how to react. It had never occurred to her that somebody might actually *die* on the island. There had been tensions in the group, of course, the petty rivalries and annoyances you would expect in this kind of situation. But nothing serious. Even the genuine animosity between Duncan and Sue had not worried Stephanie unduly. She had just assumed the woman was over-dramatising the situation.

Stephanie *had* been concerned when Sue had disappeared, and was appalled when the girl was found and it looked like she had been assaulted. But the shock of that was as nothing compared to the horror she felt now, seeing the guilty party lying dead not half a mile from the entrance to the Grotto. She stared down at the corpse of Duncan Roberts and felt empty inside. In truth, she had barely known the man. Duncan was not a particularly bright or dynamic individual, so far as she could tell, though he was always polite and he certainly knew how to work. He had been good looking, in a bland sort of way, and given the choice, Stephanie would probably have preferred spending time with him than with his mate Jeremy. But that was before she knew the whole story.

That afternoon, back at the Grotto, Sue Durrant finally felt able to fill in the blanks and the tale she told was as predictable as it was disturbing.

Duncan was a serial rapist. That much Stephanie had already deduced. The man had dragged Sue into the bedroom on their second date, held her down and forced himself on her. Afterwards, she said, she had called the police and the man had been arrested the following day. The case went to court but there were no eye-witnesses or corroborating evidence. It was his words against hers. Duncan claimed she had consented to sex and as there was no sign of bruising the jury had no choice but to believe him. He was acquitted and walked from the courtroom a free man. There were tears in her eyes as Sue told them this.

Jeremy listened silently, his face a mask of blank incomprehension, and for the first time Stephanie felt a twinge of sympathy for him. Evidently, he had known nothing about any of this.

It was only afterwards, Sue continued, that she discovered Duncan had been prosecuted before for sexual offences. Another woman had accused him of rape, two years previously, and on that occasion he had also walked free. But it made no difference. The jury had delivered their verdict. In the eyes of the world he was not guilty. Sue had had no choice but to put the affair behind her and to build herself a new life. It had not been easy.

And now, six years later, she had come to this island – which the group had innocently dubbed 'Paradise' – and Duncan Roberts had come here too.

'Why didn't you say anything?' Stephanie demanded. 'If we'd had any idea…'

'I fight my own battles,' Sue responded angrily. 'I didn't need help. Especially not from a load of gutless strangers.'

Stephanie rolled her eyes. Nobility was one thing. This was outright stupidity. What did the girl expect to happen? If she had just taken the trouble to confide in someone – perhaps had a quiet word with Clive Monroe before the director left – then Duncan would have been expelled from the island and everything would have been fine. But no, she wanted to fight her own battles, and now look what had happened. It was ridiculous. She had behaved in a stupid and reckless manner. It made Stephanie angry to think about it. If Sue had not been in such a delicate state, she would have given the woman a thorough tongue-lashing. But shouting at her now would be counter-productive and Stephanie forced herself to calm down.

Sue still hadn't told them what had happened between her and Duncan the previous evening. Steve was doing his best to draw out the information. 'I have to ask you this, Sue,' he said, gently. 'What happened to you yesterday, after I left you? Did you see him? Did you see Duncan?'

Sue did not look up but she nodded slightly. 'At the Swimming Pool. He was…drunk, I think. He raised his voice at me. Tried to grab me.' There was a brief echo of fear in her eyes as she relived the experience. 'I…dodged past him and scrambled back down onto the beach.'

Steve exchanged glances with Stephanie. *She dodged past him.* Duncan had not succeeded in forcing the girl a second time. Stephanie closed her eyes.

'I thought he was following me, but…I suppose he must have slipped.'

'You didn't go back to check?' Jane Ruddock asked.

Sue glared at the woman. 'Hardly.' There was a flash of the old venom in her voice but it was gone at once. 'I just ran and ran. I was so frightened. I stumbled through the woods. All over the place. Then I ended up in some bay on the west of the island. There's a small beach there. I…I just collapsed and… well, I – don't remember much else.' She shivered. 'I can't believe he's dead. Just like that. He was…' She paused again, her voice turning from horror to hatred in a single beat. 'I just hope he rots in hell.'

'So you weren't there when he banged his head?' Jeremy asked.

Sue blinked. 'I just said so, didn't I?'

'Hey, look, I'm just checking.' The bearded Englishman was more agitated than Stephanie had ever seen him. His usual geniality had all but evaporated.

There was one final issue that needed to be addressed. 'What are we going to do with the body?' It was Francesca who voiced the question.

Steve had already considered this. 'Well, you know, I think there are only really two options. Either we bury him straight away or we wait for Clive and get him shipped back to St. Moreau.'

'Duncan wouldn't care either way,' Jeremy said. 'He didn't believe in God or nothing.'

'I think burial would be better,' Stephanie suggested.

The group reluctantly agreed. The director was not due back on the island for several days and none of them could face the prospect of leaving the body out in the open air until then. It was not as if they had any form of cold storage. The burial, they decided, would take place the following morning.

Now, dawn had arrived. Stephanie gazed out to sea, with Steve standing silently to her left. One thing was still bothering her. Sue hadn't been surprised when the Australian had told her Duncan was dead. 'Do you think she was telling the truth?'

Steve shrugged. 'I don't know. But, you know, I think it's probably best to take things at face value.'

Maybe there had been more of a struggle than the one Sue had described. Perhaps Duncan had fallen back and hit his head on the rock. That would more adequately explain her prolonged absence. Maybe she had felt responsible. Or perhaps it had not been an accident at all. But either way, nobody could seriously blame her. Steve was right. It was better to let things be.

Andrew had never dug a grave before. It was bloody hard work, he found, and muddy too, in the aftermath of the storm. It wouldn't have been so bad, if there had been a spade between the three of them, but nobody had thought to add that to the list of essential items. If a grave had to be dug, it had to be dug more or less by hand. Andrew was not complaining, however. Some things had to be done, spade or no spade.

The grave was situated well away from the beach. Steve picked a spot of open ground a short distance from the clearing where the log cabin was being constructed. The area here was slightly less muddy, but digging out the earth still proved difficult. Every time they dug out a clump of soil, mud would rush in to fill the gap.

Jeremy was holding out his rucksack and Andrew packed the wet earth firmly inside. The hole was now a foot and a half deep and the two men were crouching at the bottom of it. When each rucksack was filled, they would hand it up to Steve, who would empty it out over by the trees. It took a couple of hours, but gradually the grave deepened.

'You know, I think we're just about done,' Steve announced, when the sun reached its apex in the sky.

Jeremy stretched out his arms above his head. 'It ain't anywhere near six feet,' he observed, his head sticking out of the top of the hole. 'But I suppose it'll have to do.' They had hit solid rock and, without a pick axe, there was no hope of digging any further.

The workers were by now caked in mud. Andrew's shorts were a uniform shade of brown and his ginger hair was invisible against the liquid earth clinging to his scalp. Jeremy's green t-shirt had all but disappeared as well, and one of his trainers had been lost in the thick mud. Hopefully they would find it later, when the place dried out a little.

'Can you give us a hand up?' Andrew called to Chris Hudson. 'I can't get a grip.' Steve Bramagh joined the Canadian, grabbing Andrew under the arms and yanking him upwards out of the hole. The young man scrabbled to find a footing on level ground. Once he was firmly beached, Chris and Steve went back to help Jeremy.

Andrew got to his feet and attempted to wipe some of the mud from his face with his hands; but they were just as dirty as the rest of him. He looked back at the grave. 'Are we going to bung his rucksack in there inall?'

Steve shook his head. 'I think we'd better keep that. Clive might want to return it to his relatives, if he has any.'

Andrew nodded sadly. A sudden thought occurred to him: they would all be going home soon. *There's no way we can stay here now.* The production company would have to abandon the whole project. They could not carry on now that one of the group was dead. *Poor bugger,* Andrew thought. Duncan Roberts had been a horrible man. What he had done to Sue was unforgivable and he deserved to spend a long time in prison. But even Duncan shouldn't have had to die in a place like this. Not thousands of miles away from home, all alone, with no-one to grieve for him. It wasn't right.

'You'd better go down to the Grotto and get cleaned up,' Steve suggested. 'I'll go and see how Stephanie's getting on.'

Stephanie and Francesca had been disassembling Duncan's A-frame. They wanted to use part of the mattress as a stretcher, to carry the body over from the beach. They had already wrapped the corpse with a few spare blankets, in preparation for the funeral. It was not a pleasant task.

Andrew was much happier digging the grave. Until yesterday, he had never even seen a dead body. When he had caught sight of the corpse on the beach, it had taken all his self control not to throw up.

After the diggers had cleaned themselves up, the ceremony proper began. Steve and Jeremy carried the makeshift stretcher from the beach to the grave site. Andrew and the others followed on behind. Stephanie had tied vines around the edge of the wooden stretcher so the corpse could be lowered into the hole. Otherwise, they would simply have had to drop him in there. Andrew and Francesca lent a hand. The vines were not long enough to lower the body the whole way into the grave, however, and the four pallbearers had to bend forward and ease the mattress down at arms length. Despite their care, there was still an audible splash when the wooden rack hit bottom.

Jeremy Fielding had agreed to say a few words.

Sue was sitting some distance away, over by the hut. She was looking up at the sky, not watching the proceedings.

Jeremy cleared his throat. 'I'm not religious or nothing,' he said. 'Neither was he. He…I hadn't seen him in years. He was…well, you know, he was the same old Duncan. Same bloke I went to school with. I didn't know nothing about…about all this stuff with Sue and him. I know he got angry quite a bit and he never could hold his drink, but…I don't know. He…he always seemed to mean well. I mean, I know what he did was wrong. There's no getting away from it, is there? But sometimes you just get screwed up inside. Sometimes you don't really understand…you don't realise…' Jeremy was struggling to find the words. He let out a sigh. 'Oh, I don't know. What can I say? He was my mate. He was…I wish he hadn't died. I wish he'd just turned round and gone straight home the day he got here.' Jeremy paused for a second, not wanting to end on that note. 'Anyway,' he mumbled, 'rest in peace, Dunc. If you can.'

'Amen,' Jane Ruddock added quietly.

Jeremy leaned over and picked up a handful of mud, which he threw awkwardly into the grave. Andrew came forward and did the same. Sue Durrant sat and watched from the clearing as each of the islanders took their turn. She did not join in, but once they had finished she got up and rejoined the group.

Steve and Jeremy stayed behind to fill in the hole. There was plenty of mud nearby. 'I'll give you a hand,' Andrew mumbled sadly.

There was no work done that day. There was not even a formal meal in the evening. Everybody collected their own food. Nobody talked. People wanted to be alone with their thoughts.

Francesca Stevens had been down to the Grotto to refill her water bottle. Stephanie had been there, smoking her daily cigarette. The girls exchanged a few words but Frankie got the impression the Australian wanted to be left alone.

She made her way back to the beach.

A few of the islanders were lying out on the sand.

Jeremy was sitting up, staring out to sea. Francesca had never seen him so lacking in animation. The man turned his head when she padded over to him. He acknowledged her presence but it was clear he didn't want to talk either. Frankie could understand that. She remembered what it had been like when her mother had died.

Sue Durrant, who was stretched out on a towel fifty yards further along, was blunter still. 'Piss off and leave me alone,' she scowled, when Francesca asked her how she was feeling. 'This is the happiest day of my life.'

Perhaps it would be better to go back to the clearing, she thought. It was unlikely to rain again any time soon and she could lie on her bunk and read for a while. There was nothing much else to do. Her book was in her backpack, which she had brought over to the glade earlier on. She only had a few chapters left, though she knew she would not be able to concentrate.

She arrived at the clearing a few minutes later. Jane was already there, sat on her mattress, her face in her hands. She looked up as Frankie came into view through the trees. Their eyes met briefly. Jane did not attempt to smile.

'Where is everybody?' Francesca asked.

'I think...I think some of the men went off to the Swimming Pool to get properly cleaned up.'

Frankie nodded. Andrew had said. The poor lamb was still covered head to foot in mud. On any other day, the sight of him like that would have made her smile.

Jane was looking up at the sky. 'At least the sun's come out. What a terrible day. That poor man.'

Francesca smiled sadly. She moved across to her bed-frame. The netting was still wet, so she pulled it up and wound it around the cross beam at the top. Then she took out the book from her pack and settled down onto the mattress.

Jane was taking a sip of water. 'What are you reading?' she asked.

Frankie held up the cover. *The Secret Garden*. It's always been one of my favourites.' She gazed up at the sky. The branches of the trees loomed over her from the edge of the clearing. 'I wish I'd brought something else,' she said.

Isabel Grant went for a walk that evening with Steve Bramagh. It was the Australian who had suggested it. It was just about the only thing they could reasonably do on a day like this. In any case, there were parts of the island still to be explored and it looked like this would probably be their last opportunity.

Isabel did not talk much, but she seemed content to walk quietly alongside him. Steve enjoyed her company. He had always been a people person, but sometimes it was nice to get away from the babble of conversation. Not that there was much to speak of that afternoon.

They cut west from the centre of the island. Steve was curious to see if he could locate the bay where Sue Durrant had found refuge from the storm.

'I think she said it was over this way somewhere.'

'Do you believe her story?' Isabel asked.

Steve tried to be diplomatic. 'Well, you know, I have no reason to disbelieve it.'

'She didn't seem surprised when you told us he was dead.'

'It's difficult to judge people's reactions in a situation like that.'

Isabel smiled slightly. 'I think you handled things very well.'

The compliment was unexpected. 'Well, you know, when you've had experience of these kind of situations, you learn how to deal with them.'

Isabel nodded. She did not ask the obvious follow-up question.

'I've certainly had to cope with a few tricky situations,' Steve volunteered. 'Over the years. You know, I had a guy working for me at Automotive a few years back. He was in what they call a "work-related accident". He'd taken the safety guard off a machine to get at some parts. Pulled the wrong lever. Got caught up in the mechanism. It was quite nasty, I can tell you.'

'He died?'

'I had to tell the family. And they blamed the company, of course. And sued us for negligence. It was understandable. It was quite an awkward situation. But you know, these kind of things happen all the time. It's difficult to apportion blame. Sometimes you've just got to say "it's no-one's fault" and let it go.'

'Sometimes,' Isabel agreed.

Steve thought he detected an undercurrent there. 'You've gone through something similar, have you?'

'Not exactly.' Isabel brought a hand up to a silver chain which she wore around her neck.

'But an accident.'

'Yes.' She looked away.

Steve could see the woman was reluctant to confide in him, but he persevered. He felt oddly keen to find out more about her. 'Who was it?' he asked.

Isabel hesitated. 'My…sister, Susanna. She was killed in a car accident. She was just crossing the road. The lights had gone red but the car didn't stop.'

'I'm sorry.'

'It was a few years ago. The doctors said she didn't suffer.'

'Still, it's not easy losing someone close.' Steve had been through something similar himself. 'My brother David died when I was just a kid. Fell out of a tree. It was nobody's fault. I think it's worse when it's like that. When there's no-one to blame.'

Isabel was silent for a moment. 'I don't think anyone will grieve for Duncan,' she said.

The Australian shrugged. 'Perhaps not. But, you know, I think we should. Everyone should grieve when someone dies. No matter what you thought of them.'

'Any man's death diminishes me.' Isabel recognised the source of the idea.

'Exactly. You know, I've always believed that each person is absolutely unique. And when something unique vanishes from the world, I think that's a sad thing.'

83

Isabel laughed. Steve looked at her in surprise. It was a beautiful, melodious sound. 'I never knew you were this philosophical,' she said. 'You always struck me as being the practical type.' Her large brown eyes were mocking him gently.

Steve grinned. 'Well, you know, you can be practical and philosophical at the same time. I like to keep active, but I like to do things that are constructive as well. And that usually requires some degree of thought.'

Isabel nodded. 'But I don't agree with you about Duncan. I think we're better off without him. He's better off dead.'

'I think that's a little harsh.'

'Not harsh. Just pragmatic. If you're really concerned about the inner-torment of a rapist, or a murderer, say, then you can rest easy knowing he's finally at peace. And the rest of us who are not so sympathetic can take comfort from knowing he's not going to hurt anybody ever again.'

'So I take it you don't believe in the possibility of redemption?'

'Not for someone like that. People are born that way. Most ordinary human beings could never behave like that.'

Steve disagreed. 'In my experience, ordinary people are capable of doing just about anything. We can all go off the rails if there's enough provocation.'

'I don't believe that.'

'Oh, I've come across quite a few examples. When I was studying psychology. And, you know, it wasn't always the poor, deprived kids who ended up committing the worst crimes. Sometimes it was the calmest, most rational people you could imagine.'

'People like you?'

Steve laughed. '*Especially* people like me.'

It was not difficult to find the bay. Sue had given them surprisingly precise directions. The beach was narrow, as she had said, and the two islanders stepped out onto near virgin sand. If Sue had been here two days earlier, her footsteps had long since washed away.

Steve and Isabel sat together facing the sea. The sun was setting in a spectacular fashion. The sky had turned a brilliant purple and the vestiges of daylight continued to play across the clouds long after their source had faded from view.

And in the fading light, the two islanders held each other gently and made love.

Chapter Six

The next day, everyone returned to work.

Several large beams had been laid across the top of the walls. Stephanie McMahon was on her knees, several feet above the ground, tying one of the beams to the triangular support on the left side of the log cabin. The group had only just started work on the roof and there was a great deal remaining to do. Clive Monroe was due back the following morning and the islanders wanted to finish the hut before he arrived. This was a tall order. They didn't have time to build a scaffold so constructing the roof was a precarious proposition. And even if they did finish it, nobody would have any time to enjoy the place. That was hardly the point, however. The islanders needed something to occupy themselves with. Working on the log cabin helped to pass the time and took their minds off other matters. That, as far as Stephanie was concerned, was justification in itself.

A large trunk of wood was lying on the ground alongside the near wall. This would stretch the length of the building and form the centre piece of the roof. Getting that into place would be the most difficult part of the whole enterprise. Every pair of hands would be needed to lift the trunk onto the top of the wall. It had taken five people just to drag it out of the forest. But the group were working well together now.

Somebody had to collect food for the evening meal, though, so Andrew and Jeremy were exempted from the grand task. At the moment, they were still in the clearing, busily making preparations for their fishing expedition. Jeremy had rallied to the idea, no doubt as a distraction, and the two Brits were working busily to prepare some make-shift fishing rods. The expedition was not an entirely frivolous exercise. They would be gathering food along the way and that would serve as the bulk of the evening meal. If they managed to catch a fish or two as well, it would be a bonus; and a memorable last supper for all of them.

Stephanie glanced down at the two men from on high. They were emptying out their packs in readiness for the trip. Jeremy was scratching his head.

'What have you lost?' Andrew asked.

'My water bottle. I left it in the Grotto yesterday. You haven't seen it, have you?'

Andrew shook his head.

'Bugger. Can't find it anywhere.'

Stephanie smiled inwardly. Jeremy was not the most organised of men. 'You can take mine,' she shouted down to him. The sooner those two got going the better. Jeremy was spending more time staring up at her arse than he was making preparations. 'It's just down there,' she said. 'I filled it up after breakfast.'

Jeremy mimed astonishment. He had obviously not expected any favours from the Australian woman. *I'm not completely heartless*, she felt like telling him. Even she wouldn't begrudge Jeremy Fielding a bottle of water. Now that the clouds had departed, the Pacific sun had returned with avengeance.

Jeremy found the spare bottle and smiled up at her. 'Thanks, love.' He winked.

Stephanie gave a disapproving tut and returned to her work.

The Englishman placed the water in his pack and glanced at Andrew Baker. 'You got your sun tan cream?' he asked, cruelly.

Andrew's face was a uniform shade of red. 'I've got me t-shirt,' he replied, with a grin.

'That'll have to do.'

He gave a quick wave to Francesca and the two men headed off. *Not before time*, Stephanie thought.

Jane Ruddock was beside her on the roof, busily tying up a piece of vine. 'Do you think they'll catch anything?'

I doubt it. They were not exactly professional fishermen and their tackle was rather basic. 'Let's hope so,' she said.

Jane was in a reflective mood. 'I suppose it will be our last meal together.'

'Very probably.' Once Clive Monroe arrived and learnt that one of the islanders had died, there would be no choice but to call a halt to the entire project. It was not as if they were doing any filming now anyway. 'That's why Steve wants to get the hut finished,' Stephanie explained.

That was why they were both balanced precariously on top of a wall some two metres above the ground. That was why they had been working so furiously since breakfast. There were only a few hours left to complete the log cabin. Sadly, it now seemed unlikely that they would succeed. There was too much left to do. *Steve will be disappointed*, Stephanie thought. The man had set his heart on finishing the hut. But the truth was the islanders would be lucky to get the infrastructure of the roof in place before sundown, let alone any kind of improvised thatch.

Stephanie looked across at Sue, who was propped up awkwardly in the far corner. She frowned. Sue had not spoken to anyone all morning. Stephanie was surprised the Englishwoman had even agreed to join the work party. Steve was passing some spare vine up to her but Sue did not meet his eye. She lifted the wood into place and continued with her work. *Stupid girl.* Stephanie looked away. *She only has herself to blame.*

Against all the odds, it was a glorious success.

They had dug out some proper bait before they had swum away from Cocoa Beach to the Rocks and in all probability this was what had made the difference. Jeremy cannibalised some of the cord from Duncan's bed-frame to use as a fishing line and even though they had no proper hooks on the end it was only a couple of hours before they got their first bite.

Andrew was ecstatic. 'Just wait 'til I tell Frankie.'

It was the first of several catches over the course of a long afternoon. Most of the fish were little more than tiddlers, but the last proved a monster. In fact, it was the nastiest looking marine animal Andrew had ever clapped eyes on. The cord had almost broken, trying to reel the thing in. 'What is it?' he asked.

Jeremy had no idea. 'Don't matter, really, does it? Ugly looking sod.' He gazed down at the creature's bulging head and winked at it. 'I'm sure it'll taste good anyway.' The Londoner was beginning to regain some of his former vigour.

Andrew slipped the fish into a small plastic bag with the others. It seemed daft, but they needed the bag to carry the fish back through the water. It would be a bit tricky having to swim with the thing in one hand but it was the only way Andrew could think of to get the food back to the mainland. On the way out, he had been able to stuff the bag under the elastic of his swim shorts.

'Tell you what,' the other man suggested, obviously thinking along the same lines, 'why don't we have a race? Last one back carries everything.' So saying, Jeremy took a step forward and launched himself into mid-air from the top of the rock. Andrew stared open-mouthed as Jeremy plunged some three metres to the ocean below. There was a huge splash as he hit the water.

'Hang on!' Andrew exclaimed. He saw Jeremy bob to the surface below, grinning broadly. The younger man fastened the plastic bag as tightly as he could and dived in afterwards. He had no intention of being beaten in a race.

It was a close call. Jeremy had a head start and was a strong swimmer. Andrew had a bag full of fish to carry and was some metres behind; but he also had youth and determination on his side. It took a little under five minutes to catch his rival and then overtake him. Ten minutes after that, Andrew ran out onto the golden sand of Cocoa Beach, laughing, a good ten metres ahead of his opponent.

Jeremy staggered forward, pulling himself up, coughing and spluttering. 'Just a fluke,' he protested, laughing.

Andrew shook his head. He was grinning from ear to ear. 'I beat you fair and square.'

Jeremy did not have the breath to argue. He collapsed onto the sand and took a succession of long, hard gulps. 'I'm not as fit as I used to be,' he gasped, looking up.

Andrew fell down next to him. 'Me neither.' He could feel his heart pounding in his chest. 'Hey, you know what we've forgotten, don't you?'

'Forgotten?'

'Aye.' Andrew closed his eyes. 'We've only gone and left the fishing rods behind!'

The two men gave themselves a short time to recover before heading back to the glade. They arrived mid-afternoon and were greeted like returning heroes. Everybody cheered when Jeremy pulled out the largest of the fish and held it aloft. The workers clambered down from the hut and swarmed around the two men. This was probably going to be their last night on the island. Everyone was determined to make the most of it.

Work was abandoned, with the roof still unfinished, and the islanders ran down to Candy Beach and threw themselves into the sea. They splashed about, played a few games and giggled like schoolchildren. Then Chris and Frankie ran off to the Grotto to fetch the radio and those who were not on cooking duty started dancing on the beach. It was a bizarre sight. The sun was sinking now and most of the group were soaking wet and barely dressed. The sand flies would be out at any moment, but no-one gave a damn. It was going to be one long party. None of them had any suitable clothes, so most of the men went bare-chested. Francesca and Isabel dug out some brightly coloured bikinis from the bottom of their packs. Jeremy did a striptease. Even Jane Ruddock got into the spirit of things and tore a couple of slits into her medium length skirt. In the aftermath of so much horror, the islanders were determined to have a good time on their last night. The bizarre, crackled music from the radio only enhanced the mood of celebration.

Andrew was in his element. He saw Sue Durrant sitting apart and with a wide grin he skipped over and asked her to dance.

'Piss off,' she said. She was still wearing a sweater and a pair of trousers. She had not been impressed by Jeremy Fielding's obscene antics earlier on.

'You might as well,' the young man insisted, proffering his hand. 'Dinner won't be for ages and there's nowt else to do.'

Sue looked up at him coldly but she took his hand and within minutes was dancing along with the others. Later on, she even took off a few of her clothes. Andrew was well pleased. He winked at Francesca and she nodded her approval.

Jeremy had by now focused his attention on Isabel Grant. No doubt he would have preferred to dance with Stephanie but the Australian was on cooking duty and the bearded Englishman seemed happy enough with the substitute. Isabel was wearing a yellow two-piece bathing costume and was proving to be an excellent dancer.

Jane Ruddock was by far the liveliest of them, however. Once she got going, the middle aged woman put the rest of the islanders to shame. Andrew had never seen her so animated. She was like a teenager on the dance floor. It was fantastic. She was really starting to let her hair down. 'I haven't danced like this in years,' she admitted. Her face was suffused with sweat, but she was smiling broadly.

'We should have done this before,' Andrew thought.

'It's too exhausting,' she protested.

The song ended and Jane moved to the side-lines to grab her water bottle. She pulled off the lid and took several large gulps. 'That's better.' She wiped her mouth and sat down on the sand. 'I'm starting to feel dizzy.'

Andrew grabbed his own canteen.

Jeremy came across. 'Dropping out already?' he laughed. 'I don't know. No stamina, kids these days.' He winked at Jane.

'We're just having a little break,' she explained, screwing the lid back onto her bottle.

Andrew offered Jeremy some water. 'I'm looking forward to dinner,' he said. 'I'm absolutely famished.'

'Me too.' Jeremy took a swig from the other man's canteen.

Andrew glanced over at the two Australians, who were hard at work over a small fire. It was a shame anyone had to cook this evening.

'I was very impressed you managed to catch those fish,' Jane said. 'I don't think I could have caught anything at all.'

'Just a knack,' Jeremy confided breezily. 'You've just got to know how.'

Andrew was more modest. 'You need a lot of luck as well.'

A jabbering voice on the radio gave way to another piece of music. Jane grimaced. If anything, the new song had an even faster beat to it. 'I really do feel exhausted,' she said. A bright red face was a testament to her exertion. 'I think I'm going to have to sit this one out.'

'Please yourself,' laughed Jeremy. 'Come on Andy. You're not giving up, are you?'

'No way!' the young man exclaimed. He was having the time of his life.

It was a couple of hours before dinner was served.

The Australians were in two minds how to cook the fish. It could not be placed directly on the fire as there was no foil to wrap it up in. Neither was there a grate to hang above the flames, so the fish couldn't easily be fried or grilled. It was possible to skewer them, of course, and hold the fish close to the flames, but in the end, Stephanie had gone for the easy option. She had cut the fish into small pieces and plopped them into the water to boil. Dinner would be a stew as usual, but stew with added fish.

Stephanie was not pleased at having to cook, while everybody else was busy enjoying themselves. She didn't like cooking at the best of times. And after working all day in the blazing sunshine on top of the log cabin the fair-haired Australian thought she deserved a bit of a break. But no, she had to slave over a hot fire instead. Such was life.

There were compensations. Steve Bramagh was helping her out and she always enjoyed his company. The two were firm friends now. Stephanie admired the man's intelligence and his ability to get things done. Steve seemed to like her strength and her forthright nature. They certainly made a good team. Stephanie had thought about taking things further but there was no point now, not when everyone was preparing to leave the island. This evening, she was content just to pass the time of day with him.

There was some fun to be had watching the other islanders making fools of themselves on the beach. The group had never been so relaxed. It was remarkable. If Stephanie had not known better, she would have sworn somebody had spiked the water.

Andrew Baker was throwing himself around like a maniac, absolutely in his element. His energy seemed unrelenting. Francesca Stevens was matching him move for move, however, and she had far more grace and poise than the uncoordinated Mancunian.

Isabel might have passed as a professional dancer. She moved with a steady, regulated precision which was fascinating to watch, though she lacked any real passion. Jeremy – dancing alongside her – was also engrossed in her performance, but it was not her necklace he was staring at as she swayed to the beat.

Arsehole, Stephanie thought.

Steve had adopted the role of head chef and Stephanie was happy to let him take charge. They chatted amiably as they worked. Steve was in a contemplative mood, oddly detached from current events. The fact that the hut had not been completed did not appear to bother him. He was more focused on the logistics of leaving the island the following day. He seemed to be in the process of mentally detaching himself. It was as if the man had already moved on. On reflection, Stephanie thought this was probably a sensible attitude to take.

'Where will you go when we leave?' she asked. 'Back home?' Steve had sold his house in Queensland, she knew, but he still had connections there; not least a string of ex-girlfriends. He had been quite open about his personal life. It was one of the things Stephanie found most attractive about him.

'Well, you know, that would be the easy thing,' he said. 'But I think I've set my heart on travelling. It's been a good few years since I spent a really long time away. I need to get back into that, I think. It's just a shame it hasn't worked out here.' He leaned forward and tested the stew. 'What about you? Have you had any thoughts?'

'I'm not sure,' Stephanie admitted. 'I've been thinking perhaps Nepal and the Himalayas. I still have a little money left.'

'You don't fancy going home either?'

Stephanie shook her head. She had nothing to go home to. 'What time do you think Clive will get here tomorrow?'

'Well, you know, I think probably quite early. He struck me as being an early bird.'

Stephanie nodded. On the morning of their arrival the director had woken them all at the crack of dawn. She remembered how angry Sue had been. It was her first memory of the girl. And of Clive, come to that. As with Steve, the Australian woman had not had a formal interview. She had met him first, very briefly, on St. Moreau, and then properly when they had flown out to the boat.

'That man's got a lot to answer for,' she muttered. Clive Monroe would not be expecting the icy reception he would receive the following morning. There were serious questions that had to be answered and Stephanie was not prepared to mince words. Someone somewhere was playing a very dangerous game, setting the islanders up before they had even arrived and then playing them off against each other. Duncan and Sue. Stephanie and Francesca. Even Steve and Andy. Yes, it would certainly be interesting to see the director's reaction when he was confronted with all this. And more importantly, when he was confronted with the news that one of them was dead.

'Go easy on him.' Steve said. 'You know, he's going to get an awful lot of flack over this. Not least of all from Sue. And I honestly don't think it's his fault.'

'You really think he's just been caught in the middle?' Stephanie peered at Steve through the smoke of the fire. Evidently, he did believe just that. 'Then he's even more stupid than I thought he was. What kind of credulous idiot doesn't notice that half his islanders are related? He was responsible for the selection process. How could he not have realised?' At least if Clive had set them all up himself Stephanie could have admired his nerve. But if the director was as gullible as Steve seemed to think then he obviously wasn't qualified to do the job.

Steve let out a sigh.

'I'll hear what he's got to say,' Stephanie reassured him. Unlike certain other people, she would never allow herself to be critical without good reason.

'That's all I ask,' Steve said. He took another mouthful of stew. 'You know, I think this is just about done. I'll turn the radio down and give the word.' So saying, he moved away and a few moments later the announcement was made: dinner was served.

The islanders gradually pulled themselves away from the dance floor – or the patch of sand that had served that function – and began to form a queue. Chris Hudson was at the front of it. He was always at the front when it came to dishing out food. He handed his bowl to Stephanie.

'I don't know what this is going to taste like,' she admitted ruefully.

'It looks great,' the Canadian said. 'I'm getting to kind of like this stuff.'

Dickhead, Stephanie thought. *Stop staring at my tits.* He was one person she was not going to miss.

Behind him, Jane Ruddock had stumbled slightly.

'Here, mind out!' Jeremy exclaimed. He extended an arm and helped Jane to regain her balance.

'I'm so sorry. I'm feeling a bit light-headed.'

'Need to get some food in you,' he advised.

She nodded. 'Yes, I'm sure that's it.' She stepped forward and handed a bowl to the cook.

Stephanie filled it from the pot. 'There'll be enough for seconds,' she said. The fish added volume as well as texture to the stew.

Jane shook her head. 'I don't think I'll be able...' She stopped mid-sentence. Her eyes had glazed over. She swallowed deeply and dropped the bowl. The hot stew smothered across the sand. Jane waved her hands uncertainly. Her legs began to fall away and suddenly her body crumpled beneath her and she thudded to the ground.

'I'm sorry to be so much trouble,' Jane mumbled as Frankie lifted her legs up onto the mattress. 'I don't know what's come over me.'

'It's not any trouble,' the girl reassured her. 'We all get a bit dizzy from time to time.'

Francesca had volunteered to put Jane to bed. The combination of frenetic exercise, heat and the stresses of the last few days had proved too much for the woman. She was probably not used to dancing like that. Jane had thrown up a couple of times on the way to the clearing, after she had fainted on the beach. No doubt the local food was partly to blame. Most of the islanders had suffered a little from the change in diet.

'Steve's gone to get you some paracetamol. He won't be more than a minute. Then you can get off to sleep.'

'I do feel tired,' Jane admitted, in a whisper. She laid back on the mattress and closed her eyes.

Frankie had to squint to see the frame of the bed. The glade was dark and the trees loomed over her, their eerie shadows silhouetted against the starry sky. *I hope Steve doesn't take too long.* She shivered. She did not envy him his after hours visit to the Grotto.

Jane cleared her throat.

'Do you still feel sick?' Francesca asked, crouching down. She was a little concerned the woman might start retching again. That was never a good idea when you were lying on your back.

'Not quite so dizzy,' Jane muttered timidly. 'But I do feel rather hot.'

Frankie put a hand to her forehead. It was soaked with sweat. 'You do have a bit of a temperature,' she observed, with some concern. 'It might be some kind of fever…'

This suggestion provoked alarm from her patient. 'Oh, I do hope not. I always cope so badly with illness.'

'I'm sure it's nothing to worry about.'

Jane coughed. 'Robert used to get so angry with me. I do get rather flustered when I'm not feeling well.' Robert was

Jane's ex-husband. Francesca had heard all about him. He had been a university professor. He'd taught history or something. They had been married for twenty years, then he had run off with one of his students. Jane had been devastated. She had still been deeply in love.

'I'm sure everything will be fine,' Frankie said. She pulled down the mosquito net and tucked it in underneath the woollen blanket. Another thought occurred to her. 'Actually, it could be sun stroke.' Jane's face was certainly a shade redder than normal, or had been when she had last had a proper glimpse of it back on the beach. 'Maybe you should drink some water. Do you feel thirsty?'

A bright light arced through the undergrowth, before Jane had a chance to reply. It flickered across the trees and onto the two figures in the clearing.

'Who's that?' Francesca called out.

'It's only me.' Steve Bramagh flicked the light upwards and Frankie caught a glimpse of the man's amiable, bespectacled face. 'I thought I might as well break out the emergency lighting while I was down at the cave.' He held a large rubber torch in his hand.

'Good idea.' Francesca brought her hand to her face to cut out the glare projecting from the pathway.

'I've brought her pack as well,' Steve said, moving forward. 'I thought she might want something to drink.' He placed the bag down next to the bed-frame and pulled a small medicine bottle from his shirt pocket. He uncapped it and shook a couple of tablets into his hand.

'That was thoughtful.' Frankie crouched down next to the rucksack. She reached inside and produced a canteen of water. It was large and metallic. She unscrewed the lid. Jane would need something to wash the pills down with.

Steve tugged away part of the netting from underneath her blanket and handed Jane the two tablets. 'I think these might do the trick,' he said. The woman sat up and grabbed the flask from Francesca. She popped the pills into her mouth and took a swig of water. She screwed up her face and swallowed the tablets with some difficulty.

97

'You know, Jane, you shouldn't over work yourself like this,' Steve said. He put a hand to her forehead and frowned slightly. 'You were well on the way to making yourself indispensable.'

The woman responded with a weak smile.

Steve glanced across at Frankie. 'I think we'd better leave her to get some sleep.'

Jane nodded. 'You go and rejoin the party. Both of you. I'll be fine.' She coughed slightly.

Francesca helped her to lie back down on the bed, then tucked the mosquito net in a second time. 'We'll check up on you a little later,' she promised. 'I'll try not to wake you up.'

'I am sorry to cause you all this trouble…'

'It's no trouble at all,' Steve reassured her. 'You just get some rest.' He moved away.

Frankie rose up from the bed to follow him. Steve swirled the torch back onto the pathway and Francesca moved into the light. The trail was a lot easier to follow with proper illumination. Coming from the beach earlier on, she had stumbled slightly and nearly walked into a tree. Now she could see the path quite clearly.

A little way along, the Australian stopped her, placing a gentle hand on her shoulder. 'Do you know if anyone's been near the medical kit recently?' he asked. The torch was still shining straight ahead.

Frankie didn't know what to make of the question. 'Not that I know of. Why?'

Steve scratched his head. 'It's just that the seal was broken on the pack. It was already open when I got to it.'

'Is anything missing?'

'Not that I can tell. But I only had time for a quick look.'

Francesca considered for a moment. 'Perhaps somebody needed a plaster,' she suggested. The islanders were forever getting minor cuts and bruises. Frankie had a dozen or more herself. 'Ask the others tomorrow.'

Steve waved his hands dismissively. 'I don't suppose it matters.'

There was no sign of Clive Monroe.

Andrew had gathered together his possessions, stuffed them into his backpack and brought it across to Candy Beach. It had taken less than ten minutes. The other islanders followed his lead and they all settled down together on the sand to wait for the director.

It was mid-morning, perhaps ten o'clock or later, but Clive was nowhere to be seen. None of the group knew if he would be coming by boat or helicopter. A boat, presumably, though according to Steve the yacht they had originally flown out to had only been rented for a few days.

Andrew stifled a yawn and rubbed his eyes gently. The balding director would arrive soon enough.

Like most of the others, Andrew had not gone to bed until the early hours and now he was having difficulty staying awake. 'Stupid-o-clock,' someone had called it. Nobody had realised they would have to get up early the next morning. The first inkling Andrew had had was when Steve came over and started shaking him. That was at six thirty. The sun had just risen but the man was convinced Clive would arrive first thing. Andrew had stumbled over to the Grotto, half asleep, and gathered his things.

He was scarcely more awake now.

It had been one hell of a night, he thought, with a smile. He could not believe it was possible to have so much fun without getting drunk. It was bloody marvellous. Everyone had got into the spirit of things. The Australians had joined in once the dinner things had been cleared away. And after a few false starts Chris Hudson had even managed to find some decent pop music on the radio. The islanders had danced and danced and danced, until most of them had collapsed from exhaustion. And then, best of all, Andrew and Francesca had fallen into each others' arms and kissed for the very first time. Everyone saw it happen. It was fantastic. Andrew had not wanted to let her go.

Part of him now was hoping Clive would not turn up. He was on a high. He wanted to stay on the island with Francesca and hold her in his arms forever. He didn't want to leave just when things were beginning to happen. The thought of it made his stomach tighten. But of course it would not be right to stay here. Not after what had happened to Duncan. And not with Jane Ruddock ill. The islanders *had* to leave. Andrew just hoped he would be able to keep in touch with Frankie when they got back to England. Manchester was not *that* far from Cambridge and he would not allow their relationship to falter just as it was getting started.

The company ate breakfast in virtual silence. They drank lime juice from one of the cooking pots and Stephanie McMahon went off for a while to gather some fruit. According to Francesca, she did this every morning for the girls in the clearing. Andrew was pleasantly surprised. He would not have pictured her doing something like that. Perhaps Stephanie was not as cold as she liked to appear. She had even gone out of her way to take some fruit over to Jane.

Andrew took a bite of his apple. It was sour but he was getting used to the taste. He had adapted more quickly to the local food than some of the others. In fact, he quite liked some of it. The bananas in Paradise tasted much nicer than the ones he got at home. And he had never eaten so many coconuts in his life.

Steve was pacing up and down the beach front, his feet grinding a deep furrow into the sand. His frustration was understandable. *Doesn't like standing around, having to wait.* The man had been so certain that Clive would arrive early; but it was nearing midday and there was still no trace of the illusive director.

Andrew heard a soft patter of footsteps from behind. He looked round and saw Francesca bounding across the sand. Their eyes met and she smiled shyly.

'How's Jane?' he asked. Frankie had just been to get her some more water. Her condition had not improved during the night. She was still resting on her bed-frame in the glade.

Francesca drew up beside him. 'Still the same. Feverish. And she's been throwing up quite a lot. Steve said not to give her any more food.'

'She's got to eat some time,' Andrew thought. He scratched his arm. A small insect had landed on him, but he brushed it away. 'Here, you don't think it's malaria, do you?' The best diagnosis anyone had come up with so far was sun stroke. It could not be food poisoning. The islanders had all eaten the same food.

'I wouldn't think so,' Frankie replied, sitting down next to him. She looked out to sea.

It was not nice being ill in such a hostile environment. No-one had any idea how to deal with it. All they could do was keep Jane comfortable and hope she got well of her own accord.

'As I understand it,' Steve cut in, 'there are no malarial bugs in this area. That's why we haven't got any prophylactics.'

'Aren't there any tablets in the medical kit?' Francesca asked.

Steve shook his head. 'Not for malaria. But, you know, I suppose it *is* just possible that Jane might have been bitten by a malaria carrying insect of some kind. I hope not, for her sake. Malaria is not a nice thing to catch.'

'Have you had it?' Andrew asked. He knew Steve had been to Africa at some point and the man was speaking with some authority.

'Well, you know, I came pretty close.' Steve drew in a breath theatrically. 'A lot of people fell under in Malawi and Zambia while I was there. But I made a special effort to be careful. I sprayed myself head to foot with DEET and the little critters didn't come anywhere near me. You know, in three months I only got four bites.'

'What's DEET? Some kind of insect repellent?'

Steve nodded. 'It's lethal stuff.'

'It would have been nice to have had some of that here,' Andrew thought. 'Even just for ordinary insects.' By now, even his bites had sprouted bites. He had so many blotches on his skin it looked like he had come down with the mumps. And there were dozens of new ones from last night. Only his sunburn competed for attention in the colouring stakes. 'That's one thing I'm not going to miss about this place,' he reflected.

Steve scratched his throat and looked out to sea for the umpteenth time. 'You know, I don't think there's much point hanging around here for another couple of hours,' he said. 'Clive's obviously been delayed.'

'Perhaps he's not coming at all,' Jeremy Fielding suggested cheerfully from across the beach.

'I'm going to head back to the clearing. I think I might try and do a bit of work on the hut.'

'I'll give you a hand,' Stephanie said, rising to her feet.

The statuesque Australian was not the only volunteer. Most of the group were bored now and the glade was a lot cooler than the more exposed sea front.

'Try not to wake Jane,' Francesca called after them.

Sue Durrant had no intention of spending any more time on that stupid log cabin. It was a complete waste of effort. Steve and the others had got the supports up for the roof and were now laying down some of the thatch, but the whole thing looked rickety in the extreme. *It can't possibly keep the rain out.* There were as many gaps in the walls as there were holes in the roof. Jeremy and Isabel were working on the supports while the two Australians laid down the grass work. *What's the point? We could be leaving at any moment.* That was Steve all over. Once he decided to do something, it was all or nothing. *Bloody Australians.*

Chris Hudson was watching from the side lines. 'It's looking kind of cool, don't you think?' His eyes were on Isabel, not on the roofing.

And bloody Canadians too.

'Actually, I think it looks "kind of" pathetic,' she shot back.

Chris stared at her, irritably. 'Man, you're always, like, so totally negative.'

Sue glared back at him. 'Hardly surprising, the company I keep.' The boy looked away in embarrassment. *What does he expect? I didn't ask him to talk to me.*

She growled. It was typical. Everyone had been treating her with kid gloves since the storm. Whatever she said. Even if she kept quiet. It was bloody annoying. The way she felt now, she just wanted to lash out at somebody and have a proper argument. Preferably with Clive Monroe, not some snotty Canadian, but she would make do. Where the hell was Clive, anyway? The stupid bastard could not even be bothered to turn up on time. *When I get hold of him...* Sue swallowed her breath. What was the point? It was all academic. This whole sorry exercise had been doomed from the start.

An unwelcome flash of memory disorientated her for a moment, but she quickly dismissed it from her mind. *It was his own bloody fault. He had it coming.* She didn't want to think about that just now. Duncan was in the past. *I want to go home. I'm fed up with this place. I wouldn't care if I didn't see any of these people ever again.* And that especially included Chris Hudson, who was still standing next to her. And bloody Jane Ruddock as well, who was coughing and spluttering a couple of yards away.

I should have guessed she'd be the first one to fall ill. If anyone was born to be poorly, it was that woman. And not with diarrhoea or heat stroke like any ordinary person. No, those they could treat. But with some indeterminate fever which would no doubt disappear as soon as they stopped paying the stupid cow any attention. Sue walked over to take a look at the patient.

Jane was lying on her back on the wooden bed. Her clothes were slicked with sweat and her body was trembling. She coughed involuntarily. Sue frowned. Actually, the woman did look in a bad way. 'Do you want your water bottle?' she asked.

Jane nodded weakly.

The canteen was lying on the ground, next to her rucksack. Sue bent down to pick it up. The bottle was all but empty. She turned it upside down in disgust. *Typical*, she thought, *I'll have to go and fill it now.* 'I won't be a minute,' she told the woman.

Jane closed her eyes.

Sue made her way back towards the beach. She glanced at the flask in her hand. It was a regulation metal thing. Most of the islanders had something similar. Hers was green. This one was blue. The initials J.F. had been scratched on the base. Sue laughed. *Stupid cow.* It was not even her bottle.

She arrived at the Grotto and quickly filled the container from out of the font. *I wonder if I should get her some lime juice instead.* She shook her head. That was not a good idea. The flies would have got to it by now.

She returned to the clearing and rummaged inside Jane's pack. Sure enough, under the clothing, she found the woman's actual canteen. It was identical to the one Sue had just filled, albeit this one was unmarked. Sue transferred the water from the one to the other. She would take Jeremy's flask back to the beach and leave it next to his rucksack. *That'll be two good deeds in one day,* she thought sourly, bending over and gently shaking the sleeping form of Jane Ruddock. 'Here you go,' she said, proffering the open bottle.

Jane opened her eyes and struggled to sit up. Her hands were shaking too much for her to grip the canteen. Sue practically had to tip the water into the woman's mouth. She was definitely not well.

'Have you taken anything?' Sue asked.

Jane nodded weakly. 'Paracetamol.'

Sue raised an eyebrow. *A fat lot of good that'll do.* Oh well. At least it could not do her any harm.

'Hey, Sue! Can you bung us up them leaves?' Jeremy Fielding was shouting at her from somewhere. She looked around angrily and saw him up on the roof. He was pointing down to a mattress of foliage lying on the ground at the foot of the near wall. It was something the islanders had prepared earlier on. Sue nearly told him where to shove it, but she bit her tongue. It was not worth the aggro. She scowled at the man instead, put down the flask and went across to gather up the mattress.

Chris Hudson stood back and watched as she struggled with the leaves. The little bastard did not offer to help.

Clive Monroe would not be coming today. That much was obvious. But it was only when the sun began to set in the evening that the islanders started to come to terms with the fact that they would be spending another night on the island. 'You sure you ain't got your sums wrong?' Jeremy asked. He had just clambered down from the roof and was dusting himself off. The daylight was fading rapidly and work was coming to a close. 'Maybe it was tomorrow.'

'I don't think so.' Steve shook his head.

'It's Friday today,' Andrew confirmed. 'I've been keeping count. And it were Friday when I first come here.'

Jeremy scratched his head. 'I don't know how you can be so sure. I lost track after the first day.'

'Well, you know, it pays to be aware of these things,' Steve said. He stood back and studied the new roof critically. The thatching didn't look at all bad. There were still some patches left unfinished, but another couple of hours would see to that. If for any reason the director did not turn up the following morning, he was determined to finish the job. Then at least one good thing would come out of their short time on the island.

'Why do you reckon he didn't turn up?' Andrew asked.

Steve could not be sure. 'Well, Andy, there might be all sorts of reasons. Transportation in this part of the world is not exactly reliable.' He was doing his best to sound optimistic. 'I'm sure the guy will get here as soon as he can.'

'I hope so,' Andrew said. He was looking with some concern at the sleeping figure of Jane Ruddock. Frankie was sitting with her, reading the last few pages of her book before the light gave out.

'But, you know, I don't think there's any point worrying about it. Clive will get here when he gets here. And until then we'll look after Jane as best we can. You know,' Steve added, optimistically, 'I think it may well be a lot less serious than it looks.'

Francesca got up in the middle of the night to check up on the patient. Jane had been going from bad to worse and Frankie was concerned she might not make it through to the morning.

She could hear the noise of the other women as they slept but as she drew close to the bed she heard no sound coming from Jane. She pulled back the mosquito net and placed a hand on the woman's forehead. It was cold. Unnaturally cold. With rising panic, Francesca searched for a pulse, but she could not find one.

Jane Ruddock was dead.

Chapter Seven

Andrew had never seen Francesca cry.

The girl had held her nerve admirably to begin with. She had woken Stephanie and Isabel, then retrieved the torch Steve had left in the glade and walked calmly to the beach to inform the men.

The islanders assembled in the square and stood awkwardly for some time, unsure how to react. The bed-frame was moved to a far corner of the clearing and a shroud was hastily improvised to cover the body. After that, there was nothing anybody could do.

Andrew returned with Frankie to the beach. They sat for a time in the pre-dawn twilight, unable to speak, and it was then that Francesca had begun to cry. He put his arms around her and tried to comfort her. He was in shock too and it upset him to see her so distressed. She buried her head in his chest and he stroked her hair gently. That seemed to calm her a little.

At length, she pulled away and wiped some of the tears from her face. 'We have to leave here,' she said, her voice a dry whisper.

Andrew closed his eyes and nodded. This was too much for any of them to cope with. He had never seen a dead body, before coming to this island. Now he had seen two in less than a week. And at least one of those two might still be alive if adequate medical treatment had been available. This holiday had become a nightmare. Frankie was right. They had to leave now, to get away from the island. When Clive Monroe arrived, as he surely must, Andrew would insist they were shipped home straight away.

Jane Ruddock, he realised abruptly, would never be going home. Someone would have to inform her relatives. If she had any. *Didn't someone say she were related to Clive?* Andrew couldn't remember. He had known very little about the woman, though he had liked her very much. She had been married, according to Francesca, but her husband had divorced her. She had probably come to the island to escape from all that. And now she was dead. It was not fair. What harm had Jane ever done anyone? She had been kind and friendly and gentle. Why would God allow someone to die like that, so far from home? And how could Andrew begin to comfort anyone else when he was so upset himself?

Frankie raised her hand to his cheek and he kissed it gently. 'I can't help blaming myself,' she said. 'If I'd done something more. If I'd stayed up with her...'

'You did your best,' he whispered, truthfully. 'There was nothing else you could have done.'

Torch light flickered unnecessarily across the sand. It was almost dawn and the gently lapping waves were becoming visible now as the tide retreated from the beach. Steve Bramagh switched off his torch and sat down next to Andrew and Francesca. He let out a heavy sigh. 'No matter how hard you try, life always finds a way to trip you up.' He took off his glasses and began to clean the lenses. 'You know, I don't think she suffered at the end. I think she just slipped away quietly.'

Frankie nodded and wiped the salt from her eyes. 'I hope so, anyway.' She placed a hand on Andrew's thigh and the young man cupped it reassuringly.

The first rays of the sun were creeping above the horizon to the east. Andrew raised a hand to shield his eyes as he looked out to sea. The warmth of a new day was spreading across the shore.

One by one, the other islanders returned to the beach. They were tired and bedraggled and very upset. Most of the group had been quite fond of Jane. She was a kindly, inoffensive woman and her death had stunned them all. And so they sat or stood or lay upon the sand, each looking out at the strangely tranquil sea.

It was several minutes before anyone broke the silence.

Sue Durrant spoke for all of them, echoing Francesca's words from earlier on. 'The sooner we get out of here, the better.'

Clive Monroe would surely come today. He would arrive, they would tell him what had happened and then they could all go home. The previous day, Andrew had felt anxious but hopeful. Now he just felt numb. And so he waited with the others on the hot sand, as the sun crept up above them; and waited there still as the seconds turned to minutes and the minutes turned to hours.

Stephanie rose after a time to gather some breakfast, but few of the islanders felt much like eating. Only Chris Hudson seemed to have any appetite. And then another long silence descended.

The Canadian was sitting on his own, chomping quietly on some fruit. Sue was rubbing her eyes. Steve was staring into the middle distance. Jeremy Fielding was drawing patterns in the sand.

All of them waited, quietly. But of the director, as before, there was no sign.

'He's got to come,' Andrew insisted, under his breath. He glared at the horizon. 'He's got to.' It was almost as if, if he wished hard enough, he could will a boat to appear. But if that was so, then Andrew was not wishing hard enough.

It must have been nearly ten o'clock when Stephanie rose to her feet a second time. The group had been sitting on Candy Beach for over three and a half hours. She dusted herself down and stretched out her legs. Andrew looked up at her. The woman's face was grim. 'He's not coming,' she said, flatly. 'We're on our own.'

Chris was not prepared to accept that. 'He's only, like, a day late.'

'A day and a half,' Sue corrected him.

'Two days,' Stephanie insisted firmly.

'But there's, like, a million things that could have held him up.'

'Maybe he's dead too,' Jeremy muttered darkly.

That suggestion made Steve Bramagh frown.

'The point is,' Stephanie continued, 'we're here and he isn't. And we can't rely on him turning up. We have to fend for ourselves. We can't sit around all day waiting for him. There are things that need to be done.'

'He'll turn up,' Andrew insisted.

'Eventually, perhaps. But he's not here *now*. And we risk losing a lot of ground if we just sit here staring at the horizon for hours on end.' She looked to Steve for support.

'I hate to say this,' he admitted, 'but, you know, Steph's right. It may be that Clive will turn up later today or tomorrow. But there's a chance he may not.'

'They wouldn't abandon us!' Chris asserted vehemently.

'I don't see why not,' Sue muttered. 'Their track record isn't exactly impressive so far. I agree with Stephanie. There's no point us just sitting here.' It was a rare thing for the two women to be in accord. Andrew did not find the fact reassuring.

'I think we'd be better served trying to sort things out for the long term,' Steve agreed. 'You know, if we're going to be here on our own for a time – even just for a little while – there are things that are going to need to be sorted. And rather than sitting here, waiting, we should be getting up and making a start.'

Jeremy rubbed his neck. 'There's no harm preparing for the worst.'

'Exactly! You know, Clive might well turn up in ten minutes and everything will be fine. But we risk losing a lot of ground if we don't act on the assumption that he might not be coming.'

'He'll come,' Andrew said. 'He's got to come.' But the young man's voice lacked conviction. In his heart of hearts, he knew that Steve was right. They had to assume the worst. He gripped Francesca tightly.

'We'll get through this,' she told him.

Andrew nodded. ''Course we will.' Though if he was honest, he did not know how.

There was a strong feeling of déjà vu.

110

Everyone was pulling together. The islanders had waited a day before making preparations for this second burial, just in case Clive did arrive and there was a possibility of shipping the body home. In the meantime, the group had worked and worked hard. They had scavenged and fished and hunted. They had put the finishing touches to the log cabin. They had stock-piled firewood. And they had done everything in their power to ignore their increasingly worrying predicament.

And then they had buried Jane Ruddock.

No-one had known what to say. Francesca probably knew the woman best, but she was too upset to speak. Isabel had some religious leanings and she spoke a few half-remembered words from the Bible. By all accounts, Jane had been a committed Christian.

They erected a wooden cross on top of the grave. It was on the opposite side of the glade from Duncan Roberts. No-one had explicitly suggested there should be a distance between the two of them, but somehow it had seemed appropriate. Regardless, the unfortunate islanders were now at rest.

Two days later, Isabel Grant fell ill.

The dark haired Englishwoman had been out foraging with Sue Durrant. She had stumbled on some bracken and then collapsed. Luckily, the two women had not been far from Candy Beach and Sue was able to summon assistance. A couple of the men had carried her the short distance back to the clearing. A cursory inspection suggested she had fallen prey to the same fever as Jane. She was nauseous, had a very high temperature and suffered periodic convulsions. She could not stand up without getting dizzy and she vomited frequently.

The girl was quickly put to bed.

Francesca was distraught. It had been upsetting enough, tending to a person she had barely known, but to see her best friend struck down with the same potentially fatal illness, that was too much to bear.

Steve shared her concern. In the short time they had known each other, he had become rather fond of Isabel. Nothing had happened between them since that day in the bay. Neither had felt the compulsion to take things any further. All the same, he had developed a deep respect for the young woman. She was intelligent and articulate, if still a little distant, and it distressed him to see her in such pain.

The fact that Isabel had fallen victim to the same illness as Jane Ruddock caused universal concern. Stephanie thought the condition might be contagious. It was possible she had contracted the disease directly from the previous victim.

'Well, you know, I don't think so,' Steve said, when Stephanie broached the idea. 'If it *was* contagious, I think Frankie would have been the person most likely to catch it. And it wouldn't have been restricted to just one of us.'

'Could it be water borne?' Stephanie suggested. 'Like cholera or typhoid?'

Steve did not think so. 'We all take our water from the same source. If it was water borne, I think we'd have all come down with it by now.'

'What about food poisoning?'

Again, Steve shook his head. 'It's difficult to see how. We all eat the same food.'

Stephanie gave a sigh. 'There must be *some* explanation.' She rubbed her arm gently, trying not to scratch any of her bites. 'I don't suppose it could be malaria after all? That would explain why we haven't all come down with it.'

Steve shrugged. 'Well, you know, if it is, it's not the same as the malaria I encountered in Africa.' In fact, it did not seem to act like any disease that Steve had ever seen, though his knowledge of such things was woefully inadequate. In many ways, he reflected, ignorance was their greatest enemy. If they did not even know what the problem was, how could anyone be expected to solve it?

Jeremy Fielding scratched his beard and watched as Chris Hudson bent over to get a firm grip on the roots. He shook his head ruefully. Sweet potatoes were always the worst. At least with the fruit, you could pull it away with one tug. With sweet potatoes, you had to dig right into the earth. 'We ain't got all day,' he teased the Canadian. Unlike Sue or Stephanie, Jeremy had no problem going out foraging with Chris. Sure, the lad was a bit work-shy if you let him get away with it, and he was certainly green around the gills, but there was no edge to him. What you saw was what you got. He was easy enough to get along with, even if he wasn't much cop when it came to digging out root vegetables.

'I'm trying,' the boy whined, squatting down and digging away some more of the soil. He tugged again, with little success, and then dropped back onto the ground, letting out a weary sigh.

Jeremy came over to him. 'You all right?'

Chris put a hand to his face. The boy's youthful stubble was gradually developing into a beard, though it was unlikely ever to challenge Jeremy's bushy mane. His hand was covered in mud, but he brought it up to wipe the sweat from his forehead. He glanced at his companion. 'Jem, what are we still doing here?'

The other man had no answer. 'Search me.' He had been as bewildered by the events of the last few days as the rest of them. Poor old Jane, popping her clogs like that, and now the same thing happening to Isabel. People were dropping like flies.

'I mean, like, Clive should have been here four days ago,' Chris said.

'There's something fishy going on, that's for sure. Look, I'm not happy about it either. But what can we do?' That girl Stephanie was right. They were stuck here. They had to like it or lump it.

'There must be, like, some way to get off this island.'

'You can always swim for it.'

Chris looked away. 'If we don't get Bella to a proper doctor, I mean, like, yesterday, she might…' His voice trailed away.

So that was what was worrying him. Jeremy grinned. *I should have known.* 'You've got the hots for her, have you?'

The Canadian did not deny it.

It was hardly surprising. Isabel was a fair looking bird. Not that Chris stood much of a chance with her. 'She'll be all right,' Jeremy said. 'She's one of the strong ones.'

'You think?'

'Yeah, of course. Take more than some tropical fever to bump her off.'

Chris was not so certain. 'I sure hope so, anyway.'

Jeremy grinned again. 'Mind you, she's out of your league.'

The youngster bristled. 'Hey, look, I don't make, like, personal remarks about you.'

'All right, mate,' he said, raising his hands. 'No offence.' Jeremy crouched down and started digging at the potatoes. He would get the buggers out, even if the Canadian could not.

'So, like, how long do you think we're going to be here?' Chris asked again.

Jeremy shrugged. 'I wish I knew, mate. I wish I knew.'

Francesca Stevens sat on the side of the bed and gazed down at the sleeping figure. Isabel had always looked beautiful in repose. She had a dark, Mediterranean complexion which seemed to suit their present location. Her skin was smooth and clear, apparently unmarked by the ravages of island life. Her brow was free of bites and her dark hair, though tangled, was fanned out evenly across the blanket. Her breathing was calmer now, her chest rising and falling with reassuring regularity. To the casual eye, she did not look ill at all, though a quick hand to her forehead was enough to prove that she was.

Frankie had resolved to nurse the girl twenty-four hours a day. She was not about to let Isabel die as Jane Ruddock had. She would do whatever it took to keep her friend alive. If that meant an all-night vigil, so be it. Francesca was adamant: Isabel would be returned to health and would leave the island along with the rest of them.

The woman coughed and opened her eyes. She seemed to be having trouble focusing. 'F...Frankie?'

'I'm still here.' She leant across and pulled a small strand of hair from the other girl's forehead.

'Now…now you know how I felt, visiting Susanna in hospital.' Isabel coughed again. Her voice was cracked and uncertain.

Francesca shook her head. 'This is different. You're not going to die.' Susanna was Isabel's sister. She had been knocked down in a car accident and had ended up on a life support machine. The girl had survived the accident but had never regained consciousness.

'Perhaps it would be better if I did,' Isabel breathed, wearily. 'It would be so easy just to slip away.'

'Don't talk like that.'

'Would anybody really care?'

'*I'd* care,' Frankie insisted. 'I'm not going to let you die.'

'I feel so hot.'

'Drink some water. Here. Sit up.' With Francesca's help, Isabel took a small sip from the canteen. 'Better?'

The girl nodded. 'A little.'

'You mustn't give up, Bella. You have to fight this. If only for my sake.'

'I'll try. But I feel so tired, Frankie.'

'You'll get through it. You have to. You're still young. You've got everything to live for.'

Isabel smiled weakly. 'You're a good friend.'

A short distance away, Chris Hudson had entered the clearing. Francesca glanced round and watched the young man for a moment. He had placed his rucksack on the ground and was starting to pull a few things out of it.

Isabel tried to focus on the Canadian. 'Where has he been?' she asked, her voice a dry murmur.

'Out foraging with Jeremy, I think.'

'That was what I was meant to be doing this morning.'

Frankie stroked the woman's forehead. 'I'm sure he doesn't mind.'

Chris stood up and came towards them. He was carrying a handful of fruit. 'I thought you might want something to eat,' he said, proffering the fruit to Isabel.

Francesca smiled. It was a kind thought, but Isabel turned her face away. 'I'm not hungry,' she muttered.

The young man was crestfallen.

'Maybe later,' Frankie told him.

'Sure.' He stood awkwardly for a moment, then returned to his rucksack and moved out of the glade.

When he was gone, Francesca turned back to her friend. 'You don't like him, do you?'

On the bed-frame, Isabel grimaced. 'I don't have an opinion.'

Frankie grinned. That was clearly not true. Few of the islanders lacked an opinion about Chris Hudson. 'You never could lie to me,' she teased.

'I admit he's not one of my favourite people.' Isabel frowned. 'I don't like the way he looks at me.'

'He fancies you, that's all. You can't blame him for that.'

The other woman gave a start. Her face was the picture of revulsion.

Francesca laughed. 'You can't seriously tell me you didn't know.'

The two girls locked eyes for a moment. Isabel seemed suddenly more lucid and Frankie could not help but play on the fact. They stared at each other, each refusing to break the gaze. It was an old game. But then a cloud seemed to pass over Isabel's face and she moved a hand to steady herself on the bed.

'You'd better lie down,' Francesca suggested, concern creeping back into her voice. Isabel laid back gently on the mattress. She was breathing more rapidly now and her body was starting to shake. Frankie gripped her shoulders and held them firmly. Then something began to bubble up in Isabel's mouth. Francesca rolled her sideways, just in time to prevent the woman from vomiting all over the blanket.

Andrew brought them dinner that evening. He had no idea whether Isabel would be able to eat anything, but it was worth a try. Her condition had not improved since he had last seen her, though she was now sitting up in bed. He handed her the bowl and she took a careful sip of the mixture. Frankie drew Andrew away from the bed. 'Is she not any better?' he asked.

The girl sighed. 'No better. No worse. But she's not going to give up without a fight.'

'I wouldn't,' Andrew said, 'if that were me.'

Frankie pressed her hands together nervously. 'Andrew, I think the crunch is going to come tonight. She'll either improve from now on or...or she'll deteriorate.'

Andrew nodded sadly. 'You're going to sit up with her.' It was a statement, not a question. He did not need to ask.

'I went to bed when Jane was ill. I'm not going to make that mistake a second...'

There was a loud clatter from behind. Isabel had dropped the food bowl. It had struck the ground, knocking over her canteen. The water was spilling everywhere. Francesca rushed back to the bed. Bits of vegetable were strewn across the earth; but it was too late to do anything about that. Isabel was hanging over the side of the frame, her body shaking once again. Frankie helped her slowly back onto the mattress.

Andrew picked up the bowl. 'Don't worry,' he said. 'I can always get some more.'

Francesca glanced back at him. 'I think water would be more helpful.'

The rains came again during the night.

Steve Bramagh had started keeping a torch by his bed in case of emergencies. As soon as he felt the first splashes of rain on his face, he sprang into life. It was a short dash from the beach to the clearing. Stephanie McMahon was already helping Francesca to get Bella out of the line of fire. Steve rushed forward to open the door of the cabin and between them they carried the woman into the safety of the hut.

A table had been set up in the larger of the two rooms. Jeremy and Chris had knocked it together the previous day. Steve gestured at it and the two women helped Isabel up onto the more-or-less flat wooden surface.

Steve swung the torch up at the roof, checking for leaks. It was the first time the log cabin had been put to the test since its completion. 'You know, I think this might be all right,' he said. There was some water dripping down in a couple of places, but the second room looked almost dry. 'We can put her in there,' he suggested.

Frankie nodded. Far better to wait out the storm here than to carry Isabel all the way over to the Grotto.

'We'll need to bring her bed inside,' Stephanie said. They couldn't leave her lying on the table all night.

The A-frame was outside in the glade. A blanket had been left on top of the mattress with the mosquito net and it was already soaking. The islanders rushed outside to retrieve the bed. The frame was awkwardly constructed and not easy to carry. Francesca grabbed one end and Steve lifted the other. He was still holding the torch, but he managed to grab the mattress with both hands and together they manoeuvred the frame towards the door of the hut.

'Can I do anything to help?' Stephanie asked.

'We'll manage,' Steve said. 'Your pack will get soaked over there. You'd better get it over to the Grotto.'

Stephanie nodded. 'If you're sure.' She stumbled off into the darkness.

The door was a fraction too narrow. 'Lean to the side,' Steve suggested, his hands gripping the A-frame as best he could. It took a bit of bumping and scraping, but eventually they got it through the open door. Together they carried the bed past the table where Isabel lay dozing and through a wider door into the second room. Here they picked a dry spot near the far wall and settled the contraption. It wobbled slightly – the ground was uneven – but Steve pushed one of the legs an inch or so into the earth and that seemed to steady it.

Frankie set about laying out the blankets and pulling back the netting.

Steve returned to the larger room and helped Isabel to sit up. The girl was barely conscious. Francesca came over and together they helped her down from the table and across to the newly established bedroom.

'I'm going to stay with her,' Frankie said, once they had got her comfortably settled.

Steve had already assumed as much. 'Good on you.' He flashed the torch around the hut a second time. 'You know, we might as well set up one of the A-frames in here permanently, when things die down.' There were a couple of beds going spare, after all.

Francesca nodded, but she was scarcely paying attention. 'I'd better go and get *my* blanket,' she realised. She had been too concerned with Isabel to think about her own bedding, which was still outside in the rain.

Before she could move to retrieve it, Andrew came crashing into the room, his face a picture of concern.

'Is Bella all right?' he asked, breathlessly. He had run all the way from the Grotto. His short ginger hair was slicked back against his scalp.

'Everything's fine,' Steve said. 'I'll get your blanket,' he added, to Francesca.

'Er…I think my pack's under the frame as well.'

'No worries.' He made his way outside.

Andrew came over to look at Isabel, who had already drifted back to sleep. 'Just our luck, it raining tonight,' he said.

'Is everyone else at the Grotto?'

'Aye. They will be by now. Running like the clappers, some of them. I just passed Steph on the way over here.'

Francesca looked down at his clothes. 'You're drenched.' Andrew's blue shirt was clinging tightly to his chest – he always wore long sleeves after dark now – and his trousers were so saturated that water was dripping from the hems and forming a small puddle on the floor.

Andrew eyed himself with amusement. 'Not the first time, eh?' He grinned.

Steve returned with Frankie's backpack, carrying her blanket under his arm. He placed the rucksack down in the middle of the room and handed the blanket to Francesca. 'I'm afraid it's a bit wet.'

'Is *your* pack still out in the rain?' Andrew asked.

'No. It's already over at the Grotto,' Steve said. 'I stowed it there before I went to bed. I had a feeling it might rain tonight.' He grinned with satisfaction at his own foresight. 'You know, I find it pays to be prepared for every eventuality.'

Andrew nodded. 'I wish I'd done that.' Foresight was not a quality the two men shared. 'I left mine out under my bunk. It's got my shorts in and everything.'

'Andy, it'll get soaked!' Frankie exclaimed. 'You'd better go and get it.'

'Actually, I were planning to stay here for the night. To keep you company, like. But I suppose…'

'You know, I can always pick up your pack on the way back to the Grotto,' Steve cut in. 'I'm heading that way anyway. I want to make sure everybody else is okay.'

'That'd be great. If you don't mind…'

'Not a problem, Andy. Just let me know if she takes a turn for the worse.'

The other man nodded.

Steve moved to the door and darted out into the rain.

Andrew watched him go. 'He's a really nice bloke, in't he?'

'I don't know what we'd do without him,' Francesca agreed.

The light of the torch flickered briefly through the gaps in the wall but then quickly faded.

'You don't mind me staying?' Andrew asked.

'Don't be silly! I'll be glad of the company. I wasn't planning on sleeping in any case.'

Andrew squinted at the girl through the darkness. 'I can't see you any more.' Without the torch, the interior of the cabin was as black as pitch. He stretched out his arms. 'Where are you?'

'Over here,' Frankie whispered.

He moved towards the voice. 'Shame we couldn't keep the torch, isn't it?' They collided gently. Andrew found her left shoulder and she handed him a blanket, which he laid out on the floor. The ground inside the hut was smooth and dry. They had done a good job levelling the area. It would be more comfortable here than in the cave.

Francesca moved back to Isabel and crouched down, feeling for the edge of the bed with her hands. She paused for a moment, listening. Her friend's breathing was quiet and regular now. She sighed. 'I wish I knew what time it was.'

'I don't think it's even midnight.'

Outside the rain continued to pour. 'I hope this weather doesn't last long,' she said. The last storm had taken more than a day to run its course.

'I don't think it will.'

'Why do you say that?'

Andrew shrugged. 'It don't seem quite so fierce. There's no thunder or nothing. It might blow itself out in a couple of hours.'

Frankie rose to her feet. Her eyes were becoming accustomed to the black. She stared down at the sleeping figure of Isabel, a faint blur in the darkness.

'A couple of hours could make all the difference.'

Chapter Eight

Her back was aching like hell. It was bad enough on the bed-frame, but another night in that bloody cave was taking things too far. There had been no room to stretch out, no soft surfaces, and water had dripped down continuously. What was that Chinese thing? Water torture, that was it. And at least when Sue slept in the clearing she did not have to put up with Jeremy Fielding and his industrial strength snoring. Even the blokes on the beach had had enough of that. They had banished Jeremy to a distant nook. It was a shame the man could not be banished from the Grotto as well.

Sue had woken in a foul mood half an hour earlier, but she had kept to the cave while the rain continued to fall. It was little more than drizzle now. The morning sky was cloudy, though a few patches of blue were beginning to peep through.

What am I doing here? she wondered, looking out from the mouth of the cave. It was five days since Clive Monroe had been due back and only four since the death of Jane Ruddock. The whole reason for them being on the island had simply evaporated. They had long since stopped using the video cameras. The batteries were dead now in any case. There would be no documentary, so what was the point in carrying on? *They must have been mad, setting everything up like this. Did they honestly think we'd just sit back and calmly film it all when everything was falling apart?* Another, more disturbing thought struck her. *Maybe they never intended us to film it. Maybe the documentary was just an excuse to get us all out here.* She frowned. Why would anyone go to all that trouble? *It's not as if...*

Chris Hudson was hurrying across the rocks towards her. Sue scowled. He had probably only left the cave to answer a call of nature. The lanky young man had been up a couple of times in the night. He could not move quietly to save his life.

'I hope you washed your hands,' she snapped.

He stared at her for a moment, but the comment was lost on him.

How that idiot got into Cambridge I'll never know.

'I've just been to see Bella,' he said.

Oh, not dead then. 'How is she?'

'She's, like, sitting up and eating. It looks as if she may be on the mend.'

'Good for her.'

The Canadian sounded relieved, anyway. *Stupid sod.*

Sue had not been to see Isabel since the girl had fallen ill. It was rather callous, she knew, but there was no point exposing herself unnecessarily. God knows what kind of virus the young woman had contracted. *Steve might be certain there's no danger, but I'm damned if I'm going to take the risk.* Isabel was a survivor. She would get through it somehow. Actually, Sue rather admired her. The woman knew how to handle herself, even if she was a bit stuck up. And anyway, there were plenty of people looking after her. Frankie had stayed with her during the night and Steve Bramagh had got up first thing to see how she was. He was paying *particular* attention. Sue wondered if Stephanie had noticed that. After all, hadn't Steve and Bella disappeared off together, the day after... 'Where's Stephanie?' she asked Chris.

'She's over at the hut as well.'

Out of the rain. Very sensible. 'It makes a change having two dry spots.' Sue scratched her neck. She was feeling a bit hungry now. 'I think the rain's about to stop.'

'I guess so,' Chris agreed, peering upwards.

She stepped past him out of the cave and wound her way across the wet earth to Candy Beach. She walked slowly, trying not to slip on the mud.

The beach itself was deserted, the tide halfway out, most of the footprints washed away. Only the line of A-frames gave any indication that the area was inhabited. The furthest one belonged to Jeremy Fielding. It was set apart from the others, a good twenty metres down the beach.

Serves him right, Sue thought. *If it rains again tonight, I'm sleeping in the hut.*

'You know, it's only a suggestion,' Steve said.

Jeremy scratched his beard. 'No, I think it's a good idea. We can't get much of a fire going anywhere else. Not when it's raining.' A little beach hut would serve them well. It didn't need to be anything elaborate. Just a roof to keep the rain off while they were cooking.

'We could store some wood under there an'all, to keep it dry,' Andrew suggested.

'I was thinking that very same thing,' Steve said. 'You know, we could be here for a while yet, and I think we owe it to ourselves to prepare for every eventuality.'

'It gives us something to do, anyway,' Jeremy added.

'Well, you know, there is that too.' Steve smiled. Now that the rain had cleared, the islanders would be looking for something to occupy themselves with, beyond the usual foraging.

'So what do we need?' Jeremy asked. 'Just wood and palm leaves?'

The Australian nodded. 'A few poles to carry the weight and some branches to support the roof.'

Jeremy surveyed the edge of the beach. 'How big do you reckon?'

'I was thinking about three metres squared. That ought to do it. We're not going to be sleeping underneath.'

'Won't it catch light,' Andrew asked, frowning suddenly, 'if the roof is made of grass and stuff?'

Steve shook his head. 'We only use small fires for cooking, Andy. Less effort and more heat. So the flames aren't going to get up very high in the first place. And, you know, there won't be any walls, so we'll have plenty of ventilation.'

'Anyway, it's only for emergencies,' Jeremy pointed out. 'Just when it's pissing it down.'

It had rained twice so far, in the two weeks they had been on the island, but that was a lot less than average for the time of year. Steve had looked up the figures before he came away.

'Hey, maybe we should make some sort of dining area as well,' Andrew suggested. 'So we can all eat without getting wet at the same time.'

Jeremy laughed. 'Why don't we just build a five star restaurant and have done with it?'

'It were only an idea…'

'No. Straight up. Posh little number. A la carte menu. The works. We could get some of the girls to dress up as waitresses. Short skirts. Little black numbers…'

'What we *need*,' Sue Durrant cut in, emerging from a clump of bushes a short distance away, 'is some kind of latrine.' She glared at Jeremy, her lips curling in distaste. 'I'm getting sick and tired of having to squat behind a bush every few hours. If you want to make something useful, make that.'

Jeremy lifted up his hands. 'Sounds like a good idea. Unfortunately, Andy and me are just off collecting wood. Perhaps you'd like to make a start, digging the hole? Then maybe we'll give you a hand when we get back.' He winked cheerfully. 'Come on, Andy.' And with that the two men marched away.

Sue stared after them, speechless.

'You know,' Steve admitted, 'that man is definitely getting worse.'

By mid-afternoon, the clouds had vanished and the island was once again bathed in glorious sunshine. Stephanie McMahon retrieved her rucksack from the Grotto and carried it across to the glade. It was more convenient to store it here, close to her bed-frame, now that the roof of the log cabin had shown its worth. After a night of heavy rainfall, the interior of the hut had remained mostly dry, with just a handful of damp patches close to the walls.

As Stephanie approached, the main door swung open, revealing the tall, slim figure of Isabel Grant. Her dark brown hair was a tangle of knots, but the girl was up on her feet again, at long last. Stephanie greeted her warmly. 'You must be feeling better!'

'A little,' she admitted, supporting herself on the frame of the door and blinking in the harsh sunlight. 'I wanted to get a bit of fresh air. But I'm starting to feel dizzy again now.' She clutched the side of the door and swayed slightly.

The Australian swung her pack off her shoulder. 'You're bound to be a bit disorientated, lying in bed for so long.' She placed the rucksack on the ground and gazed at the other woman. 'Are you sure that's all it is, though?'

Isabel nodded. Her eyes were properly focused now and she had stopped shaking. 'I have been feeling a lot better.'

'You certainly *look* better,' Stephanie agreed. For all her dizziness, she did seem reasonably alert, for the first time in days. 'Even so, it's best not to rush these things. Perhaps you should go back to bed.'

Isabel sighed. 'I suppose I ought to.'

Stephanie held out an arm and the woman allowed herself to be guided back into the hut. Francesca Stevens was lying in a small bundle on the floor in the far room, fast asleep. Isabel sat down on the edge of her bunk and looked fondly across at her friend. 'She must have been up all night. I didn't want to wake her.'

'Andy must be shattered too.'

'Was he here?' Isabel lifted her arms above her head and stretched herself out. 'I wasn't terribly lucid. I don't even remember being carried inside.' She pulled back the mosquito net and swung her legs up onto the mattress.

'Is there anything I can get you?' Stephanie asked. 'I think Sue's just started dinner, but it won't be ready for an hour or so.'

'I'm fine. I don't want to start throwing up again.'

A muffled hiccough from the floor indicated that Frankie was beginning to stir.

'I'll leave you be then. I only came to stow my pack.'

Stephanie smiled as Isabel adjusted her blanket and lay back on the bed. She turned and strode out of the hut to collect her bag. Returning to the main room, she pushed it under the table, beside the other two rucksacks. Those belonged to Francesca and Isabel. She crouched down and retrieved her cigarettes from the backpack. There were only seven left. And no lighter, she realised. Of course. She had lent that to Sue earlier on. The Englishwoman had misplaced her own matches. *I'll get it off her on the way back*, Stephanie thought.

Frankie was standing by the bedroom door, rubbing her eyes. 'What time is it?'

'Late afternoon.'

The girl yawned and gestured back to the bed-frame, where Isabel was now quietly dozing. 'I think she's going to be all right.'

Stephanie nodded. 'It's nice to have a bit of good news for a change.'

The next morning, work began on the roof of the cooking hut.

Poles had already been erected, well away from the tide on the near side of Candy Beach, and the three workers had quickly laid out a basic framework for the roof. Now it was just a question of covering it over.

The project had turned into an all male affair. Chris and Jeremy were helping Steve Bramagh and Andrew Baker.

Stephanie and Sue were away foraging and Francesca was keeping an eye on Isabel, making sure the young woman didn't suffer any kind of relapse. She was taking it easy today, reading Frankie's battered paperback, though Francesca said she had read it before.

The thatch the men had prepared for the roof was turning out better than any of them had expected. 'You know, I think we're really getting the hang of this now,' Steve declared.

Andrew was pleasantly surprised at their progress. This time the roof looked as if it would be completely waterproof. There would be no damp patches on the sand underneath.

'Always the way, isn't it?' Jeremy laughed. 'We should have done this one first.'

A ladder was propped up against the near edge of the roof. It was a rickety contraption of wood and vine, which they had thrown together the previous evening. They hadn't really needed one before, as they had been able to scramble up the walls of the log cabin and grab onto various branches. Here there was no such purchase.

Jeremy and Steve took turns at the top of the ladder. The beach hut was a much simpler affair than the log cabin. The roof didn't need to be as thick and it was covering a much smaller area. Andrew wound the vines and prepared some of the thatch on the ground, while Chris Hudson manhandled the various pieces up onto the roof.

The four men chatted amiably as they worked.

'I reckon we'll be finished by sundown,' Steve affirmed, after they had taken a short break for lunch.

The others did not share his confidence.

'You'll be lucky!' Jeremy chortled.

Candy Beach was not an ideal place to work. The heat of the sun was punishing and the men were soon bathed in sweat.

Andrew's skin had roasted now to the point where it could not be roasted any more. It was no longer painful – all feeling had long since burnt away – but he couldn't help worrying about the long term damage the sun was doing to him. He was wearing a t-shirt, of course, which was dark and wet with perspiration, but that didn't offer him any real protection.

'You all right down there?' Jeremy called, from the top of the roof.

'Aye, I were just thinking about that bloody sun.'

'Yeah. We're crazy being out like this.' Jeremy wasn't even wearing a t-shirt. His body was stretched across the thatch, his feet barely kissing the top rung of the ladder. 'Probably all die of skin cancer. Talk about Mad bloody Dogs. Here, Chris, pass us up some juice, will you?'

'Sure.' Chris was on ladder-holding duty. Nobody had been surprised when he had volunteered for that, though it was an important job. If anyone fell off the steps and broke their leg, they would all be screwed. He grabbed a bottle and handed it up to Jeremy.

'Thanks, mate.'

Chris nipped back beneath the ladder, where a small amount of shade had now become available.

Andrew grinned. *Trust him to nab it first.* Andrew was one of the few people who actually liked Chris Hudson. They were of a similar age and the two of them got on well, though

Chris had seemed rather withdrawn of late. It was hardly surprising, what with Isabel being ill, but there was probably more to it than that. The fact of being marooned here was enough to upset anybody, but by all accounts the Canadian had led a particularly sheltered life. He was used to having everything laid out for him. His father was stinking rich, apparently, and had always been on hand to sort out any problems. Here, on his own, he was completely out of his depth. *I'll have to cheer him up*, Andrew thought. 'We should go for a swim later, if we've got time. Maybe see if we can find that bay Steve said about.'

The young man's face lit up. 'That'd be kind of cool.'

Andrew grinned. Actually, he was curious to find the bay himself. If it was nice, he thought, maybe he could take Francesca there one afternoon. She needed cheering up as well.

There were three cigarettes left in the packet. Stephanie lit the fourth and took a long, slow drag. She closed her eyes and inhaled deeply. *I needed that.* She had got into a routine now. Whatever she was supposed to be doing, she would make a point of going to the Grotto a couple of hours before sunset and having a smoke. Steve came and sat with her occasionally, but the others usually left her alone. It was an all-too-brief period of solitude which Stephanie had managed to set aside for herself. She didn't want to think about what she would do when she had smoked her last cigarette. It was difficult enough coping with the petty irritations of day to day life, without having to give up smoking as well. Perhaps the withdrawal symptoms would not be so bad this time. One cigarette a day was practically not smoking already.

Nearly a week had passed since the death of Jane Ruddock and outwardly everything seemed calm. The boys had built a hut on the beach and Sue and Francesca had dug a latrine, a little way from the clearing. The sickness that had struck Jane and Isabel seemed to have burnt itself out and the fact that Bella had recovered from it was reassuring. Nevertheless, a sense of unease pervaded the group. The islanders were working as

129

diligently as before – indeed, they were getting along now better than ever – but there was an unspoken understanding that things could not continue as they were. It was not just the expectation that someone, somewhere would eventually come by and check up on them; it was the irrational belief that their run of bad luck could only continue; that some other misfortune was waiting in the wings.

How long can we scrape by like this? Stephanie wondered. Their diet was not good. Even the fish some of the men occasionally caught did not improve matters, shared as it was between eight people. They had all lost weight. Stephanie had had a few pounds to spare, but Chris and Isabel now looked painfully thin. In Bella's case, the illness was probably partly to blame; but the diet was not helping either.

Hard work was the best distraction, but there was a limit to how busy they could all keep and constructive activities were becoming thin on the ground. The more free time they had, the greater the opportunity for people to worry. As Steve had said the other day, the group was like a powder keg waiting to go off. Which one of them would be the first to crack?

The cigarette had burnt to almost nothing. Stephanie looked down at her fingers in surprise. Surely she had only just lit it. Reluctantly, she stubbed out the end and threw the extinguished butt to the back of the cave. She sat for a moment, considering whether to pull out the radio and listen to the news. The batteries were probably running low by now. She would save it for another day. *Perhaps as a substitute for the cigarettes,* she thought sadly. *A very poor substitute.*

She pulled herself up with some effort. She was beginning to feel old. Her bones were aching. The insect bites, bruises and burnt skin didn't help. *And it's down hill from now on,* she thought. It was days since she had last dared to look at her reflection in the rock pool. She was still a very attractive woman but island life was doing none of them any favours. She unscrewed her water bottle and began to fill it up from the font.

A nervous cough sounded from behind her. Stephanie did not have to look round to know who it was. Chris Hudson. She grimaced. What was *he* doing here? She acknowledged his presence with a nod of her head, but she didn't bother to smile. Chris was carrying the cooking pot from the fire. On duty, obviously. He did not meet her eye. He was a nervous young man, even at the best of times. He would glance at her sideways or out of the corner of his eye, but he would never meet her gaze directly. Evidently, there was something about her he found intimidating. *And rightly so*, she thought. The bronzed Australian had better things to worry about than the sexual frustrations of a socially backward adolescent.

'You're cooking tonight?' she asked him, politely.

'I…yeah, I…it's my turn.'

'Anything nice?'

Chris could barely stammer a response, 'I…I guess, kind of the usual type of thing…'

It was sad, really sad. Andrew Baker was a little in awe of her but at least Stephanie could have a decent conversation with him. 'I'll look forward to it then,' she responded dryly, screwing the top back on her flask.

Now where did I put my lighter?

The young British couple had stopped short of consummating their relationship; but they had kissed and cuddled up together and then fallen asleep on the crisp white sand of West Bay.

By the time Francesca roused herself, some hours later, it was beginning to get dark. The sun had just set and the sky was an orange glow. Andrew's head was resting tenderly on her chest, his arm on her midriff. He had the look of a contented child. Frankie smiled. It was a shame to wake him. But they had not thought to bring a torch and darkness descended quickly in Paradise. 'Hey, you!' she whispered gently. Andrew opened his eyes. 'It's getting late.'

He gazed up at her fondly. 'I wish every day could be like this.'

Francesca smiled again. 'Me too.' She kissed the top of his head. His ginger hair had grown remarkably in the two and a half weeks they had been on the island. She liked it longer. It made him look more mature. 'Come on, lift yourself up!'

Andrew moved reluctantly. He scrambled to his feet and put out a hand to help her. The girl rose up and drew close to him. They kissed for a moment. She could feel his body pressed tightly against her. Then they pulled apart.

She bent down to retrieve the blanket. When she shook it out, a cloud of sand enveloped her. Frankie started to cough and Andrew laughed good-naturedly. 'You've got to sleep on that tonight,' he pointed out.

'If you were a gentleman, you'd offer me yours.'

He shrugged. 'You can have it if you like.'

'I was only joking, silly. Come on, let's get back.' She took Andrew's hand and the couple walked arm in arm into the jungle, leaving a set of footprints behind them on the slender beach.

Francesca was happier than she had felt in quite some time. No doubt this was what Andy had intended. He was good that way. At first she had suspected his motives in bringing her to the bay, but not any more. The afternoon had done her the world of good.

She closed her eyes and held his arm closely.

West Bay was less than a mile from Candy Beach, as the crow flew, and it did not take them long to come within hailing distance of the clearing.

The light of the sky had all but vanished now – the stars were starting to appear – but another bright light was flickering through the trees ahead of them. There was an acrid smell too – smoke, billowing towards them – and it was obvious at once that something was terribly wrong.

A searing heat radiated outwards from the glade.

Francesca glanced anxiously at Andrew and the young man dashed forward to get a closer look.

It was not difficult to see what was going on.

The log cabin was on fire.

Chapter Nine

'Is anyone inside?' Jeremy Fielding yelled.

Steve Bramagh was dragging one of the bed-frames away from the clearing. 'I don't know. Where's Bella?'

A voice cried out from behind him. 'It's all right! I'm over here.'

Sue Durrant moved past her and pulled open the front door of the hut. Steve grabbed her arm and hauled her away. 'My pack's in there!' she exclaimed.

'There's nothing you can do!' Steve shielded his eyes. The heat from the fire was excruciating. How could the whole building have ignited so quickly? It was an inferno. 'Has anyone seen Andy and Francesca?'

Isabel came up beside him. She grabbed onto the one remaining bed-frame. 'They went to the bay. They should…'

Andrew sprinted out of the trees and stopped dead in his tracks. He stared at the blazing wood cabin, his mouth wide in disbelief; then he brought an arm up to shield his face. 'Bloody hell!' he cried.

Francesca came to a halt beside him. 'What happened?' she yelled, struggling to be heard above the roar of the fire.

'We don't know,' Steve shouted back. 'It just went straight up. None of us was here.'

'Can't we get some water or something?' Andrew asked, urgently.

Just then a huge section of roof collapsed inwards and sparks flew up into the air.

Frankie ducked instinctively.

'Everyone get back!' Steve yelled. 'The walls might go at any time!'

Stephanie appeared from behind the building. Her face was bright red and covered in soot. 'The wind's blowing the flames over the other side. If any of the trees catch light, we could have a real problem.'

Steve wiped his face. It was just like the bush fires back home. He glanced around, trying to assess the situation properly.

The glade was large and the gaps between the hut and the trees were probably wide enough to keep the fire contained along the front and the sides. But as for the back... He looked across at Andrew. The man had a blanket clutched tightly to his chest. 'Andy. See if you can get some more blankets. Go down to the beach and soak them, then bring them back here. And somebody get the cooking pots and fill them up with water.'

'That won't do any good!' Sue Durrant sneered.

'We've got to do something!' Stephanie snapped back.

Steve was already making his way around the edge of the log cabin. He darted between the trees, trying to avoid the worst of the heat, and moved back into the clearing at the rear of the hut. It was just as Stephanie had said. The evening breeze wasn't particularly strong, but the gap between the wall and the tree line was narrow enough that a stray spark or a falling log might carry the flame across. If that happened, the whole island could catch light.

He came to a halt at the far corner of the cabin. Here the gap was at its narrowest. If he could find something to prod with, perhaps part of the wall could be pushed inwards, directing the flames away from the forest. The roof would have to come down first though. He moved in towards the wall, trying to see if he could get close enough to push against it with a stick. The heat of the flames scalded his face, but he found that if he pulled his shirt up over his nose he was able to get close to it, at least for a brief time. All he needed now was a good piece of wood to attack it with.

Andrew arrived back with the blankets. Chris Hudson was following behind. 'The water's coming!' the Mancunian yelled across.

Steve had found a suitable stick. He rushed over to meet the two men. 'If you see any sparks hitting the ground, or if any of the branches catch light, I want you to try and smother them.'

Andrew nodded. 'I understand.'

Chris was staring wide-eyed at the flames. 'That is, like, totally awesome,' he breathed.

Another section of roof imploded. A plume of sparks shot into the sky and showered the three men. They ducked down and threw their hands over their heads. A small patch of flame hit the bottom of a nearby tree. Andrew leapt to his feet and smothered it with a wet blanket.

The near corner of the hut was now bereft of roofing. Steve pulled up his face mask and moved towards it. He kicked at the corner post, trying to get it to fall inwards, but the foundation was too deep. The heat was too much for him as well; he had to pull away for a second. Then, lifting his stick, he moved in again and kicked and prodded at the other parts of the wall. Some of the meshing broke. He thrust the stick again and a portion of wall fell inwards as he had intended. He dragged himself away, with glowing embers catching the base of his trousers. He shook his legs and stamped his shoes heavily on the ground.

'Hey, be careful!' Chris warned. Steve looked round, but the boy was not yelling at him.

Andrew had pulled himself up onto one of the nearest trees. A high branch poked out from it, the closest point to the top of the burning hut. Some of the flames were flickering within a few inches of the wood. The Englishman scrambled along and manually bent the branch away from the danger zone. Fortunately, it was thin enough to pull round but, try as he might, Andrew could not snap it off. He held the branch fast with one hand and called down to Chris to get him a knife. Luckily, the Canadian had one to hand. Andrew could not let go of the branch, so Chris had to clamber part-way up the tree to hand it across. Andrew grabbed the knife tightly and began to saw. It would take him a few minutes to cut through the wood and detach the branch.

In the meantime, the women had arrived with the water. There were only two cooking pots and the amount of liquid they could carry was pitiful; barely more than twenty litres between them. Nonetheless, Stephanie and Sue had filled both containers to the brim and brought them around to the back of the hut. Frankie and Isabel arrived moments later with a couple more blankets they had found in the Grotto.

Sue came forward with one of the pots, intent on throwing it at the fire. 'Not on the hut!' Stephanie yelled.

'Stay back!' Steve added. 'Keep it for the trees.' The water would be more use smothering any embryonic bush fires. He moved across to join the women.

By now, they were all sweating and raw faced. The sun had set over an hour ago but the light of the fire was such that nobody had any difficulty navigating the area, even back among the trees. Acrid smoke was funnelling upwards away from the glade.

'I've nearly got it!' Andrew called. He twisted the branch around and finally succeeded in detaching it from the mother tree.

'Be careful!' Francesca warned, squinting up at him.

The youngster threw the branch down into the undergrowth, well away from the hut, and then began to clamber down the tree himself.

The last support strut gave way just as Andrew hit the ground. The roof of the log cabin disintegrated in front of him, as Chris yanked him into the safety of the undergrowth.

'That's it,' Steve said, from back among the trees. 'We should be able to contain it now.' He looked across at Stephanie. 'Keep the water ready. There might still be the odd spark jumping across.' She nodded. But the worst of the danger was over. The fire would continue to blaze for some hours, probably even into the morning, but the core of it would most likely die away quite quickly now.

Half an hour passed with no further trouble.

'You know, I think we might as well head back to the beach,' Steve suggested, wearily. 'We could probably all do with something to eat.'

Chris nodded eagerly.

'I'll keep an eye on things here,' Andrew volunteered.

Jeremy offered to keep him company. 'Better to be on the safe side, ain't it?'

'Good on you,' Steve said. But his face was grim.

Sue had lost almost everything; her clothes, her water bottle, her backpack. *What an idiot,* she scolded herself. *Why did I put it all in there in the first place?* That hut had been a disaster waiting to happen. Any stray spark might have set it off. *Did set it off,* she corrected herself. That was why they did the cooking on the beach. What kind of idiot took a lighted match into a log cabin?

Sue was not the only one to have lost her rucksack. The men had got off scot-free, but Stephanie, Isabel and Francesca had all left their bags inside. Frankie had returned from West Bay wearing nothing but a t-shirt and her bikini bottoms. Everything else had been left in the hut. The poor bitch had lost everything.

'You'd better wrap a blanket around those legs,' Stephanie suggested, looking with concern at the barely dressed young woman. Insects were buzzing madly around her exposed limbs. 'The sand flies are worse than ever tonight.'

'I've noticed,' Francesca said, scratching her legs with some anxiety. 'But all the blankets are being used.' Andrew and Jeremy had them piled up in a big heap in the clearing, just in case.

Poor cow, Sue thought, watching the girl slap herself again as another insect attempted to draw blood. *At least I was covered up.* Sue had lost a few pairs of knickers and a pale green swimsuit, but at least her trousers were safe. She had already changed into her evening wear before the fire had started. *Thank god for a long sleeved sweater.*

'What else have we lost?' Isabel wondered. She was wearing leggings rather than trousers but like Sue she was at least covered up. Her face was smothered in soot, however. She had been in the thick of the action earlier on and the smoke had taken its toll. She coughed heavily and reached for some water.

Chris Hudson, ever attentive, answered her question. 'I guess the work bench and one of the torches.'

'We've still got the medical kit and the radio,' Stephanie pointed out, from over by the cooking fire. She was helping Steve to prepare dinner. 'I was planning to put them in the hut. I suppose it's just as well I didn't.'

'Who cares about the bloody radio?' Sue spat. The stupid thing might just as well have been added to the bonfire. 'You do talk drivel sometimes.'

137

Stephanie pursed her lips. She was too tired to be provoked.

'Has no-one got a spare pair of trousers?' Francesca asked.

Chris shook his head, staring at the sand flies swarming around her legs. 'Hey, but Jeremy might have.' The bearded Londoner was the only one to have brought a second pair with him. It was meant to be one pair of trousers and two pairs of shorts each but Jeremy had broken the rules.

Steve had another idea. 'You know, I wouldn't suggest this at any other time. But there are two rucksacks full of clothes over in the Grotto that aren't being used.'

Francesca took a deep breath and nodded. Those were the ones that belonged to Duncan and Jane. It felt rather ghoulish, stealing their clothes, but there was little alternative. 'I'd better go now,' she said.

Steve waved his torch. 'Here, take this.' The cooks could manage for a few minutes without light. Frankie accepted it gratefully. 'You might want to grab another one while you're down there.' The fire had destroyed a second emergency torch but there were two more in the Grotto.

'Do you want me to come with you?' Isabel asked.

Francesca shook her head. 'I'll be all right.' She flicked the light on and headed off towards the cave.

Rather you than me, Sue thought, watching her go. Sue had already made a couple of trips to the Grotto this evening but it hadn't been quite so dark the last time. It was a pity there was no moon. She turned back to the group. 'So do we know how this thing started?'

Chris didn't want to get caught up in a slanging match. 'Can't we, like, wait until after dinner?'

'Dinner's going to be ages. Haven't you been paying attention? They've only just got the fire started again.' Preparations for the group's evening meal had been abandoned because of the blaze. Afterwards, Sue had brought one of the cooking pots back from the clearing and refilled it, but hot food was still a long way off. The broth wasn't even bubbling yet.

The Canadian changed tack. 'I'm feeling really tired.'

That was typical, Sue thought, always putting himself first. 'Well I'm sorry, but this is something we need to discuss. If some idiot left a lighted match on the floor of the log cabin…'

'Where *are* the matches?' Isabel asked, out of curiosity.

Sue shrugged. 'I've no idea.' She had brought the matchbox to the island, but it had gone walkabout a couple of days earlier.

'You know, I think it would take more than just a match,' Steve asserted, stirring the soup. 'That hut went up like a rocket.'

'It must have started *somehow*,' Sue insisted. 'Unless you think one of us did it deliberately.'

That got a snort from Stephanie. 'Hardly,' she said.

'So how did it start?'

'Well, you know, Sue, there might be a dozen perfectly straight-forward explanations,' Steve declared.

'Name one.'

Chris had an idea. 'It might have been struck by lightning.'

Sue laughed. 'Yeah, right!'

'Hey, there's been a lot of that stuff around just lately…'

The guy was an idiot. 'Yes. Thunder, lightning. Storms. You don't get one bolt of lightning on its own!'

'Leave the boy alone,' Stephanie snapped.

'What are you, his mother? Anyway, *Stephanie*…' Sue articulated her name in the most insulting manner she could muster. 'You're the one with the lighter. Perhaps you dropped one of your cigarette butts next to the wall. That's a far more convincing explanation, if you ask me.'

Stephanie glowered but still she refused to be provoked. 'In the first place,' she replied, with icy calm, 'I have never lit up anywhere near the log cabin. I have one cigarette a day and I smoke that at the Grotto in the afternoon. As you know full well. Secondly, I lent my lighter to Chris this evening so that he could start the cooking fire, because you have lost the one box of matches we did have between the eight of us.'

Lost them? 'I didn't lose them!' Sue protested. 'Someone walked off with them. I told you. Anyway, you wouldn't have any matches at all if it wasn't for me.'

'We haven't got any now,' Stephanie pointed out.

'I left them on the workbench in the hut,' Sue reiterated, speaking slowly, as if to an idiot. 'I went back later and they weren't there. So somebody took them without asking. Maybe it was you.'

'Why would I need your matches? I've got a lighter.'

'Hey, look, can everybody just, like, calm down…' Chris was becoming agitated by all the raised voices.

'Piss off!' Sue growled. 'This is nothing to do with you.'

'You know, I think this is something to do with all of us,' Steve interjected calmly. 'I don't think throwing accusations around is going to help matters very much. Most likely there's a perfectly innocent explanation for all this, but you know, I don't think we'll discover what it is by shouting at each other. I suggest everybody cools down and gives me a hand with dinner. You know, young Chris here is right. We should let this drop for now. We can discuss everything later when everyone is in a more rational frame of mind. And when the whole group is here.'

Sue glared at the curly-haired Australian. 'All right, have it your own way. But if I find out who stole those matches, I'm telling you: I won't be responsible for my actions…'

Jeremy Fielding had dragged a bed-frame back into the glade and placed the backpacks in a row on top of the mattress. The mosquito net and bedding had been removed temporarily. Four of the group's rucksacks had been destroyed in the fire but the six remaining packs had been brought over from the Grotto first thing after breakfast. Sue had insisted every one of them was thoroughly searched. Lengthy discussions over the cause of the blaze had got them nowhere and the Englishwoman would not be satisfied until they had at least discovered the whereabouts of her matches.

Smoke continued to rise from the ashes of the log cabin. The charred embers were still giving off heat a good fifteen hours after the fire had started. The four women, who normally slept in the clearing, had been forced to join the men on the beach for the night. And Francesca had had to borrow some clothes from the late Duncan Roberts.

Frankie stepped forward now, a little embarrassed, in a pair of black jeans that were far too long for her. She had tried on Jane Ruddock's trousers first, but they had been too tight around the waist. The others watched as she tentatively opened the first rucksack, the one belonging to the dead man. She emptied out the contents, placing each item methodically on the blanket next to the pack. She already knew what was inside; she had rummaged through it the night before. Once everything was laid out, she held up the bag for everyone to see.

Steve took charge of the second pack. This was the one that had belonged to Jane Ruddock. It was smaller than Duncan's but contained a similar mix of clothing and personal items. Her only luxury had been a travel pillow. Sue watched carefully as Steve laid out each item.

The third pack belonged to Jeremy. Isabel opened the top of it and started to remove the contents, trying to be as circumspect as possible. The rucksack had two side pockets. She unzipped one of them and found a few boxes of contraceptives, which she placed down on the bed without comment.

'Got to be prepared, ain't you?' Jeremy laughed. He winked at Stephanie. The Australian rolled her eyes.

Jeremy was not the only one carrying contraceptives. Most of the men and all of the women were equally well-prepared. Condoms were one item that had not been on the prohibited list.

But still there was no sign of the matches.

Chris Hudson's rucksack was the last in line. 'The zip's kind of awkward,' the young man volunteered.

Frankie unhooked the cover. There was precious little in the main section, apart from the usual set of clothes. At the bottom of the pack was a tin of powdered orange – his chosen luxury – alongside the regulation metal flask. Francesca picked up the canteen, which was the same colour as Jane's.

'Looks a bit like my one,' Jeremy remarked.

Chris stared at the water bottle. 'That isn't my flask,' he declared, blankly. The others glanced at him in surprise. 'I've got mine here.' He lifted up a yellow canteen. The one Frankie had was metallic blue.

She looked at it again. 'Is it yours?' she asked Jeremy.

The Englishman shook his head. 'No. I've got mine here, look.' He flipped it over. 'It's got my initials on the bottom.'

Francesca frowned. 'So this must be...must have belonged to Jane. What's it doing in your rucksack?'

'I...I don't know,' Chris responded, awkwardly. 'I didn't put it there. I...I've already got a water bottle.'

'I could do with a spare one,' Isabel said. She had lost her own bottle in the fire.

Frankie lifted the flask to her ear and shook it. There was still a bit of liquid left inside. She unscrewed the top and sniffed the contents. 'It smells like...I don't know.' She handed the bottle to Steve.

'It's kerosene,' he said, in surprise.

'*Kerosene?!?*' Sue Durrant exploded.

'Just a trace,' Steve confirmed. 'But the smell is unmistakeable.'

All eyes focused on the Canadian.

'I...I don't even know what that is,' he mumbled.

'It's lighter fuel,' Francesca said. 'Paraffin. You use it to...' Her voice trailed away.

'You use it to start fires,' Sue finished angrily. 'You little bastard. It was you, wasn't it? You did it deliberately. You set light to the hut...'

Chris was speechless. 'I...I...no, I...'

'You don't *know* it was him,' Frankie observed, defensively.

Sue strode forward and grabbed the backpack from the A-frame. There was an underside pocket which had not yet been searched. She ripped at the zip mechanism and pulled the fabric apart. Inside there was a large box of matches. *Her* matches. She pulled them out triumphantly and spun around to confront the boy. 'What more evidence do you need?'

Chris stared at the matches in horror. 'Sue, I…I swear…' He seemed genuinely bewildered.

'You bastard! You vindictive…'

Steve stepped forward. 'Sue, calm down!'

'Calm down? Why should I calm down? Eight days that bloody hut took to build and then this little bastard razes it to the ground.' She advanced menacingly on the Canadian, who quickly backed away. 'Why did you do it?'

'I…look,' he protested. 'I…I didn't do anything. I worked as hard on that thing as anyone else. Like, why would I…?'

' *"Worked hard"* ?' Sue sneered. 'You've never worked hard in your life. Poor little rich boy. Everything you ever wanted and this is how you show your gratitude!' She threw the box of matches to the ground. 'Well, daddy's not going to get you out of this one, you spiteful little bastard!'

She launched herself at him. Chris stumbled backwards and tried to scrabble away but Sue was already on top of him and smashing at his face with her fists. The others rushed forward to restrain her, but the woman managed to land several blows before the two of them were dragged apart.

'For goodness' sake!' Steve exclaimed.

Jeremy had swung his arm around Sue's neck and yanked her back onto the ground. Chris flipped over and found his feet. The woman pulled herself up but Jeremy had locked her arms behind her back. The Canadian bolted into the forest.

'That's it! You run!' Sue jeered, struggling to free herself from Jeremy's iron grip. 'Run away! There's nowhere to hide, you little…' Steve slapped her hard across the face.

For a moment, nobody spoke. Sue stared at the Australian in disbelief. 'You hit me!'

'Yes I did. Now are you going to calm down or would you like me to do it again?'

Sue glared at him. Their eyes remained locked for several seconds but Steve would not break the gaze.

'All right,' she grunted at last. 'I'm calm. Just let me go.'

Steve nodded to Jeremy and the Englishman released his grip.

'You didn't have to be so bloody rough!'

'Susan…'

'All right! I'm calm. I'm calm.' Sue lifted her hands and closed her eyes for a moment. 'But that boy is definitely guilty. And he's going to pay for it. One way or another.'

Steve bent over and picked up the matchbox. 'How do you know he's guilty?'

'What do you mean, "how do I know"? Have you not been following all this? I found the matches in his pack. And the lighter fuel. You said yourself, it must have taken more than a match to get that thing going. The little bastard…'

'…was on the beach preparing the fire for dinner,' Steve pointed out quietly. 'Don't you remember?'

Sue blinked; then she frowned. She hadn't thought about that. Chris *had* been on cooking duty and she remembered seeing him there. Steve had only taken over when the fire had gone out. Before that, the young man had been tending to the food.

'I lent him my lighter to get it going,' Stephanie confirmed. 'We all saw him there.'

Sue shook herself angrily. They were right, the bastards. But the glade was not that far from the beach. 'He might have slipped away for five minutes. We weren't watching him all the time. And if he had your lighter as well…'

'…then he wouldn't need the matches,' Stephanie finished, with impeccable logic.

Sue glowered at her.

'There was no call to attack him like that,' Francesca admonished, appalled at the other woman's behaviour. 'You frightened the life out of that poor boy.'

'I thought…'

'You didn't think at all,' Stephanie snapped.

Steve strolled back to the A-frame and picked up the metal flask containing the kerosene. 'You know, sometimes, Sue, it might be helpful if you stopped and thought a little before you jumped to conclusions.' He was too tired now to be diplomatic.

'All right,' she admitted, reluctantly. 'So he was on the beach at the time. That doesn't explain the flask. Or why he stole the matches.'

'Someone might have planted them there,' Isabel suggested.

Sue laughed. 'Yeah, sure.'

'You're right about one thing, though,' Frankie said. 'The fire must have been started deliberately.'

'The kerosene,' Stephanie agreed. 'It couldn't possibly have been an accident.'

'Where did they get it from?' Isabel wondered. 'And why would they hide it away?'

Sue had an answer. 'Ask Chris. He's still the most likely suspect, no matter what you say.'

Steve sighed. She was right, at that. The evidence did point towards the Canadian. 'What do you think, Andy? You know him better than anyone.'

Andrew considered for a moment. 'I don't think it were him. I mean, I know the stuff were in his pack, but...he's not vindictive or nothing. Wouldn't harm a fly. And anyway, if everyone saw him on the beach...'

'He was there,' Jeremy confirmed. 'We all was, so far as I could see. Except you and Frankie.'

'We were down at the bay,' Andrew reminded him.

'And Chris was certainly bewildered when I took out that flask,' Francesca added. 'I don't think he could have faked that reaction. Especially not when Sue produced the matches.'

'I don't think it were him,' Andrew repeated, with growing confidence.

Steve was inclined to agree. 'But regardless of that, you know, we still have to face a rather unpleasant fact. One of us here is an arsonist. One of us deliberately burnt down the log cabin, and maybe tried to pin the blame on young Chris.' He shook his head sadly.

'It might have been an accident,' Andrew said.

'I'm afraid not, Andy.' Steve looked down at the Canadian's pack. There was a slight bump underneath he had not noticed before. He slid his hand inside the pouch. 'Just a minute,' he said. 'I think there's something else in here.'

A small container had been stuffed right down inside. Steve pulled it out. The bottle was dark green and had a plastic lid. He unscrewed the top and pulled out a small rubber pipette.

'What is it?' Stephanie asked.

'I don't know. It was tucked in pretty firmly.'

'Probably just something personal,' Andrew suggested.

'Looks like nail varnish,' Jeremy thought, grabbing hold of the bottle and taking a sniff. 'Well, maybe not.' He shrugged. 'Better ask Chris, I suppose. If he's not halfway to Timbuktu by now.'

'I'd better go and find him,' Andrew said.

'Tell him not to bother coming back.'

Steve shot Sue a warning glance.

'All right. Sorry! We'll give the little sod the benefit of the doubt.'

Andrew took the glass bottle from Jeremy. 'I'll ask him what it is. I won't be long.' So saying, he turned and disappeared into the forest.

Frankie watched him go. 'I wish I understood why anyone would want to do this,' she said, staring at the charred ashes of the log cabin. 'Why would anyone burn down the hut? We all worked on it. It doesn't make sense.'

Stephanie pursed her lips. 'It obviously makes sense to someone.'

It took Andrew three quarters of an hour to locate Chris Hudson. The young man had darted off in one direction, but had then forked west. It was difficult tracking anybody through the forest. Andrew was not the most observant of people and the island was almost four miles across. He might not have found him at all if the Canadian had not responded when he had started shouting out his name. 'Chris!'

'Over here!'

Andrew followed the sound and arrived at the base of a thick tree trunk, not far from West Bay. The two of them had come this way before. They had played football together on the beach, using an unripened coconut as a ball. Now Chris was balancing comfortably on a branch about six or seven metres up, his body partially obscured by leaves and other branches, though Andrew could still make out his fair hair and ever-reddening skin. 'What are you doing up there? I've been looking for you all over.'

'I…didn't want anyone to find me.'

Andrew grinned, peering upwards. 'I don't suppose they would up there. What's the view like?'

'I…I haven't really been looking.'

He grabbed a branch. 'Do you mind if I join you?'

Chris shrugged. 'If you like.'

Andrew found a foothold and began to haul himself up. It was not an easy climb, but he was good with his hands and after a couple of minutes he had pulled himself up to the same level as his friend. There was no room on the branch where Chris was perched, however, so Andrew manoeuvred himself a little further, finally resting his back on the trunk of the tree and dangling his legs over the side. 'Good up here, in't it?'

Chris nodded non-committally.

A brief moment of silence followed. Andrew was practically the only person the Canadian ever talked to, apart from Jeremy, but it often took a while to draw him into a conversation.

'I've always loved climbing trees.' Andrew said, breaking the silence. 'Especially big ones like this.' He peered at the ground, which now seemed quite some distance away. 'I don't like looking down, though. It gets me all dizzy.' His mum had often compared him to next door's cat; he'd scramble up anything, without ever thinking about how he was going to get down. 'At least I'm not hanging over a bonfire this time.'

Chris was staring straight ahead, at the gently swaying canopy and the calm sea beyond it. 'They all think I did it, don't they? They think I burnt down the hut.'

Andrew shook his head. 'No they don't.'

'Sue does. Hey, I don't blame her. It's, like, it was all there.'

'Everyone saw you on the beach, preparing dinner. They know it couldn't have been you.'

Chris looked up. 'I didn't do it,' he declared, simply.

'I know.' Andrew slid a hand into his pocket and produced the small bottle Jeremy had handed to him. 'We found this at the bottom of your pack. I don't suppose it's yours, is it?'

The young man peered up at the bottle. 'I've...never seen it before. What is it?'

Andrew shrugged and handed it down. 'I don't know. We found it in the bottom of your pack, where the matches were. I thought it were yours.'

Chris shook his head, taking a close look. There was no identifying label on the glass. 'This is really freaky. I mean, like, all this stuff in my pack. How did it get there? Where did it come from?'

Andrew shrugged. 'Somebody must have put it there.'

'But that's it. It's like, who could have done that? I mean, there's no-one, is there? Okay, sure, none of us are close, but Christ, someone might have been *killed* in that fire.'

'I know. That's what I don't get.'

'I can't believe anyone here would do something like that. Not one of us. Not unless they were, like, schizo or something.'

'I still reckon it could have been an accident,' Andrew said. 'Somebody dropping a match or maybe a spark drifting over from the beach.'

The Canadian shook his head. 'It was deliberate, Andy. Someone must have, like, put all that stuff in my pack. The kera...whatever it was. The matches. And if someone did that...'

'Then they must have started the fire.' Andrew could not fault the logic.

'I mean, like, Jesus, why are we even still here? People dying. It...' Chris put a hand to his face. 'This is really freaking me out, Andy. You know? I just...I want to go home.'

The other man nodded. 'I know. Me an'all. I don't reckon we should ever have come here.' Andrew shook himself. *Don't get all gloomy on him.* 'But we won't be here much longer,' he added, trying to sound optimistic.

'I sure hope not, anyway.' Chris glanced up again. 'Everyone thinks I did it though, don't they?'

'It's only Sue. Everybody else is keeping an open mind. Like I said, half of them saw you on the beach in any case.'

'And you believe me?'

'Course I do.' Andrew grinned. 'You'd have to be pretty bloody stupid to leave all that stuff lying around in your rucksack for us to find.'

Chris smiled. 'Hey, I've done some pretty stupid things in my time. But...thanks.' He handed the bottle back and gave out a loud sigh. 'I wish my pop was here. He'd sort everything out. He's kind of cool like that.'

'You get on well with your dad?'

'I guess. He can be kind of distant sometimes. But he's always been there for me.'

'How old is he?'

'Sixty two. A lot older than my mom.'

That made sense, anyway. 'Is he as rich as what everyone says?'

'Yeah, he's pretty solvent.'

'Lucky sod.' Andrew wondered what it would be like to have rich parents. His mum and dad had never had two ha'pennies to rub together.

'It's funny. Like, you'd think it would make life easier. But...it doesn't, somehow.'

Andrew nodded. 'I know what you mean. I knew a bloke at school. His dad were in films and stuff. Didn't do him no good. Mind you, his parents were divorced.'

Chris smiled sadly. 'I guess I'm kind of lucky my parents stuck together. I'd like to have a family of my own one day. Maybe in a few years. Like, when I'm twenty-eight or something.'

'That'd be nice,' Andrew agreed. Settling down with someone. 'Once we get away from here.'

'How old's Frankie?' Chris asked.

'Twenty-four.'

He paused for a moment. His mood seemed to be improving. 'Have you, like, done it with her yet?'

149

Andrew laughed. 'You mind your own bloody business!'

Jeremy Fielding was scrabbling across the southern side of the Rocks. He and Andrew had swum out together but Jeremy had cut his legs clambering up the north face. 'There must be another way onto this thing,' he had complained, staring out to sea. 'I'm going to go take a look.' Jeremy had gone off in search of an alternative route, while Andrew broke out the fishing rods. The equipment was kept here permanently now. It was too much of a hassle carrying everything back and forth.

Andrew attached the bait and cast out his line. It would probably be some time before he got the first bite.

Jeremy returned after twenty minutes, breathing heavily from all the exertion. 'Here, Andy, have you got your pen knife with you?'

The Mancunian shook his head. 'No, I left it in my pack.' The bags had been dumped on Cocoa Beach as usual. There was no point trying to swim out with them. 'Did you find another way up?'

Jeremy nodded. 'Yeah, but it's right on the other side. It's not easy to get at from over here.' The island was scarcely ninety feet across but it was difficult to navigate. He looked down at his legs and winced. They were crusted in blood. Some of the stones on the south face were razor sharp. 'You're better off swimming round and fishing on the other side. There's a small beach there, all pebbles and stuff. It might be worth trying the next time we come out here.' There was a sudden tug from Andrew's line. 'Oy! Pay attention!' Jeremy laughed. 'You've got a bite there!'

Andrew grinned. 'Feels like a big 'un an'all.' The cord was already taut. He stood up and yanked the rod backwards over his head. The fish came flying halfway towards them but then flopped down onto the side of the boulder. Andrew grabbed the cord and pulled it the rest of the way up. The fish was flapping about desperately. He unhooked the beast from the spike and held it down on the rock beside him; then he picked up a stone with his other hand and bashed the creature on the head. The fish stopped moving at once.

Jeremy chuckled. 'I keep telling you, they don't feel nothing.' There was no need to put it out of its misery.

'I know. But when it's wriggling like that…any road, it makes me feel better.'

The other man picked up the fish and placed it in the plastic bag. It was their first catch of the day. 'Well, that's one anyway.'

Andrew quickly checked the end of his line and cast it back out to sea. 'So what did you want a penknife for?' he asked.

'Oh, nothing. I'll show you later, if we've got time. I think you probably need a bit of help here.' The Londoner grabbed his own fishing rod and sat down next to Andrew. He draped his legs over the side of the rock and cast out a line. 'Just call me Mr Fish,' he said.

Stephanie McMahon pulled herself up onto a rock and dug out her cigarettes. Every day, it seemed, there was someone in the Grotto when she wanted to take a break. Today it was Francesca Stevens, filling up the cooking pot. 'I won't be a minute,' the girl said, sloshing the water from the pot and refilling it from the pool.

Stephanie took out her last cigarette, sighed and lit it slowly. There had been twenty cigarettes in the pack to start with, which meant they had been on the island for nineteen days. She had smoked an extra one the evening before last, when the hut had burnt down.

Since then, an air of suspicion had descended upon the camp. Chris Hudson was keeping an understandably low profile. Most of the islanders were reluctant to point the finger, but the frustration they all felt at the non-appearance of Clive and at the deaths of Jane and Duncan had now been given an involuntary focus. Not everyone was convinced Chris was responsible, however, and this only fuelled their collective paranoia. If not him, then somebody else. The only thing they could all agree on was that the hut had been burnt down deliberately.

Stephanie took a long, slow drag from the cigarette. Frankie was watching her with some curiosity. 'My last one,' she explained, closing her eyes. 'Just when I'm really starting to need them.' She took another long drag as the younger woman moved away, carrying the now full cooking pot.

Steve had been badly affected too. He was masking it well, but Stephanie could see the signs. He had always tried to keep everyone busy, but that was not possible now. No-one was going to pull together and rebuild the hut if they thought it was just going to be burnt down again. Everybody had an excuse for being apathetic and Steve was running out of ideas. *I suppose I should try and come up with something constructive to do, to help him out.* But the only thing Stephanie could think of was to distract him in other, more personal ways. Steve had been too busy lately to pay her much attention so she would have to make an extra effort. But now that they had the time, there was no point in holding back. Steve knew she was interested and if nothing else, it would take her mind off having to give up the cigarettes.

Forget that bloody log cabin, Jeremy thought. Going without sex was the worst thing. He was not used to abstinence and he resented it when there were a couple of good looking birds going free. It wasn't natural. They were usually fighting over him. He was a fair looking bloke, wasn't he? What was the matter with them? *Stupid cows.* They didn't know what they were missing.

He had started dreaming again; the kind of dreams he hadn't had since he was a teenager. It was embarrassing. *I hope we're not going to be here for the whole bloody year. I can't go without a shag for that long. It'll drive me crazy.* He had been so sure something would turn up. Ten people. Bound to be someone. *What an idiot.*

Oh sod it, he decided. He was not going to let it worry him. *It's their funeral.*

He turned over and adjusted himself. *What time is it?* he wondered. He must have been in bed a couple of hours by now. *Have I been asleep yet?* He wasn't sure.

He had been thinking about that bird he knew in Doncaster. *What was her name? Jenny. That was it. Bloody hell, she was gorgeous. Legs up to her armpits and tits like you wouldn't believe. She'd put any of this lot to shame.* He grinned at the memory. *What a night that was!* He could see her now, smiling at him. Undressing. Reaching down. He could feel…

A hand grabbed him across the mouth. Jeremy jerked in surprise. His eyes flicked open. *What the…?* There was a flash of steel across his throat and then blood pouring from the wound. Somebody had…pain flooded his senses. He tried to scream but no sound came out. He tried to move but he was being held down. There was a figure looming over him, but his eyes were unable to focus. And all at once his mind fogged over.

Jeremy blacked out and his shoulders slumped back onto the bed-frame.

Chapter Ten

Isabel Grant discovered the body the following morning.

Steve was piling wood under the small roof on Candy Beach. He had been awake for some hours, having risen at the crack of dawn for his usual early morning run. On his way back, he had collected some wood and was now stacking it up under the roof of the beach hut, where it could be kept nice and dry. It didn't look like rain, but there were a few wisps of cloud in the distance and it was as well to be prepared.

Isabel was lifting the netting on Jeremy's A-frame, a little way down the beach. Steve watched as she drew a hand to her mouth and dropped the fruit she had been carrying. A few seconds later, she was running across the sand towards him.

'What is it?' he asked. The girl was not exactly in a state of panic, but it was clear that something had upset her.

Isabel glanced around, making sure no-one else was within earshot. Thankfully the other bed-frames were empty; most of the islanders were up and about by now, taking care of their morning ablutions. 'It's Jem. I just went over to wake him up.' The Londoner liked to have a bit of a lie-in before breakfast. 'I think you'd better come and see.'

Steve frowned, abandoning the firewood in his hands.

Jeremy's A-frame was twenty metres down the beach. When the other men had politely suggested he move away from them, Jeremy had dragged the bed right across the sand, until it was almost out of sight behind some foliage. He hadn't been offended – he knew full well how loud his snoring could be – but he had managed to gain some comic mileage out of pretending that he was.

Steve and Isabel drew close to the bed. Even from a distance, it was obvious something was wrong. Red stains were visible on Jeremy's throat and upper torso. Steve moved in for a closer look. There was a gash across his neck. His eyes were wide open, his face a frozen image of shock and bewilderment. Steve lent over and closed the eyelids with his fingertips.

154

'Someone must have cut his throat,' Isabel breathed, with a shudder.

That much was obvious. Steve felt the muscles tense in his back. 'You know, I was half expecting something like this to happen.' He took another breath and examined the wound more closely. The blood was stodgy and congealed, the stains on his shirt completely dry. He lifted an arm, which was cold and inflexible. Death must have taken place some hours ago. 'I think he must have been killed during the night. Can you see a knife lying anywhere? Or broken glass?'

Isabel looked around. 'Not that I can see.' Apart from their footprints and Jeremy's pack, the sand was unmarked.

Steve removed his glasses and rubbed his eyes. 'This is not good.'

'What are we going to tell the others?'

Steve shrugged. 'The truth. What else can we tell them?'

'That one of us is a murderer?'

He looked down at the corpse sadly. 'This wasn't a spur of the moment thing, Bella. It was obviously planned.'

The girl clutched her hands tightly together. 'Someone had a grudge against him?'

'Not just him. You know, I think someone must have a grudge against all of us.'

Isabel did not understand. 'You don't think…you don't think this has something to do with us being here in the first place?'

Steve glanced up. 'How can it not? First the hut, then this. You know, I never believed Clive Monroe had the first idea what was going on here. And the fire the other day got me thinking. What if it was one of us? What if someone *on the island* had brought us all together?' He gazed down at the body a second time. 'You know, I think this proves it. One of us did this. Somebody wanted Jeremy Fielding dead, right from the start. And whoever it was, they must have organised the whole thing. Brought us all to the island in the first place.'

'But *why?* What could they possibly…?' Isabel stopped herself mid-sentence. A new thought had struck her and her eyes widened in horror. 'You don't think…the other deaths?'

155

Steve pulled himself up abruptly. 'Duncan and Jane?'

'Is it possible?'

The Australian was staring straight ahead. 'I don't know,' he admitted cautiously. 'But we're going to have to find out…'

'What's this all about?' Stephanie McMahon asked him calmly.

The blonde woman had gathered up the remaining islanders, as requested, and they had assembled in the forest glade a little way from Candy Beach. Sue and Francesca had already gone out foraging and it had taken a good fifteen minutes to track them down. Nobody knew why Steve had summoned them all together like this. The group stood uneasily in the dusty ruins of the log cabin.

'Is everyone here?' Steve asked.

There were a few coughs and nervous glances.

Andrew shook his head. 'Jem's not.'

'Apart from Jeremy.' Steve made a quick mental count of the group. Seven people, including himself. That was everyone.

Sue did not appreciate being kept in the dark. 'Look, are you going to tell us what's going on, or are you just going to stand there and smirk? I for one have got better things to do.'

Steve suppressed the urge to sigh. 'You know, Sue, I wouldn't have asked you all here if it wasn't important.'

She snorted. 'Fine, so tell us. Have you found out who burnt the hut down, is that it?'

'It's not about the hut,' Isabel replied, sadly.

Frankie picked up on the mood. 'Something else has happened. Why isn't Jeremy here?'

'Jeremy's in bed,' Sue spat. 'He hasn't got up yet. I'll go and wake him, the lazy sod.'

Isabel shook her head. 'I think you should stay here.'

'I don't take orders from you!'

Steve raised a hand. 'Please, Sue. There are a couple of things we need to look at before anyone goes wandering off.' He turned back to the group. 'First of all, can everyone please turn out their pockets?'

Sue grimaced. 'What is this? What's going on here?'

'Just do as he asks,' Stephanie said. 'I'm sure there's a good reason.' She reached inside her shorts and produced a lighter and a penknife from her pockets, which she placed down on one of the beds. Steve watched her closely, paying particular attention to her hands.

When she had finished, he emptied out his own pockets, under Isabel's careful scrutiny. The Englishwoman then proceeded to do likewise and the other islanders followed suit, with Sue the last in line. When everyone had finished, Steve took a step back. There was a small pile of bric-a-brac on the mattress, but nothing incriminating that he could see.

'So what did that little charade achieve?' Sue demanded.

'Well, not what I'd hoped for,' he admitted. 'Look, Susan, I need to ask you a question and I want you to answer me honestly.'

The woman took a step back. She didn't know where this was leading. 'I can't stop you asking,' she muttered, not meeting his eye.

'Is there anything you haven't told us about Duncan Roberts? Anything you saw or heard the day he died that you might have missed out?'

Sue bristled angrily. 'What is this? I've already told you! He was alive when I left him. What, you think I killed him or something?'

'You know, I didn't say that, Sue.'

'No. You never say anything, do you? You insinuate. You just stand there smugly, pretending you know everything. But you're just a loser like the rest of us. Why else would you be here? If you had a proper life you wouldn't want to spend a whole year with a bunch of total strangers.'

Steve didn't flinch under the verbal assault. His voice was as calm as ever when he spoke again. 'Sue, if you know something, just tell us. No-one will blame you.'

She met his gaze; then she looked away. 'I...there's nothing else, all right? He was alive when I left him.' But her voice lacked conviction.

Francesca stepped forward. 'Steve, I think it's about time you told us what's going on. Has something happened to Jeremy?'

The Australian nodded. 'Jeremy's dead. He died during the night.'

There was a collective shudder. The group exchanged confused glances. 'What happened?' Stephanie asked.

'He was murdered. Somebody cut his throat with a knife.'

Frankie let out a gasp. A shocked silence descended upon the glade.

'He's really dead?' Andrew mumbled, incredulously.

'I'm afraid so.'

Only the previous day, the two men had been out fishing together.

Francesca rubbed her eyes in bewilderment. 'So…what happens now?'

'I wish I knew,' Steve said. 'You know, I hate to say it, but this whole expedition seems to have been cursed from day one.'

'And you think it was one of us who killed him?' Stephanie asked.

'It must have been. There's no other explanation.'

Another silence descended, as the islanders struggled to digest the information. Andrew's mind raced back over the questions Steve had just been asking them. 'Here, you don't think Duncan were murdered an'all?' Duncan and Jeremy had been old friends.

Steve shrugged. 'It's a possibility. I hope I'm wrong, but – not just Duncan. You know, I'm beginning to think Jane Ruddock might have been murdered as well.'

'Oh man!' Chris Hudson exclaimed, shifting his weight from one foot to another. 'We have to get off this island!'

Frankie was doing her best to maintain her composure. 'I was with Jane all the time. She had some kind of fever. I don't think…'

Steve reached into his rucksack and pulled out the small green bottle they had discovered in Chris's backpack. 'You know, it's only a guess, but I think this may well be some kind of poison…'

'Hey, now look…' said Chris.

'No-one's accusing anybody of anything,' Stephanie reassured him.

'I'm just speculating,' Steve agreed. 'But it's possible that Jane might have been poisoned using the contents of this bottle.'

'If that *is* poison,' Isabel said. 'You've got no way of knowing. And anyway, even if it is, how would it have been administered?'

Francesca nodded. 'That's true. We all eat the same food and drink.'

'I know how it was done,' Sue volunteered, quietly. The others looked at her in surprise.

'You know who poisoned Jane Ruddock?' Andrew asked, unable to hide the scepticism in his voice.

'No. No, I don't, but…' Sue paused, collecting her thoughts. 'It was the water bottle. It wasn't Jane's, it was Jeremy's. Someone must have poisoned *his* water.'

'Jeremy's?' Frankie didn't understand.

'It was a mistake. Jane was using Jeremy's water bottle. I picked it up, the night she died. I went to fill it up for her. Then I noticed it wasn't actually hers. It had Jeremy's initials scratched on the bottom. Someone had spiked it. But not to kill Jane. To kill Jeremy.'

Steve considered this for a moment. 'So somebody really *was* planning to murder him, right from the start.'

'Yes, but…'

'Why did Jane have someone else's water bottle?' Isabel asked.

'How the hell should I know?' Sue snapped back. 'It was the same colour. She must have picked it up, thinking it was hers. She was a dappy cow at the best of times.'

'Jeremy did misplace his bottle,' Stephanie recalled, thinking back to the morning they had started work on the roof. 'I lent him mine. You remember? That must have been the day Jane fell ill.'

Andrew remembered that too. But there was something else. 'He left all his stuff in the Grotto. The day before, when we buried Duncan. We were using his rucksack to pile up the earth. Perhaps she picked it up then.'

Steve scratched his head. 'You know, that does make a kind of sense.'

'And the poisoner must have got to it at around the same time,' Isabel concluded.

'But what about you?' Stephanie asked. 'Was that an accident or was someone trying to kill you as well?'

'Why would anyone want to poison me?' Isabel seemed utterly baffled. 'I've not done anything to upset anyone. I'd never even met anybody before I came here, apart from Frankie.'

'And whoever the murderer is, they wouldn't have made the same mistake twice,' Steve pointed out, 'mixing up the water bottles. If Bella was poisoned, it must have been deliberate. One of us here must really want her dead.'

Isabel swallowed hard, scanning the group. Francesca took her hand and gave it a reassuring squeeze.

'Somebody here wants us all dead,' Sue muttered.

'Well, you know, we can't be certain of that,' Steve thought. 'All we do know is that someone has some kind of grudge against young Bella here.'

'But who?' Frankie wondered.

'And, like, why isn't she already dead?' Chris added.

'Perhaps there wasn't enough poison,' the woman herself suggested, trying to consider the matter dispassionately.

Francesca disagreed. 'The water bottle got knocked over when you dropped your food. Don't you remember?'

'Not really.' Isabel frowned. 'I must have been delirious.'

'The bottle was still half full. I got Andy to go and refill it.' Frankie stared at her friend. 'If you'd carried on drinking that water…'

Isabel's eyes widened. The implication was clear. 'You saved my life,' she whispered.

Francesca nodded, scarcely believing it herself.

The two women embraced.

Stephanie turned back to her fellow Australian. 'None of this explains *why* she had to be killed. Why kill any of us? Why burn down the log cabin?'

'Hey, it looks kind of obvious to me,' Chris said. 'There's a psycho on the loose. Somebody's, like, completely deranged and they want to kill us all, one by one.' The young Canadian was becoming seriously agitated.

'It's all right,' Frankie said, attempting to calm him. 'Nothing more can happen now. Not if we all stick together.'

'But it's one of us!' Chris exclaimed. 'Man, it could be you! It could be any of you!' He backed away.

Andrew shared his anxiety. It was difficult to believe even half the things people were suggesting. It was insane. Nobody here could be a cold blooded killer. 'It can't have been one of us,' he asserted. 'It must have been somebody else. There must be someone here on the island we don't know about.'

Sue scoffed. 'What, for three weeks? Running around without being seen? Don't be stupid.'

'You know, I don't think that's likely,' Steve agreed. 'But, look, let's get a sense of perspective. You know, everything we've been saying so far has been a matter of conjecture. It seems to me that the only constructive way forward is to find out as much as we can about all the different events. And we should start from the beginning.' At this point, he turned back to Sue. 'Now I think you understand why I was asking you about the Swimming Pool.'

The woman stared at him in dismay. 'You don't think I...'

Chris glared at her. 'Hey, like, she was there when Duncan died. Maybe she hit him with something.'

'You don't know anything!' Sue snarled. 'I didn't kill Duncan.'

'But you know who did,' Steve suggested, quietly. Sue did not reply. 'Susan, if you know something, you've got to tell us.'

'There's a man lying dead on Candy Beach,' Stephanie pointed out, tartly.

'I don't know anything,' she said. 'I'm sorry.'

161

Chris did not believe her. 'She's lying!'

'You're the one who burnt down the bloody hut!'

'I did no such thing!'

'You had the matches. The kerosene. And Stephanie's lighter. And you were the one carrying the poison in your rucksack!'

'All right! That's enough!' Stephanie snapped.

'Don't you shout at me!'

'For God's Sake,' Francesca cried. 'Jeremy's just been murdered. Can everybody please calm down!'

Sue opened her mouth to reply, but then thought better of it.

'I think we should all go and take a look at the body,' Stephanie suggested.

Andrew remained in the glade while the rest of the group moved off. He couldn't bear the thought of seeing yet another corpse. It was too much to deal with just now. His head was already spinning. Frankie stayed behind and they sat next to each other on her bed-frame, their hands grasped together. Chris Hudson had darted off somewhere, in anger or fear, but the other islanders had followed the two Australians to Candy Beach.

'I don't understand any of this,' Andrew said, when they had all left. He wanted to cry but he was too bewildered. He held Frankie closely instead and she buried her head in his shoulder. He wasn't quite sure who was comforting who. 'I just can't believe it. I mean, if it were all planned from the start. How could anyone...? His voice drifted away.

'We'll get through this, Andy,' she told him, looking up. 'You and me. I promise. I won't let anyone hurt you.'

'I know.'

'You didn't find the murder weapon?' Stephanie asked, looking down at the body on the mattress. The group had gathered around the A-frame on the far side of Candy Beach. Insects were buzzing around them as Isabel pulled back the blanket to expose the dead man. She shuddered again at the sight of the gash across his neck.

Steve shook his head, in answer to Stephanie's question. 'But, you know, it must have been some kind of knife. That's why I wanted everyone to empty out their pockets. I figured there might be a bit of blood on someone's hand, or maybe on their clothing.'

Stephanie moved around to the other side of the frame. 'If I had my hand here,' she said, holding her right arm above Jeremy's throat, 'and I cut like this...' She frowned. 'I can't see how I could avoid getting some blood on my fingers at least.'

'You'd think so, wouldn't you?' Steve agreed. He waved his arm to discourage the flies in front of his face. 'But no-one had any marks on them that I could see, and we're all dressed the same as we were yesterday.'

'Perhaps they stripped off,' Isabel suggested. 'If they crept out of bed after dark, they might have been in their underwear.'

'That's true,' Steve said.

'They'd still have blood on their hands,' Stephanie asserted. 'Literally as well as figuratively.' A fair chunk of Jeremy's shirt had been stained red, below his throat. Some of that blood must have spurted onto the killer. 'And if everyone's got clean hands now, then they must have washed it off afterwards.'

Steve looked out to sea. 'If they ran into the ocean from here, they'd risk being seen. They'd have to go to the Grotto to get properly cleaned up.'

'Can you remove that kind of stain without soap?' Isabel wondered.

Steve gestured to the pathway on the other side of the beach. 'Let's go see.'

Sue glanced nervously around the forest, making sure the two of them were alone. She had been itching to talk about this properly from the moment Jeremy's death had first been announced. But they needed to be away from the rest of the group first. 'Tell me you had nothing to do with it,' she said.

Her companion boggled. 'You surely don't think I killed him?'

'I don't know what to think.' Sue gritted her teeth. The death of Jeremy Fielding had taken everyone by surprise.

'I'd never even met the man before.'

'You killed Duncan,' Sue pointed out.

'And if I hadn't, he might have killed *you*. It was an accident. You know that. I was just trying to stop him from hurting you.'

'Yeah, right.' Sue shuddered, remembering it all. It had taken just one hammer blow and Duncan had thudded onto the rocks. She had known at once that he was dead. She could still see him lying there, in her mind's eye. 'But you never said what you were doing there in the first place.'

'I told you. I was concerned. I heard raised voices and I came to see what was going on.'

Sue was not convinced. 'You're a bloody good liar,' she said. 'I know that much.'

'You think I'm lying? You think I killed Jane and Jeremy? And then poisoned...? Why? Why would I do that? What do I have against any of them?'

'I don't know,' Sue admitted.

'There's nothing *to* know.'

Sue glanced down at her feet. 'Don't worry. I believe you. If I thought otherwise, I'd be having this discussion with the rest of the group, not with you.' She looked up. 'Perhaps we should just make a clean breast of it. No one would blame you.'

'Sue. You promised.'

'All right, so I promised! I haven't broken my word, have I?'

'And I'm grateful. Believe me.'

'But I'm warning you. If you're lying to me...'

The two Australians returned to the beach to collect the last of the A-frames. The rest of the beds had already been dragged over to the clearing. The girls and boys would be sleeping together from now on. There was safety in numbers and fewer biting insects away from the sand. Steve's frame was the last one to be moved. Jeremy's bed would be left where it was for the time being. The man himself was laid out respectfully on the mattress where he had been found, a blanket serving as a makeshift shroud.

The islanders had paid a visit to the cave just before midday, to see if anybody had been there during the night. A small bar of carbolic soap had been abandoned just inside the entrance. The soap had been taken from the medical kit and its wrapper casually discarded. Steve picked up the wrapper, which was covered in red smudges, and examined it closely. A couple of bloody prints had been left on the lid of the medical box as well, which doubtless could have been used to identify the guilty party, if anyone had the first idea how to go about it.

Hands were inspected a second time but none of the group seemed particularly well-scrubbed or fragrant. If one of them had used the soap in the early hours of the morning, it wasn't evident now.

There was no blood on the pathway leading up to the Grotto from the beach and no indication of the route the murderer might have taken to get to the cave. Whoever the killer was, he or she must have moved about in complete darkness. The emergency torches were all accounted for and the moon had been nothing but a slender crescent.

Andrew thought he had heard somebody getting up to go for a pee during the night, but whoever it was he didn't think they had been gone for more than a couple of minutes. Steve was pretty sure this was Chris Hudson, although the Canadian was too frightened to admit it. Over in the glade, none of the girls had heard anything at all, though Francesca confessed to having got up once, probably a couple of hours before dawn.

Steve sighed and pulled back the netting on the A-frame. He had been on his feet now for almost eight hours and he was still no closer to the truth. He sat down wearily. It was time for a bit of a break. Stephanie seated herself next to him and unscrewed the top of her water bottle. She offered him a swig, which he took gratefully.

'You know, what we really need is a team of forensic scientists,' he said. With the proper equipment, the whole case could probably be cleared up in a matter of minutes. 'Those fingerprints would tell us everything we needed to know. But I don't have the first idea what to do with them. We haven't even got a magnifying glass between us.' He handed the bottle back to her.

Stephanie smiled. 'You can't be expected to solve everything.'

Steve watched her drink. 'Maybe if we sprinkled some flour on the soap wrapper. We must have some left.' Absently, he swatted a fly which was hovering over his left leg. 'You know, whoever did this, I don't think they really care what happens next. They must know someone in authority is going to come along and examine the evidence at some point. Otherwise, why be so careless?'

Stephanie nodded. 'Perhaps they were in a rush to get back to their bed, in case they were missed.'

'No, I don't think that's likely. It's easy enough to slip in and out of bed without being noticed, especially on such a dark night. You could be away for hours without anyone noticing. No, I think our killer left the evidence behind deliberately. Everything that's happened here has been worked out in advance.'

'But for what reason?'

Steve rested his hands on the blanket behind him and stretched out his legs. 'Well, that's just it. I've been trying to think of a possible motive. But, you know, there doesn't seem to be one.'

'Sue had an obvious motive,' Stephanie suggested. If anyone had good reason to bludgeon Duncan Roberts to death, it was the bad-tempered Englishwoman.

'Yes, but only in isolation. It doesn't explain Jem or Bella.'

'Sue has the temperament for it,' Stephanie insisted. 'She's not exactly stable, even at the best of times. And she's certainly hiding something from us.'

'Agreed. But this whole thing was meticulously planned. The poison, the kerosene, even the soap. And I don't believe Sue Durrant has the aptitude for any of that.'

Stephanie considered for a moment. 'Perhaps she's good at hiding things. Maybe she's more clever than we think.'

'I don't think so.'

'Well, somebody has to be responsible.'

There at least they agreed. 'And someone with a fair amount of money, too.'

Stephanie frowned. 'Why do you say that?'

'Well, think about it.' Steve looked at her. 'Whoever killed Jeremy and Duncan must have set up this whole expedition. The island, the yacht, the interviews. Bringing us all out here. That would take quite a bit of capital.'

'Renting an island,' Stephanie conceded. 'Even just for a couple of months. I don't think Sue is particularly well off.'

'And I don't think she has the organisational skills either. But, you know, *we* do – you and I. And both of us are well off, at least in comparison to the Brits.'

'But neither of us…' Stephanie protested.

Steve smiled, raising a hand. 'We've got to be methodical,' he said. 'We have to consider every possibility. We both have the resources to set up something like this. And so does Chris Hudson. Why not start by considering the people with the money?'

Stephanie frowned again. 'If you think it will do any good.'

'You know, I think it's worth trying.' Steve was becoming animated now, as the possibilities began to flow. 'Let's start with me. All right, say I was the murderer. I've got the capital to back it up. But did I have the opportunity?'

Stephanie pursed her lips. She really didn't want to play this game. 'Well, I suppose you were with Sue when she went swimming, the day Duncan died. You could have doubled back after she left and then attacked him. And I suppose you could have poisoned the water too. And you were on the beach last night, so you could have slipped across and…'

'Okay. So I had the opportunity.' Steve adjusted his sunglasses. 'What about motive?'

Stephanie shrugged. 'None, that I can see. Unless it was some kind of grotesque psychological experiment.' Steve raised an eyebrow and she stifled a laugh. 'I'm just hypothesizing'

'No, that's good. We've got be rigorous here.'

'And I suppose *I* had the money and the opportunity as well. I could have used my inheritance to set everything up. If I hadn't already spent most of it…'

'But you could be lying about that.'

'Well, yes.' She looked down at her feet.

'So what about motive?'

Stephanie grimaced. 'I can't think of anything. If Francesca had been the victim, then possibly…' The two women had clashed in the courts, but that was over and done with now. Neither of them bore a grudge and, of all people, they had probably suffered the least since arriving on the island.

'Let's try someone else,' Steve suggested.

'Well, how *about* Francesca?' Stephanie gripped the mattress. 'Not that I think for a minute…I – I really like the girl,' she insisted.

Steve waved away her discomfort. 'We've got to consider everyone. Is there anything we know about Frankie that might link her to any of these deaths?'

Stephanie struggled to think. 'Didn't she work for a pharmaceutical company before she came here?'

'I think so. Yeah, I do remember her saying something about that.'

'So she might know a little about poisons.'

Steve scratched his head. 'It's a bit tenuous. In any case, from what I recall, I think she only worked on the admin side of things. She wouldn't have had access to any of the chemicals.'

Stephanie shrugged. 'I can't think of a motive anyway.'

'Well, only the same one you might have. And you haven't been murdered either.'

The blonde woman flinched. She didn't like to think of herself as a murder victim, even hypothetically.

'Besides,' Steve added, 'I don't think she would have had the resources to set any of this up.'

'She might have inherited something when her mother died. I know Bella did.'

Steve blinked in surprise. 'Isabel inherited some money?'

'From her mother. So Frankie said. A fair amount, by the sounds of it.' Stephanie took another gulp of water from her canteen. She handed it across to Steve.

'So Bella would have had the wherewithal to organise things here.' He raised the bottle to his lips and took a quick mouthful.

Stephanie stared at the man blankly. 'Well, yes. But it can't be her. She was one of the victims.'

'Well, you know, we did say we'd consider everyone. And unlike Jane, she *is* still alive.' Steve took a second swig of water and passed the canteen back to Stephanie.

'Yes, but...I mean, why would the girl poison herself? It can't have been an accident.'

Steve shrugged. 'Maybe she wanted to distract our attention, to throw us off the scent.'

Stephanie screwed the lid back on the bottle and put the canteen down on the ground. 'But we didn't know any of this was going on when she was ill.'

'Perhaps she was being clever.'

'That's not clever. That's just stupid. The girl very nearly died.'

'Do you think she might have faked it?'

Stephanie was adamant. 'Nobody could fake those kind of symptoms.'

'But she does have the resources,' Steve maintained. 'And she's certainly an intelligent girl.'

Stephanie raised her hands. 'All right. You win. We'll consider her a suspect. But, let's be honest, the most likely person other than Sue has to be Chris Hudson.'

Steve agreed. 'In terms of resources, certainly.'

'He was caught red handed, with a half empty bottle of kerosene, Sue's matches and probably the poison as well.'

Steve considered this for a moment. 'But, you know, that really doesn't make sense. Why would he be so clumsy? If Chris had the wits to organise everything here, then surely...'

'Maybe he had some help. His father *is* on the board of that company. What was it called? CNL?'

Steve nodded. 'That's the one.' CNL had taken over the company he had worked for back in Australia. 'So, yeah, you have to admit there is a strong *prima facie* case against Chris. Even if his personality doesn't fit.'

'But not enough to convict him,' Stephanie thought. 'Not unless Sue was on the jury.'

Steve smiled. 'So...we have strong evidence against young Chris. Sue has a motive. You, Bella and I, and possibly Frankie, have the resources. Who does that leave?'

'Andy.'

Steve laughed. 'Now he has to be the unlikeliest person of all...'

It was Andrew who discovered the murder weapon, later that afternoon. He had been out scouting for a suitable burial place for Jeremy Fielding. Steve had wanted to leave the body where it was so that the authorities could mount a proper investigation, when they finally arrived, but the others felt that leaving him out on the beach, with all those insects buzzing around, would be disrespectful. A shallow grave was a reasonable compromise and the sooner it was dug the better.

It was a shame none of the video cameras were working; then at least they could have documented the crime scene.

Walking north-west away from the clearing, in the vague direction of Candy Beach, Andrew had stumbled across a bit of cloth, stained red, lying abandoned in the undergrowth. He had lent over and picked it up. It was part of a t-shirt that had belonged to Duncan Roberts, but it was torn now and had been wrapped around a slim metal object. Andrew pulled the cloth apart and stared horror-struck at the bloodied knife within. This was almost certainly the blade that had killed Jeremy Fielding.

Isabel and Francesca were following behind. He showed them the knife. 'Who does it belong to?' he wondered. It was not a penknife. It was far too big.

'Duncan had a blade like that,' Frankie said. 'He lent it to me a couple of times.' She recognised the t-shirt, too. It had been pulled out of Duncan's pack during the search the other day. She had tried it on, over in the Grotto, but it had been too baggy for her. 'Someone must have ripped it up and...' Her voice faded away.

'We'd better tell Steve,' Isabel suggested.

The two Australians followed them back through the forest to where the knife had been found. This was scarcely twenty yards from the far end of Candy Beach. 'You know,' Steve said, looking through the trees towards the sand where Jeremy's A-frame was positioned. 'If someone were coming from the clearing and didn't want to be noticed, I think they might have chosen exactly this route.'

'Or if they didn't want to be seen walking across the beach afterwards,' Stephanie added. 'It's not conclusive either way.'

Andrew had already shown them the knife, with its twelve inch steel blade. Like the cloth, it was stained with blood. 'We'd better keep that safely under wraps,' Steve said, thinking ahead. The Englishman had already deposited it in a clear plastic bag, the one he usually used when he went out fishing. He offered the bag to Steve but the Australian waved it away. 'You might as well keep hold of it.'

Sue had joined the others as soon as she had heard the hue and cry. 'Why trust him with the knife?'

'Somebody has to look after it,' Stephanie snapped. 'Would you rather we give it to Chris?'

'Where *is* Chris?' Francesca wondered, looking around.

'Probably hiding up a tree again,' Sue growled.

'He shouldn't go wandering off on his own. It might be dangerous.'

'He's the only dangerous one,' the older woman scoffed.

Steve was surveying the ground. The undergrowth here was thinly spread and there was a sizeable gap between the trees. The earth didn't seem too hard either. 'You know, I think this is as good a place as any for the grave. At least we won't have to carry the body far.' He glanced at Andrew. 'We might as well get started, while we've still got plenty of light.'

'Only a foot or two, you reckon?' the other man asked, happy to begin work. Steve nodded. The body would have to be dug up later, so there was no need for a big hole.

'I'll give you a hand,' Frankie volunteered.

Andrew was already down on his hands and knees, clearing a space.

'We need a couple of people to prepare the body as well,' Stephanie suggested.

'I'd better take care of that,' Steve said. 'I want to have one last look at him before the funeral. There's a chance I may have missed something.'

'You mean you're not God after all?' Sue laughed, coldly. But she gestured for him to lead the way.

Andrew looked up at Francesca, as the others departed. 'Here we go again,' he said.

It was the same dream as before. Usually it faded as Sue woke each morning, but this time it lingered in her memory. She had been reliving the final moments with Duncan. Every night, she must have been revisiting these events, without even realising it. Now her memory was crystal clear. She could hear his voice and see the blank expression in his eyes, over and over again.

'Is that what you wanted to say to me?' he sneered.

'Say? I never wanted to speak to you again as long as I lived.'

'Is that a fact? Then why all the cloak and dagger stuff?'

'What are you talking about?'

'Don't play the innocent with me. You asked me here. I came. So say what you wanted to say.'

'I didn't...'

Sue lay awake for some time, going over the words again and again in her mind. She had almost forgotten them, the memory had been so deeply buried. But the words were still there in her dreams and she was forced to confront them now.

'You asked me here.'

Duncan had thought she had asked him to come to the Swimming Pool. But Sue hadn't spoken to him at all. And no-one had known she was going to be there. How could they? It was a spur of the moment thing. So someone else had arranged for him to go and fooled him into thinking Sue herself had made the request.

Only one person could have done that, she realised. The person who had supposedly come to her aid. The person who had killed Duncan Roberts when he was trying to attack her. The person who had convinced Sue not to tell anybody about it, even before she ran off on her own.

'You asked me here.'

Sue brought a hand to her face. There was no doubt. Everything fitted. Duncan had been brought to the rock pool in order to be killed. And the same person who had ended his life was responsible for everything else that had happened on the island.

Sue shuddered.

She knew who it was. She knew who had murdered Jane Ruddock and Jeremy Fielding. She knew who had burnt down the hut and who had poisoned Isabel Grant.

But she did not for the life of her know why.

Chapter Eleven

Stephanie felt a hand on her shoulder. She had been dozing gently, her head cushioned in a rolled up blanket, vaguely aware that dawn was approaching but not yet fully conscious. Her eyes snapped open when she felt the unexpected touch. Steve Bramagh was looming over her. She frowned up at him, struggling to focus. He put a finger to his lips and gestured to one of the other beds in the clearing. Stephanie blinked away the sleep in her eyes, unsure what he was getting at. He lifted her mosquito net over the top of the cross beam as she pulled herself up. 'What is it?' she whispered, swinging her legs over the side of the bed. There was nothing amiss that she could see. The gentle snores of the other islanders drifted peacefully across the glade. Everybody was fast asleep. It had been a good idea, she thought, bringing all the beds into the clearing like this. There really was safety in numbers.

Steve motioned her over to the A-frame he had just indicated. It was Sue Durrant's bed. Stephanie moved across to take a proper look. The netting had been pulled back but the mattress was empty. She peered down at the ruffled blanket. Where on earth had the woman gone, at this hour? It was not even dawn yet and Sue wasn't normally an early riser.

Steve's face mirrored her concern. He gestured to the edge of the clearing and the two of them crept quietly towards the line of trees. 'Sorry to wake you like that,' Steve said, now that they were out of earshot of the others.

Stephanie stretched out her arms and stifled a yawn. 'That's okay.'

'I've only just got up myself.' Steve was always the first out of bed, though Stephanie was usually not far behind. 'I made a quick check of the group, just as I was heading off to the beach, but as you can see, Sue isn't here.'

Stephanie looked back into the glade. 'Maybe she's gone to the toilet.' A latrine had been dug within stumbling distance of the hut, not far from where they were standing now.

'I thought of that already. But I checked, just before I woke you. She's not there either.'

Stephanie grimaced, wiping the grit from her eyes. It was a little chilly this morning, she thought, shivering slightly. It was a long time since she had last felt cold. Mind you, she was only wearing a t-shirt; one of Jeremy's over-sized tops, which he had lent her after the fire. She had not had time to get properly dressed. She pulled the t-shirt down over her legs, trying not to expose herself unnecessarily.

'You know,' Steve said, 'Sue might just have gone walkabout. But I didn't want to rouse anyone else before I made sure. I thought you and I could go and check the Grotto, before anybody else wakes up. She might just be over there, filling up her water bottle.'

At this time in the morning? That didn't seem likely. 'Hang on,' Stephanie said. If they were going to go blundering about in the forest, she wanted to put something on her feet. 'I won't be a minute.' She slipped back into the glade and grabbed a pair of thongs from the side of the bed.

The early morning light barely illuminated the trail as the two islanders made their way towards Candy Beach. Unlike Stephanie, Steve was already fully dressed. He had risen a good twenty minutes before the sun, in preparation for his usual early morning run. Island life suited him, Stephanie thought. He had a compact, firm torso which belied his shorter stature.

The beach was less than two hundred metres from the sleeping area. The roar of the ocean was ever present, but more so as the Australians moved out onto the sand. Wood was piled up in the little beach hut and Jeremy's A-frame lay abandoned to the west but otherwise, the place was deserted. The man himself had been buried the previous evening. It had been a brief, sad affair and everyone had been glad to get it over with.

'This is getting worse, isn't it?' Stephanie remarked. 'If something's happened to Sue as well...'

Steve did not want to jump to conclusions. 'You know, we don't really know if anything's wrong yet. It's best not to worry.'

'You're always so calm,' she observed, with approval.

He smiled at that, his teeth a brilliant white. 'Well. Only on the outside.' His eyes were twinkling behind his sunglasses. 'You know, you're pretty even tempered yourself, most of the time.'

That was not true. Stephanie had lost her cool on a number of occasions over the last few weeks, usually with Sue. 'I try not to let myself get angry without good reason.'

'Well, actually, you know, I quite like it when you get angry.' Stephanie laughed and Steve grinned at her mischievously. 'You know, if things weren't so...' He looked away.

'I know.' She placed a hand on his shoulder. It was not the time for that.

They made their way east, towards the Grotto, but there was no sign of Sue there either.

'Where could she have got to?' Stephanie wondered, in dismay.

Steve was standing at the entrance to the cave. 'Nobody dragged her out of bed, that's for sure. If there'd been any kind of struggle, we'd all have heard it.'

That was certainly true. If anyone had attacked her in the clearing, Sue would have screamed blue murder. *She must have gone off on her own.* Stephanie shook her head. *That girl never learns.* 'I suppose we should go back and tell the others.' She sighed, not relishing the prospect. It was the second time Sue had disappeared like this. The third, if you counted that day on the beach when they had first arrived. 'We'll have to organise another search.'

Steve remembered the last time they had gone out looking for her. 'At least it's not raining this time,' he said.

It took a moment for Sue to remember where she was. Her body was propped up against a large tree trunk, her legs sprawled out in front of her. It did not seem possible that sleeping rough in the forest could be more uncomfortable than lying on her mattress back in the clearing, but somehow it was. She arched her back and flinched as an arrow of pain shot through her already bruised body. She growled. There were a dozen new bites to contend with, including several on her face. She brought a hand up to her cheek and scratched a couple of them irritably. Sleeping without a mosquito net was never a good idea. Falling asleep in the middle of the forest had not been part of the plan.

Not that there had been much of a plan.

Sue had been lying awake on her A-frame during the night, reflecting upon the events of the last few days, when all at once an image of Jeremy Fielding had popped into her head, unbidden. He had been lying on his bed as well and somebody had held him down and cut his throat. A sudden fear gripped her. The murderer was dozing not more than five metres away from her. At any minute she might be garrotted, like Jeremy. Sue had made an instant decision: she needed to get away from the clearing; she had to find somewhere safe, to hide.

If she had been thinking more rationally, she would have stayed where she was and woken the others. It would have been a simple matter to expose the killer in front of the whole group, even in the middle of the night. But Sue had not been thinking rationally. Her only thought had been to get away and after stopping to snatch her trousers she had bolted from the clearing with barely a second glance. She hadn't even thought to grab a blanket, which had proved something of a mistake. It was surprisingly chilly in the early hours of the morning.

Her intention, such as it was, had been to return to the glade at day break and to confront the murderer. Once everyone was awake, there would be no danger in revealing the identity of the viper in their nest. But once she had found a place to bed down, Sue had promptly fallen asleep; and now it was well after dawn.

'Oh hell,' she muttered, pulling herself up. She had no idea how far she had come or in which direction. It had been dark when she had left the camp site and she had not brought a torch. *I have to get back*, she realised. *All hell will break loose when they find out I'm missing again.*

Francesca was already awake when the Australians returned to the clearing. She had guessed that something was up. 'What's going on?' she asked, standing up and stretching out her legs.

'Susan,' Stephanie said, gesturing to the empty A-frame.

Frankie eye's flashed with concern. 'Is she...?' The prospect of another death was too terrible to contemplate.

'We don't know,' Steve admitted, reaching down into his pack and grabbing his water bottle. 'We can't find her anywhere.'

Isabel was sitting up in bed. 'Find who?' she asked, staring across at Steve as he took a quick swig from his canteen. Francesca explained and Bella rolled her eyes. 'That's all we need.'

Steve was making plans already. 'I want to start a search right away. Frankie, can you get Andy and Chris up? I'm going to take the short cut to the Swimming Pool.' He bundled his water bottle back into his pack and rose to his feet. 'If someone else can head to Cocoa Beach, and maybe someone to the bay...?'

'Should you go off on your own?' Francesca asked, nervously.

'I'll be all right.' The Australian exuded confidence. 'The sooner we find her, the better for everyone.'

Frankie nodded. 'All right. I'll wake the others.'

As soon as Andrew heard what was wrong, he took off across the island at a breakneck speed. He had been out of bed less than three minutes, but a quick splash of water over his face had roused him properly and then he was gone, running as fast as he could, even passing Steve on the way to the beach. If Sue was on the other side of the island, he would find her, and quickly. Andrew could not bear the thought of any more deaths.

He arrived at Cocoa Beach in record time.

'Sue!' he bellowed, crashing out onto the hot sand. 'It's Andy. Are you there?' He glanced up and down the shoreline and took a moment to recover his breath. Apart from his own footprints, the beach was unmarked. This in itself proved nothing. If Sue had come here during the night, the tide would have washed away the evidence by now.

Andrew looked out to sea. The Rocks loomed above the surface of the water, a good half a mile out. *She wouldn't have swum out there, would she?* He dismissed the idea at once. Sue had slipped away in the dark. There was no way she would go swimming at night, not on her own. He stared at the waves crashing against the rocks and grimaced. It was the first time he had been back this way since Jeremy had died.

I suppose she could have swum out first thing this morning. 'Sue!' he called again, at the top of his voice. It was doubtful the sound would carry all that way but it was worth a try. Andrew squinted. If she *was* out there he was bound to be able to see her, unless she had swum around to the far side, like Jeremy had done.

A random memory bubbled up in his head; something Jeremy had said, the day before he'd died. He had asked to borrow Andrew's penknife. What had that been about, he wondered? They had been over at the Rocks, preparing to catch a few fish. Perhaps Jeremy had found something hidden away on the other side; maybe something important. But Andrew couldn't worry about that now. For the moment, all that mattered was finding Sue.

Sadly, the girl wasn't anywhere in sight and there didn't seem much point swimming out to the Rocks on the off-chance that she might be there. *Better get back to the others*, he decided.

Sue had learnt enough from Steve to know she was heading in the right direction. If the sun rose in the east – and she could see it now, between the trees – then all she had to do was keep it to her right and eventually she would hit Candy Beach, or at least some other point along the northern coastline.

In the distance, a voice called out her name. It was too far away to determine where it was coming from, less still who it belonged to. *Oh hell!* She had already been missed. *Isn't that typical? Days go by and they don't pay me a damn bit of attention, but I'm away for five minutes and they call out the army.* Not that anybody really cared. They just didn't want another corpse on their hands. *Mind you, neither do I,* she reflected soberly, *especially not if it's going to be me.*

Sue had no intention of replying to the call. Better to keep quiet, she thought. She couldn't be sure at this distance, but it might well be the murderer. And it would be easy enough to return to the clearing under her own steam.

She continued on, stumbling unexpectedly on a clump of bramble, which scraped at her ankle and drew blood. 'Bloody hell!' she swore. 'I've had it with this island!' The sooner they got away from here, the better. And once she had revealed the identity of the killer in their midst, getting away would not be a problem; not unless somebody was behaving very stupidly indeed.

'Sue!' a voice called out, much closer now.

She froze. The voice was far *too* close and Sue recognized the caller. She spun around and her suspicions were confirmed. A figure was moving towards her through the grass. 'It would be you,' she observed, dryly.

'What were you thinking of, running off like that?' The figure came to a halt in front of her.

'I...I got scared,' Sue admitted. 'I thought...somebody might slit my throat during the night, like they did with Jeremy.'

The islander regarded her suspiciously. 'And so you ran away?'

'Just for the night.' Sue nodded.

'I don't believe you.'

'It's true. I...'

'Sue, don't lie to me.' The figure moved closer. Only now did Sue notice the mallet being gripped firmly in one hand. This was the hammer that had killed Duncan Roberts. She had not seen it since that day at the Swimming Pool.

'Look, I…' Sue held up her hands. 'All right, I know,' she said. 'I know you killed Jeremy Fielding and Jane Ruddock.'

'How do you know?'

She sighed. 'Because of what Duncan said, that day at the pool. I…I had a dream last night. He thought…he seemed to think I'd *asked* him to go there. He only got angry because I denied it and he thought I was playing games with him. But it wasn't me. I hadn't even spoken to him. I'd been doing my best to avoid the little bastard. But you had; you'd spoken to him. And you must have asked him to come.'

'Sue, that doesn't follow.'

'You were there, weren't you? At the Swimming Pool? It must have been you. You told him I wanted to speak to him, so you could lure him away from the others. And when he turned up at the rock pool you were going to kill him, hit him over the head with that.' She gestured to the hammer. 'But you didn't expect *me* to be there. So you improvised, came to my rescue. And I fell for it, hook, line and sinker. But you would have killed Duncan whatever happened.'

'And all this you deduce from a dream?'

'It wasn't a dream. It was a memory. I'd tried to block it out, like when I ran away. But then when Jeremy died and everyone started having a go…then it came back.'

'Sue, I did you a favour.' The islander sounded exasperated. 'Duncan would have killed you, if I hadn't intervened.'

'So you said. But he wouldn't have been there at all if you hadn't told him to come. He wouldn't even have been on this island. You brought Duncan here and you killed him deliberately in cold blood. And that means you must have arranged everything else.' Sue stared at the figure defiantly. 'You're the one who brought us all here in the first place.' She took a deep breath. 'Well, aren't you?'

There was a pause. 'Yes. Yes, I'm afraid I am.'

Sue's eyes widened. To suspect was one thing, to have her thoughts confirmed so casually… 'Why? Why did you do it?'

'You wouldn't understand.'

181

'Try me. Come on! What did any of us ever do to you?'

The islander hesitated momentarily. 'Nothing, Sue. Nothing at all. And that's the point. Everyone on this island is either a victim or a predator. You're a victim. Jeremy was a predator.'

'But…'

'Jane Ruddock was an accident. I never intended to kill her. If I could bring her back, I would.'

'But what did Jeremy ever do? I know he wasn't exactly…'

'He got a fourteen year old girl pregnant.'

Sue made a face. 'So? Under-age sex. That's hardly a capital offence…'

'The baby was put up for adoption. Her mother committed suicide a year later. Jeremy didn't care one way or the other.'

'Did you know the girl?' Sue asked.

'No. I never met her.'

'Then how…?'

'I've done a lot of research, on everybody he…'

A cry rang out, interrupting their conversation. Somebody else was calling Sue's name. A woman, by the sounds of it.

'I'm sorry. There's no time…' The figure advanced again, lifting up the mallet.

Sue drew in her breath. She stumbled backwards and tried to run, but the other islander leapt at her. Sue crashed to the ground, struggling to get away. The figure had kept a grip on the mallet and lifted it now a second time. Sue screamed out, but she could not escape. The hammer smashed hard into her skull. It was over in a second. She slumped to the ground, blood pouring from the back of her head.

The islander looked down at her sadly. 'I'm sorry, Sue. I never intended for this to happen.' The voice was barely more than a whisper now. 'But I couldn't let it finish here. I have to see this through to the end.' The figure dropped the mallet and disappeared into the undergrowth.

Chris Hudson was sitting in the clearing, all alone. He gave a start when Stephanie appeared behind him. 'It's only me,' the woman barked. Chris had risen to his feet and was starting to back away. The kid looked terrified. *Dickhead.* 'I'm not going to hurt you.'

'Yeah, like I'll take your word for it.'

Stephanie clenched her fists. 'Listen!' she hissed. 'I've just spent the past forty-five minutes searching this island for someone whose life might very well be in danger. I suppose it would be expecting too much for you to offer to help in some way?'

'I...' The Canadian relaxed slightly. 'Frankie said to stay here. In case she, like, doubled back or something. Did you...did you find her?'

'Does it look like it?' the Australian snapped. 'We'll have to hope Steve has more luck over at the Swimming Pool.'

Francesca came to a halt. She was sure she had heard a noise, somewhere close by; voices of some kind. She had been on her way back to the camp site. She had tried to follow the sounds but they had stopped abruptly. Now she was beginning to wonder if she had imagined them.

A twig snapped nearby and Frankie saw a figure moving through the bushes. 'Who's there?' she called.

Isabel Grant had returned to the main trail.

Steve was making his way back to the clearing when he came across the woman. 'No luck?' he called.

The girl shook her head. 'Did you go to the Swimming Pool?'

Steve nodded. 'No sign of her. I scouted the whole area.'

The group had split itself across the island fairly evenly. Andrew was investigating the southern region around Cocoa Beach. Stephanie had the south west, mainly forest with a few rocks. Isabel had been out east, in an area consisting almost entirely of woodland.

'Perhaps she went to the bay,' the Englishwoman suggested.

'Well, if she's over there, Frankie will have found her.'

They were a good five minutes from the camp site. A rough trail had been trodden out between the clearing and Cocoa Beach and it wouldn't take them long to follow it home. Steve gestured for Isabel to take the lead.

'Did you see Andy at all?' she asked him, as they started off.

'Only on the way out. He ran right past me. You know, I'm a pretty good runner, but…'

A piercing scream reverberated through the trees.

'That's Frankie!' Isabel exclaimed, in horror. She bolted sideways into the densely packed forest. Steve was right behind her, but after a few metres she stuttered to a halt. 'Frankie?' she called out, unsure of the direction.

There was a muted response. 'Over here!'

Steve spotted some movement in the distance. He pointed a finger but Isabel was already moving off.

Andrew and Francesca were standing together about a hundred yards from the main track. 'We were too late,' Andrew said, as Steve and Isabel came into view. He indicated the body of Sue Durrant, which was lying spread-eagled on the ground in front of them.

Steve knelt down to examine her. The blood was warm on the back of her neck. 'She's still breathing!' he exclaimed, in surprise. He tugged at the woman's shoulders and rolled her onto her back.

Frankie was bewildered. 'I thought…when I saw her just lying there…'

Isabel got down on her knees to take a closer look.

'We need to staunch the bleeding,' Steve told her. 'She's been quite badly hurt.' He pulled off his t-shirt and began to rip it into strips.

'Are you going to use that as a bandage?' Francesca asked, looking on.

'That's the idea. Andy, head back to the Grotto. Get the medical kit. We'll meet you at the clearing.'

The Mancunian nodded and rushed away.

Steve finished tying the bandage around Sue's head. The woman was out cold, her eyes firmly closed. 'Susan?' He tapped her gently on the face but there was no response. Steve looked across at Isabel. 'She's lost a lot of blood.'

'We should get her back to the clearing,' Frankie said.

Steve wasn't sure that was a good idea. 'You know, it might be better to leave her where she is. If we move her, it could make things worse.'

'We've got to try,' Francesca insisted. 'The killer might still be out here somewhere.' She glanced anxiously around. The group was rather exposed, out among the trees. 'We should be able to carry her between us. We have to get her back to the others.'

The Australian bit his lip. 'All right. But, you know, we're going to have to be careful...' He stopped abruptly, catching sight of something out of the corner of his eye. A hammer was lying discarded in a nearby bush. Steve pulled himself up and retrieved the blood-soaked weapon. 'You know, I think this must have happened pretty recently,' he said, wielding the short but heavy mallet.

Isabel was of the same opinion. 'If she'd been bleeding like this for more than a few minutes she'd probably be dead by now.'

Steve looked from the hammer to the two women. 'Who got here first?' he asked Frankie.

'Andy did, but only a second before me. We were both...' Her voice trailed away. 'You don't think...?'

Steve was saying nothing.

'Andrew has nothing to do with this,' Francesca insisted. 'You can't possibly think...it's preposterous. Andy wouldn't hurt a fly. You know that.'

'Agreed,' Steve said. 'But you know, this whole thing is preposterous. It's almost like one of us is schizophrenic.'

'Or a very good actor,' Isabel thought.

'And the only person who has any idea what's going on has probably just paid for it with her life.'

'Let's get her back to camp,' Isabel suggested. 'Before anything else goes wrong.'

Chapter Twelve

So the worst had happened after all. Stephanie was not in the least surprised. Andrew had crashed back into the clearing and delivered the news. Sue had been attacked by one of the islanders and was now in a critical condition. *She should never have wandered off like that,* Stephanie thought. But that was Sue all over; act first and think later. It was too late now for recriminations. 'How badly hurt is she?'

Andrew shrugged. 'I don't know. I thought she were dead, but Steve said she was still breathing. I'm going over to the Grotto to get the medical kit.'

'I'll come with you,' Stephanie volunteered, glad to get away from Chris Hudson for a minute. The Canadian had been struck dumb by the news and was now of no practical use to anybody.

'It was awful,' Andrew told her, as they made their way along the path towards the Grotto. 'There were blood pouring out of her head and everything. Steve was trying to bandage it up with his t-shirt when I left.'

Stephanie raised an eyebrow. *Resourceful as ever.*

The medical kit was at the back of the cave with the other supplies. Most of the equipment had been taken over to the log cabin and lost in the fire, but a handful of items had been left behind in the Grotto. Video cameras, dead batteries. Nothing useful, apart from the medicine. Stephanie grabbed the box and handed it across to Andrew. He placed it on the ground and offered her a hand as she clambered back out of the cave.

Together, the two of them made their way back to the camp site.

Transporting the unconscious body through the forest was not easy. The islanders had had no choice but to pick the woman up and carry her between them. There wasn't time to manufacture even a rudimentary stretcher. Steve threaded his arms around Sue's upper body, cushioning her head against his chest, while

Francesca grappled with her legs. Isabel moved ahead of them, clearing a trail through the ragged woodland and directing Steve as he stumbled backwards. The main path was not far away and, as soon as they reached it, Steve was able to quicken the pace.

The bandage around her head seemed to have staunched the bleeding, though it was not clear how much blood Sue had already lost. The hammer blow might well have fractured her skull. There could be internal bleeding, brain damage even. But Steve was not going to worry about that just yet.

Chris was waiting in the glade to assist them. Andrew and Stephanie arrived back from the Grotto at the same time. Together, they manhandled the unconscious figure onto one of the mattresses on the nearside of the camp site, resting her head carefully on a pile of blankets. Stephanie put the medical kit down on an adjacent A-frame and, once Sue was settled, Steve came over to take a look at it.

The man was still sweating from the exertion of carrying the body. Stephanie squatted beside him as he opened the lid. The box was far more than a First Aid kit. It was chock-full of useful items: antibiotics, sterilising fluid, needles, antiseptic wipes, bandages, scissors. Stephanie lifted up a plastic bottle and squinted at the label. 'What do you think we should we give her?'

Steve adjusted his glasses, conscious more than ever of his own ignorance. 'Well, some kind of pain killer to start with. But first of all let's sterilise the wound and change that bandage on her head.' The ripped up t-shirt had been a good idea but it was no substitute for the real thing. He pulled out a fresh bandage and removed the plastic wrapping.

Francesca set to work unwinding the stained cloth from the top of Sue's head. She flinched at the sight of the hair, which was encrusted with blood.

'What did they hit her with?' Chris asked, curiosity getting the better of his usual squeamishness.

Isabel lifted up the bloodied mallet, which she had carried back to the camp site. The young man recoiled in horror.

Stephanie opened a packet of antiseptic wipes and handed them to Frankie, who dabbed the wound as best she could. Steve came over with the new bandage and while the girl gently lifted Sue's head the Australian began to wind it around the top.

Meantime, Stephanie was examining some of the other bottles in the medical kit. There were quite a few pills in there, including pain killers, but those would be of no use while Sue was unconscious, as she would not be able to swallow them. A couple of smaller bottles contained opiates, which could be injected directly into her bloodstream. That was probably the best option, Stephanie thought, though she had never given an injection in her life. *There's a first time for everything, I suppose.*

Isabel was watching Francesca tying off the end of the bandage. The material was already stained red, though as much from the smudges on Frankie's hands as from the wound itself. 'What she really needs is a blood transfusion,' Bella observed. But that, of course, was out of the question.

Stephanie had filled a syringe from one of the bottles. 'Pain killer,' she said, moving across to administer the injection.

'Hey, just a minute!' Chris protested. 'Shouldn't we, like, check what bottle that came from?'

Stephanie glared at him.

'It's all right,' Steve said calmly. 'I watched her do it.'

She held up the empty bottle anyway, allowing the Canadian to read the label. 'Satisfied?'

He nodded. 'Hey, look, I'm just trying to be careful. You could have been, like, trying to finish her off.'

Stephanie gritted her teeth and gestured to Sue's wrist. 'Frankie, can you hold that steady for me?' The other girl nodded, taking hold of the arm. Stephanie searched for a suitable vein. 'I don't suppose anyone else knows how to do this?' she asked, looking up. 'No, I didn't think so.' She pressed the needle into the flesh and emptied the syringe. She had to stop herself from closing her eyes before she pulled it out again. She had never liked needles. Steve was ready with an antiseptic wipe and a plaster.

Andrew peered down at the unconscious woman. 'How long will it take to work?'

Stephanie wasn't sure. 'Not long, I shouldn't think.'

'But you know, it *is* only a painkiller,' Steve pointed out. 'It won't do anything to stabilize her condition. It'll only reduce the pain.'

'Perhaps we should give her some antibiotics as well,' Stephanie suggested, looking to Steve for approval. 'It might prevent infection.'

The man shrugged, as much in the dark as she was. 'Well, Steph, we haven't exactly got anything to lose.'

'We've got everything to lose,' the blonde woman assured him, 'but here goes anyway.' Chris and Isabel watched closely as she filled another syringe and emptied it into Sue's forearm. The injured woman was looking a lot calmer now. Her body had already stopped shaking.

'She is, like, still breathing, isn't she?' Chris asked.

'She's doing fine,' Francesca reassured him. She had acted as a nurse before and was fast becoming accustomed to the role.

Stephanie withdrew the needle and stepped back as Steve applied a second small plaster. The group stood silently for a moment, observing the rhythm of Sue's chest as it rose and fell.

'So what happens now?' Andrew asked.

'Well, you know, we've done just about all we can for her,' Steve said. 'I always thought it was a bad idea not to have at least one person out here with a bit of medical training.'

'First Aid even would have helped,' Frankie agreed, tidying the bandage on Sue's head.

'But is she going to be all right?' Andrew asked again.

Steve did not have an answer. 'Well, let's hope so,' he said. 'You know, all we can do now is wait.'

The sun was on the verge of clearing the tree tops. Soon the glade would be bathed in sunlight, but there were always corners of the camp that could be relied upon to provide a little shade. Sue's bed-frame had already been shifted across to one of these areas so that the woman wouldn't be exposed unnecessarily as the day drew on. By mutual agreement, there were never less than three people in attendance around her. The islanders were keeping careful watch on each other as well as the patient, determined to prevent anything untoward from happening to her. If Sue was going to die, it would be as a result of the hammer blow, not anything that happened here.

Stephanie and Steve were sat a short distance away from the others, talking quietly. Francesca and Isabel were looking after the patient, with Chris watching them both suspiciously. 'That girl is such a fool,' Stephanie muttered, staring across at them. 'You'd have thought after Duncan's death she'd have learnt the danger of keeping secrets. She could have confided in us then and none of this need have happened.'

Steve was inclined to give the woman the benefit of the doubt. 'You know, she probably thought she was doing the right thing.'

'It's difficult to see how. If she knew who'd killed Duncan she had an obligation to tell us.'

'Perhaps she thought she was protecting them. If Duncan attacked her and somebody came to her rescue, she was bound to feel grateful. Especially if it seemed like a spur of the moment thing, someone leaping to her defence. And if that person asked her to keep quiet – pretended to be upset – you can see why she might have agreed to it.'

'Yes, but not after Jeremy was found dead.'

'I know,' Steve agreed. 'I can't explain that. But she was lucky the first time.' When they had found her, shivering in the rain. 'Perhaps she'll be lucky again.'

Stephanie glanced across at Frankie, who was pouring some water onto a cloth and wiping Sue's face. The unconscious figure looked almost peaceful now, stretched out on the shaded mattress.

'Either way, I've got a feeling things are coming to a head,' Steve said. Stephanie shot him a questioning look. 'Well, you know, whoever is doing this has been very lucky so far. They've managed to avoid being seen. But after this morning's debacle, and with the possibility of Sue waking up at any time, he or she will be feeling very nervous. And that means they're more likely to make a mistake. Also, we're none of us going to

191

be going off on our own from now on and that gives our killer very little room to manoeuvre.'

'Do you think the intention is to kill us all?' Stephanie asked.

'No I don't. You know, I think certain individuals were targeted right from the outset. Duncan and Jeremy, for example. They weren't the most popular people on the island. And neither is Sue, come to that. Jane we know was a mistake and Bella, if we're honest, has never really integrated that well.'

Stephanie scratched her neck, trying to hide her anxiety. 'So who's going to be next?'

'I wish I knew. You know, I don't understand why they haven't had a second crack at Isabel.'

Stephanie considered for a moment. 'Perhaps she wasn't important. Maybe there's only one victim, and the rest were just...for effect.'

Steve frowned. 'I'm not sure I follow you.'

'Well, look.' She turned to face him. 'Nobody here could have known everybody else beforehand, could they? So no-one can bear a grudge against all of us. Perhaps everything so far has just been a distraction. Maybe the real victim hasn't even been touched yet.'

Steve rubbed his chin. 'You know, I think you may be on to something there. They create a climate of fear to distract attention, and then...' He paused for a minute, thinking the idea through. 'If that's the case, then who's the real victim?'

'Somebody who hasn't been touched so far.'

Steve's gaze flicked briefly across the clearing. 'In that case, as far as I can see, there are only three possibilities: you, me or Andy.'

Stephanie took a last swig of water from her canteen. She stretched out her legs and pulled herself up from the mattress. It was two hours later. Steve was taking a power nap, while Francesca continued to minister to her patient, under the watchful gaze of Chris Hudson. The youngster was in a state of extreme agitation. He looked as if he might bolt into the forest at any moment, despite the obvious danger. He had always been a nervy young fellow, but now he looked absolutely petrified. Every few minutes, he would jump to his feet and pace up and down.

It was getting close to midday and the sun had all but flooded the glade. Stephanie arched her arms above her head. It would be hotter than ever this afternoon. She fastened the lid back onto her canteen and called across to the others. 'Does anyone else need more water?'

Steve was lying on his back nearby. 'You know, I was just going to ask the same thing.' He pulled himself up and grabbed his flask, checking to see if there was anything left in there. 'I think we could all do with a bite to eat as well.'

Chris was toying nervously with his own water bottle. 'Nobody is leaving the camp site,' he declared, with quiet determination. 'That's, like, not an option.'

'We can't go without water,' Francesca pointed out. Not everyone had had a chance to refill their canteens this morning and even those who had were now running low. 'At the very least, someone should go to the Grotto and fill up all the flasks.'

'Not on their own.' Chris was adamant and Stephanie was inclined to agree with him. There was no point taking unnecessary risks.

'I'll go,' Andrew volunteered. 'If someone wants to come with me?'

Isabel was sitting cross-legged on the ground to his right. 'I could do with stretching my legs,' she said. 'All this hanging around, I think I'm starting to get cramp.' She winced as she untangled her limbs and clambered unsteadily to her feet.

'I'd better come too,' Stephanie suggested. 'We did say at least three people at all times.'

Steve nodded. 'Three here, three away. That should be safe enough.' That way, whoever the killer was, they would always be outnumbered.

Andrew was glad of the company. 'Makes it easier to carry all the bottles, anyway.' He grinned.

Stephanie helped Isabel to gather the flasks, which they packed away in Andrew's rucksack. Chris hesitated before handing his over.

'You do trust me, don't you?' Isabel asked, mocking him gently.

'I suppose.' He gave her the bottle.

'Don't worry,' she said, seriously. 'We'll all keep an eye on each other.'

His eyes flicked reflexively to her body as she moved away, and then he glanced at Andrew.

The Mancunian smiled broadly, picking up his pack. 'Maybe she does fancy you after all,' he whispered.

Chris looked away in embarrassment.

Stephanie was already heading off towards the beach. 'We won't be more than ten minutes,' she called.

They arrived at the Grotto a short time later.

Andrew hauled the rucksack off his back and began to rummage inside. The pack was a lot fuller than he remembered. He pulled out a couple of bottles and handed them to Stephanie. Isabel came up behind him and he passed the rest to her, one by one. The flasks were more or less identical, regular two litre canteens, though in a variety of colours.

Stephanie lined the bottles up along the edge of the rock pool. 'I suppose we should keep an eye on each other while we're doing this,' she remarked, glancing at Andrew.

'I reckon so,' he agreed, crouching down. It was as well to be careful, though he had no suspicions of these two girls. He picked up the first canteen, which was a metallic green, and unscrewed the lid. He submerged the bottle in the pool of water. It only took a moment to fill it up. Then he replaced the lid and handed the flask back to Isabel.

He was midway through filling the second bottle when he heard a sudden commotion behind him. It took him a moment to balance himself so that he could look round, but before he could do so Stephanie called out his name. Andrew glanced back and found himself staring into the barrel of a gun.

Sue Durrant was dreaming.

Duncan Roberts lay sprawled on the rock, the wound on his head shockingly visible. She could feel the blood spilling out from his skull. She could taste the pain, almost as if she were inside his head. And as Duncan's life oozed away, so *she* seemed to drift also. But she did not want to go with him. Duncan was dying – he was dead, in fact, lying there by the Swimming Pool – and Sue was very much alive.

A woman stood above them. She was tall and beautiful. In her hand she held a hammer which was stained with blood.

She was saying something, the woman.

A voice whispered in her head.

'She's saying something…'

Isabel Grant stumbled back into the clearing.

It took a moment before anyone registered her arrival. The islanders were congregating around Sue's bed. The woman had cried out a few seconds before and the group was trying to determine what was wrong. Chris looked up first and caught sight of Isabel. His mouth dropped open. Francesca followed his gaze.

'Bella!' she exclaimed, noting the shocked expression on her friend's face. 'What's happened? Where's Andrew?' Nobody was meant to be walking around on their own.

Steve moved across to find out what was wrong.

'It's Stephanie,' Isabel muttered, barely coherent. 'She's…she's gone crazy. She's waving a gun around.'

'*Stephanie?*' Steve could not hide the incredulity in his voice.

Andrew was lying face down on the rock, his hands tied behind his back, the cord digging tightly into his wrists. His ankles were roped together as well. Stephanie had done a good job. There had been some cord stowed away in his rucksack. Andrew did not know how it had got there. He shivered involuntarily.

Where did she get that gun? he wondered. The revolver had appeared from nowhere. He had been taken completely by surprise. And then…

I don't believe this. His mind struggled to focus. *Not Stephanie.*

Isabel's voice was little more than a whisper. Steve had sat her down on a mattress and tried to calm her. 'She's got Andrew tied up. She's gone completely mad.' Isabel was shaking with fear. 'I thought she was going to shoot me.'

Chris and Francesca exchanged anxious looks.

Steve placed a calming hand on Isabel's shoulder. He was sitting next to her on the A-frame, his face an image of fatherly concern. He would have offered the girl some water, if any had been available. 'How did you get away?'

Isabel swallowed hard. 'She…forced me to go. I tried to refuse. I didn't want to leave Andy behind. But she said she'd kill him if I didn't do what she said.' She blinked nervously. 'She wanted me to bring you a message. To tell you…it's not Andrew she's after. She doesn't care about him. It's you, Frankie. It was you she was after all along.'

'*Me*?' Francesca was dumbfounded.

Isabel clutched her hands together. 'She says if you want to stop her killing him, you have to go to the Grotto yourself. Alone. Then she'll let him go.'

The other girl let out a gasp.

'I think she's serious, Frankie. I'm sorry. I didn't want to leave him like that, but there was…there was nothing else I could do.'

'It's not your fault,' Steve reassured her.

'She says she doesn't want to harm him, but she will if you don't come to her. She said she'd wait a quarter of an hour and if you weren't there then…she'd kill him.'

'But if *you* go, she'll kill *you*,' Chris asserted, unhelpfully.

Francesca covered her mouth. 'Oh, God!'

'I won't let that happen,' Steve declared, looking up. 'I promise you. We'll sort this out. Nothing's going to happen to you or to Andy.'

'You can't know that!' the Canadian snorted.

Frankie was insistent. 'I can't let Andrew die.' Her voice was barely audible now. 'I have to go. I won't let him die because of me.'

Chris stared at the girl in disbelief. 'Are you, like, totally out of your mind? You heard what Bella said. She's tooled up. She'll blow your brains out!'

Francesca nodded unhappily. 'But what else can I do?'

'Forget it!' Chris said. 'Like, save your own skin. We're better off here, together.'

'I can't leave him to die!' she exclaimed, with sudden anger.

'Frankie, think about this.' For once, Isabel was siding with the Canadian. 'She's serious. She *will* kill you if she gets the chance. She's insane. I saw it in her eyes.'

But Francesca had already made up her mind. 'I'm going,' she said, with an air of finality.

Steve looked on in admiration. 'You know, you're a very brave woman. But if you *are* going, then I'm coming with you.'

'She said only Frankie,' Isabel protested, in alarm. 'If you turn up as well…'

The Australian scratched his head. 'You know, I think we should take the chance. If I stay back and cause some kind of distraction…' Francesca was willing to consider the idea.

Chris stared at the two of them. 'You're out of your minds. You'll both be killed!'

'Nothing that puts Andrew in any danger,' Frankie warned.

'Granted,' Steve said, attempting a smile.

'All right,' she agreed, bracing herself. 'We'd better go.'

For several minutes Andrew hadn't dared to move. His mind was numb with fear and his body seemed to have undergone complete paralysis. For a time, with that gun being waved about, he had seriously believed he was about to die. *I'm sorry, mam,* he had screamed inside. *You were right. I should never have come here.* But now several minutes had passed without anything happening and Andrew began to hope he might get through it after all. *I've got to see Frankie again.* He held onto that thought as he lay helpless on the ground. His face was beginning to go red. Without realising it, he had been holding his breath. He expelled the air quickly and listened for any sign of movement, but there was none. All he could hear was the angry sea and the sound of his own breathing. She had gone then, as promised.

Tentatively, Andrew opened his eyes. He breathed in and swallowed hard. Then he rotated his head to face the light. He was lying close to the entrance of the cave. He could see outside now, but there was no-one there. He moved his head again. Carefully, he rolled his body onto its other side and the interior of the Grotto came into view. He steeled himself to look, even though he knew exactly what he would find.

Stephanie McMahon lay stretched out on the rocks. She was naked and as beautiful as ever. Her lips were parted, her eyes open, but she stared lifelessly at the roof of the cave. The hilt of a dagger protruded from the centre of her chest. It was the same knife that had killed Jeremy Fielding, the knife that Duncan Roberts had originally brought to the island. The knife that Andrew Baker had placed in his backpack for safe keeping.

The young Mancunian let out a cry.

'What did she ever do to you?' he had screamed.

The reply, when it came, was incomprehensible.

'Absolutely nothing,' she said.

Chris Hudson was dumbfounded. 'I can't believe it,' he muttered. *I mean, like, Stephanie?!?* 'I can't believe it was *her.*'

Isabel stood opposite the young Canadian, on the other side of the A-frame, with Sue Durrant lying unconscious between them. The girl lifted her head and looked Chris straight in the eye.

'It's not her,' she told him. 'It's me.'

Chapter Thirteen

Francesca had no idea what she would find at the Grotto. Steve had doubled back, saying he would join her there shortly. There hadn't been time to ask him what he was planning, but it was important that they did not arrive together. 'Andrew!' she yelled, stumbling along the pathway from the beach, anxious to arrive before she lost her nerve.

'I'm in here!' the young man called back.

The cave mouth came into view and Frankie's heart leapt as she saw the Englishman lying on the ground. He was tied up but very much alive. Then she saw the naked body of Stephanie McMahon spread out across the rocks behind him, a knife imbedded in her chest 'What happened?' she breathed, drawing closer. Blood was splashed across the woman's breast and neck.

'It was Isabel,' Andrew told her. 'She pulled a gun on us.'

Francesca did not understand. 'Bella? But she said…'

'She threatened to shoot me. Got me to lie down here.' Andrew was struggling to make sense of it. 'There was some rope or something in my pack – she must have planted it there – and she got Steph to tie me up.' He pulled on his wrists, to demonstrate. 'Then she got her to strip off, and while she were doing it Bella must have hit her over the head. I couldn't see very well. I think she must have used one of them water bottles.' There was a canteen lying on the ground between him and the dead woman. 'Then she laid her out over there and…and… stabbed her. There was nothing I could do, Frankie. I screamed at her, I yelled, but there was nothing I could do.'

Francesca shuddered, unable to take it all in. Bella was her best friend. It was not possible for her to have done this. She stared at the lifeless body of Stephanie McMahon. It made no sense at all.

'She murdered them, Frankie,' Andrew declared. 'Duncan, Jane, the rest. She must have done. She's stark raving mad.'

'She came back to the clearing. She told us Stephanie was waving a gun around, that she was holding you hostage.'

'It weren't Steph. It was Bella all along.'

Isabel slid a hand into one of her pockets, which was hidden beneath an over-sized t-shirt. She drew out the small revolver, flicked off the safety catch and aimed the weapon squarely at Chris Hudson. The Canadian stared back at her, horrified, unable to speak. The two of them were scarcely six feet apart.

'Where did you get the gun?' Steve asked. The Australian had doubled back along the pathway and returned to the camp site.

Isabel stood on the near side of the clearing, holding the revolver at chest height, well above Sue's unconscious body. Her eyes were locked on Chris, who was standing on the other side of the A-frame. Steve had arrived on the outer edge of the glade, out of the woman's field of vision, but not close enough to risk rushing her. 'I have a few things hidden away,' she said, in reply to his question. It had been a simple matter to collect the revolver from its hiding place, when they had all been out looking for Sue that morning. She had picked up the mallet at the same time. 'If you move so much as a muscle, he's dead.'

Steve raised his hands cautiously. 'I'm not moving, Bella.'

Chris could not take his eyes off the barrel of the gun. The revolver was dirty and mud-spattered; and the hands clasping it were no less grubby.

'My little charade didn't fool you then?'

'It was very convincing,' Steve admitted. 'You're an excellent actress. But you overlooked one thing.'

'What was that?'

The Australian smiled to himself. 'This time, you forgot to wash your hands.'

Andrew was utterly bewildered. 'Why would she do it, Frankie? Why would she do all this?'

Francesca had pulled a penknife from her pocket. 'I don't know,' she admitted, sawing rapidly through the cord binding his wrists together. 'It's absurd. She has no reason to hate anybody. The only person...' She stopped. *No. It's not possible.* Isabel's sister had been killed in a road accident a few years before. Bella had been devastated by the loss. But there couldn't be any connection between that and anybody here. Steve had never been to Cambridge and as for... *No, wait a minute,* she thought. Chris Hudson had been to Cambridge. He had gone to University there. She shuddered. *It can't be. He can't have been the one who...*

Frankie had freed Andrew's hands. He pulled his wrists apart and she moved quickly to untie his ankles.

'We have to get back to the camp site,' she said.

There were smudges of blood on the palms of her hands. Steve had half-spotted them earlier on, when he had been trying to comfort her, but he had not immediately grasped their significance. Now he understood all too well. 'Was it Andrew or Stephanie?' he asked, quietly.

Isabel did not look round. 'Who do you think?'

The Australian closed his eyes. *Stephanie.* He took a few quick breaths to calm himself.

'I...I don't understand.' Chris had found a voice at last. 'Like, what did I ever do to you?'

The girl regarded him coolly with her large brown eyes. 'You really don't know, do you?' He shook his head and she gazed at him with what looked like benign amusement. All at once, he understood and panic gripped him anew. 'You didn't even visit her in hospital,' Isabel spat. 'After you knocked her down in the street.'

Chris was shaking now, unable to hold himself still. 'I...I couldn't. I...'

'You make me sick.' She glared at him contemptuously.

'I...I...'

'Two minutes,' she said.

'Wha-?'

'Two minutes. And then I'm going to kill you.' Chris closed his mouth, not quite grasping what she was saying. Between them, on the mattress, Sue Durrant gave out a low moan. 'One minute fifty-five seconds. I suggest you start running.'

Even these words took a moment to penetrate the Canadian's fogged consciousness; then he stumbled backwards and bolted from the glade.

Isabel dropped the revolver and turned to face Steve. The Australian had not moved an inch from the edge of the clearing. 'Don't try to stop me,' she warned.

Steve was still trying to come to terms with what was going on. 'All this,' he asked, uncertainly. 'Just because of a road accident?' He remembered the girl telling him about it, that evening in West Bay, but it hadn't seemed important at the time.

Isabel inclined her head. 'He should have rotted in jail. He should have spent the rest of his life there. But what did he get? A slapped wrist and his licence revoked. He can probably still drive in Canada. Is that fair? Is that right?'

'Bella…'

'And you know what the worst thing was?' Her eyes flashed with pain and regret. '*She didn't die*. My sister. Just lying there, for almost a year. Do you know how that made me feel? Seeing her there every day, alive physically, but knowing she was dead inside. And I had to finish the job, Steve. I had to kill my own flesh and blood. Chris made me do that. He turned me into a murderer. And now I'm going to kill him.'

'Bella.' Steve spoke very calmly. 'I can't let you do this.' He took a step forward cautiously, his hands raised in front of his chest. 'Too many people have died already. Give me the gun, Bella.'

She shook her head, lifting the weapon and pointing it straight at him. 'I think the two minutes are up. You'll have to excuse me. I have a Canadian to kill.'

Steve moved closer.

'I don't want to hurt you,' Isabel warned, stepping backwards. 'But I'm not going to let you stop me.'

'We have to hurry!' Francesca insisted, as the two friends made their way along the path towards Candy Beach. Andrew was utterly bewildered. He could not get the image of Stephanie McMahon out of his mind. What could possibly cause anyone to do something like that? To strip her down, humiliate her in that way, and then to plunge a dagger into her chest? *Why?* he had screamed. *What did she ever do to you?* But Isabel had not given him an answer.

Frankie seemed to know, if not about Stephanie, then about Isabel. But there was no time for questions.

They pelted out onto the sand and arced left, desperate to reach the camp site before anybody else was killed.

In the distance, a shot rang out.

Steve crashed to the ground, clutching his leg. Blood began to spurt from the wound. The pain was excruciating. *I mustn't black out*, he told himself urgently. *I have to concentrate.* But the man could barely focus his eyes. With a supreme effort, he managed to pull himself up from the ground into a sitting position, using one hand to prop his body while the other staunched the bleeding. The bullet had hit his right thigh, just above the hem of his shorts, and it looked to be imbedded there. The pain was indescribable – Steve gritted his teeth and made a mental effort not to scream – but gazing down at the bloody gash, he realised with relief that he was not in mortal danger. And there were other, more important concerns. *Chris.* He had to stop…

Steve looked across the glade. Barely half a minute had passed since Isabel had shot him, but the woman herself was long gone.

Chris Hudson was running for his life. He had no idea where he was going, he just knew that he had to get away. He had followed the pathway southwards, stumbling over the uneven terrain. The sound of a gunshot from behind did nothing to slow him. He did not dare think of what it might mean. Had Steve incapacitated the woman or had she murdered him too?

I should have known, he kept telling himself, over and over, as he ran. *I should have known.* The Cambridge connection, the links between the different islanders. He had thought it was the company thing, his father taking over Automotive. Everything else he had put out of his mind. But there it was all along, coming back to haunt him, as it had haunted his dreams every night for a year or more after the accident. The one mistake he had made. The one error of judgement that could never be undone, no matter how confidently his father tried to intervene.

Orange lights moving to red. He had put his foot on the accelerator, hoping to slip through at the last moment, and then...

A life lost.

He could never have visited the girl in hospital. It would have been unbearable. He could not have coped with the guilt.

And now he was going to pay for that cowardice with his life.

Francesca reached the camp site ahead of Andrew and took in the situation at once. Steve was sitting on the ground, clutching his leg. Sue was lying on her back on the A-frame, but there was no sign of Chris or Isabel.

She rushed across to the Australian and knelt down in front of him. 'Are you all right?' she asked, anxiously. When she had heard the gun shot, she had automatically assumed the worst.

'Just a flesh wound,' he said. 'I don't think she meant to kill me.'

Andrew was more concerned with the others. 'Which way did she go?' he asked, thumping down his rucksack as he pulled up alongside them.

Steve gestured to the path on the far side of the clearing. 'Over there. She took off after Chris.'

Andrew was perplexed. 'What, to Cocoa Beach?'

'I think so. You know, I don't think young Chris was in any state of mind to think logically. He'll have bolted straight for the sea.'

That made matters simple. 'I'd better go after them,' Andrew said.

'She gave him a two minute start. Once he gets to the beach, he'll either have to swim for it or find a place to hide.'

'I reckon he'll just jump in the water.'

'Well, I hope he's a fast swimmer.' Steve winced. 'You know, she's a pretty good shot.'

Frankie was examining the wound. Steve gritted his teeth as she pulled back the hem of his shorts. Blood was congealing across the whole of the upper leg. 'Andy, get the First Aid kit, and some water,' she told him.

Andrew shook his head. 'I'm going after Chris.'

Francesca rose to her feet. 'Sterilize the wound and dress it.' She pointed to the medical box, over by Sue. 'Try and staunch the blood. *I'm* going after Isabel.'

'But…'

'She's my friend, Andy. If anyone can handle her, it'll be me.' She gazed down at Steve. 'Are you going to be all right?'

The Australian nodded. 'Andy will look after me. You know, if you want to catch them, you'd better make a start. She'll have a couple of minutes on you by now.'

Frankie drew in a breath, then turned and started to run.

'Good luck!' Steve called after her.

Another small clearing loomed into view. Chris had passed this way several times before, on the way to Cocoa Beach. There were a few trees further on and then the beach itself. He sprinted out into the glade and halted, looking left and right speculatively. The trees either side of him were straggly and widely spaced. If Isabel was close behind, she would see him sprinting off, whichever direction he took. There was no time to consider his options. The beach was a dead end, but he pressed forward regardless, hitting the trees at the southern edge of the clearing and darting out onto the hot sand. An idea struck him and he ran forward into the water. The Rocks were in view now, a good half a mile out to sea, but Chris had no intention of swimming out there. He kept to the shallows and ran along the edge of the sand, to where the beach narrowed on its western-most edge. Here the sand mixed once again with trees and greenery and he was able to hop from the water onto dry grass. There were no boulders on this side of the beach. Rapidly, he disappeared into the undergrowth.

The notion of fair play had been far from Isabel's mind when she had given the Canadian a head start. There were other, more personal reasons for this particular game of cat and mouse. It was not enough simply to kill the man. He had to suffer, he had to endure, he had to live with the knowledge of his death and understand the reasons for it. Only then would she allow him to die. It was a calculated risk, allowing Chris free rein across the island. The young man would be scared out of his wits – that was the point, after all – but his fear would work to her advantage. Isabel had watched him closely in the three weeks they had lived together on the island. The boy had no imagination and did not cope well in a crisis. In a situation like this, he would behave in an entirely predictable manner. There would be no difficulty tracking him.

She paced herself as she ran, keeping her breathing calm and regular. The Canadian had dashed furiously to begin with. Too quickly, without thinking. He would burn himself out and have to slow down. An even pace would keep her level with him and give her an advantage when she finally caught up. She listened closely as her feet padded across the ground, her eyes scanning ahead. He would not have left the trail, but it was as well to be sure. A clearing loomed. She was almost at the beach. Chris had narrowed himself into a corner, just as she had expected, and he would not have the imagination to escape.

She moved through the trees and out onto the sand. There, as clear as a neon signpost, were the footprints that led across the beach into the sea. And beyond, less than a kilometre in the distance, were the Rocks that Isabel considered to be her home away from home.

She smiled to herself. *So he's not so stupid after all.*

'I should go after her,' Andrew said, looking anxiously at the gap in the trees. He had done his best to clean Steve's leg and to bandage up the wound, though he'd had to make do with the remnants of the man's t-shirt as all the proper dressings had been used up. Once it was done, he helped Steve to his feet and sat him on an A-frame adjacent to Sue Durrant. The injured woman was awake now, a little groggy, but drinking greedily from a bottle of water Andrew had brought back from the Grotto in his rucksack.

'It's too late,' Steve told him. 'Whatever's going to happen, there's nothing we can do about it.' Events would have to run their course.

Andrew sat down next to him.

The Australian had greeted the news of Stephanie's death with admirable calm. 'She's a clever one,' he reflected. 'She almost had me fooled.'

'Why would she do it? Why kill Steph of all people?'

Steve shrugged. 'I don't know. Because of Frankie, maybe.'

'And killing all them others.' Andrew shook his head. 'It don't make sense.'

'Oh, it makes sense,' Sue said, propping herself up on the bed opposite. The woman had been awake for some minutes now and her strength was slowly returning. 'But only to her,' she added, with a cough. She lifted the canteen to her mouth and took another gulp of water. 'The little bitch explained it all, just before she hit me with that hammer. She said she only killed people she thought "deserved" to die.'

Steve nodded. He could see the logic in that. 'Duncan was a rapist. I suppose a lot of people wouldn't blame Bella for murdering him. And Steph was a thief, in her eyes. She robbed Francesca of her inheritance and probably helped Frankie's mother to an early grave.' He let out a sigh. 'But as to the others…'

'Bella said something about Jeremy.' Sue steadied herself on the mattress, clutching one hand to her head as a wave of nausea threatened to overcome her. 'Something…something about a fourteen year old girl and an abortion, I think.' It was difficult to remember exactly.

'It would have to be something like that,' Steve said.

'And it were Chris she were after all along?' Andrew asked, incredulously.

'You know, it certainly looks that way. She must have wanted to scare the boy out of his wits. Have him blamed, panic him, then pull the gun and tell him exactly what she was going to do.'

'Why didn't she just kill him straight off?' Andrew wondered.

Steve shrugged. 'It obviously wasn't enough.' He told them briefly about the accident that had killed Isabel's sister. 'Chris must have been driving the car.'

'And all this, because of some stupid mistake?' Sue grunted in disbelief. 'That girl must be deranged.'

Steve could only agree. 'She'll kill him, if she finds him. I only hope Francesca gets there in time…'

Frankie was not used to running at such a pace. She arrived at the beach out of breath, clutching the sides of her stomach and looking down at the sand. There were two trails of footprints. One led directly across the beach and into the sea, the other curved right and continued along the western shoreline. The footprints overlapped at the nearest point and Francesca could see that the ones cutting across the beach were the more recent of the two. *They must belong to Bella,* she thought. *But if Chris…* She peered out to sea. Even if the young man had been swimming like mad, he could not have reached the Rocks yet. But there was no sign of him in the water.

All at once, she saw what he had been trying to do. She shook her head. A good idea, but not good enough.

Chris grabbed onto one of the branches and began to pull himself up. He had been thinking about the other day, when Sue had accused him of burning down the log cabin. He had run away then, though not in fear of his life, and he had found refuge in one of the larger trees. That had been on the same side of the island, though further north. Andrew would never have found him if he had not called out. *If I can get up above ground...* His ruse on the beach had probably bought him a couple of minutes. Moving away from the sand, he had already found a suitable tree, but Isabel cut him short. 'That's far enough!' she cried.

Chris lost his grip on the branch and smashed to the ground. He scrabbled up and tried to scurry away, but Isabel was too fast. She kicked him in the back and he sprawled out across the grass. Her foot flashed a second time and came down hard on his back, preventing him from moving any further. The nub of a gun pressed firmly into the back of his skull.

'Bella!' Francesca yelled.

Isabel looked round, keeping the revolver jammed tight against the young man's head. 'Just in time for the end,' she muttered.

'You don't have to do this.' Frankie was breathing hard. Her face was red with exertion and her eyes were wide with fear. 'It's not his fault. He never wanted to hurt her.'

Isabel regarded her friend blankly. 'Maybe not. But he did, didn't he?' On the ground, Chris was beginning to whimper. 'He never even visited her in hospital.'

'Bella, you've got to let it go. You've got to forget the past. If my friendship means anything to you...'

Isabel shook her head sadly. 'You don't understand, Frankie. If I let him go then it will all have been for nothing. All those people who died. It won't mean anything at all.' She closed her eyes. 'This is the end which justifies the means.' And with that, she pulled the trigger.

There was a jolt as the Canadian's body reacted to the force of the bullet. It was over in an instant.

Frankie screamed.

Isabel removed her foot from the man's back and took a step sideways. With her free hand, she unclipped a thin chain from around her neck and threw it forward into the dirt. 'The Rocks,' she said. 'You'll find everything you need.'

Francesca looked down at the necklace, bewildered.

'I'm sorry,' Isabel said. She lifted up the revolver and placed the barrel in her mouth.

Chapter Fourteen

A second shot reverberated across the island.

Andrew leapt to his feet and bolted for the trees without another word.

Steve watched him go. *Two shots*, he thought. In all probability, two more people dead. Frankie would not have been harmed. That meant Isabel had taken her own life, after killing the Canadian.

Sue had reached the same conclusion. 'She did it. She actually did it.' She threw up her hands. 'The stupid bitch.'

Steve was sitting on the edge of an adjacent A-frame, his upper leg bandaged and covered in blood. 'I should have realised what was going on,' he berated himself. 'I should have seen the signs.'

'Yeah, right,' Sue laughed, bitterly. 'It was obvious all along.'

'It *was* obvious. You know, Isabel was the only one here I never really sussed out. I never got…' He gritted his teeth, as a fresh arrow of pain shot through his leg. 'I never got a sense of what was going on inside her head. I could have helped her. I'm sure of it.' She had opened up to him a little, that afternoon at West Bay, but he had not pressed her further.

'Steve, she was too far gone. To arrange all this…she must have been a monomaniac.' Sue shook her head. 'And rich too. I mean, bringing us all together like this. It must have cost a fortune.'

'Not a fortune,' the Australian reflected, sadly. 'But she must have inherited a fair amount when her mother died. Enough that she didn't have to work, at any rate.' According to Francesca, Isabel had given up her job soon after moving to Cambridge. 'You know, I think she must have pretty much devoted herself to all this after her sister died.'

'What did she do before?'

'A stenographer, so Frankie said. A shorthand typist. I think she worked for some kind of legal company.'

Sue swung her legs over the edge of the bed. 'You don't think...?'

'What?'

'No. I'm being stupid.'

Steve looked across. 'Go on.'

'I was just thinking...if she was working for a legal firm, could that be how she knew about Duncan and me? If the company was connected in some way with...I don't know, with the prosecution?'

Steve considered that. 'It's possible, I suppose. How long ago was Duncan's trial?'

'About six years. A little more.'

The Australian shrugged. 'We'll have to ask Frankie. But she certainly worked in that area. She might well have handled some of the records when your case came to court. I suppose it's not beyond the bounds of possibility that she was even there in court the day you gave evidence.'

Sue snorted. 'Now you're just taking the piss!'

'Well, you know, stranger things have happened. Who'd remember a stenographer in a case like that? And she must have been doing something before she moved to Cambridge. She's only a year younger than you. *Was* only,' he corrected himself, sadly.

'So how do *you* think she knew so much about all of us? She did say she'd done a lot of research.'

'Well, I think it's more likely she brought in an agency of some kind, to do the donkey work for her. They could have produced a list of names, people of dubious character, who she might have wanted to bring out here alongside Chris.' Steve frowned. 'You know, I'm pretty sure she wouldn't have got everyone she wanted, however she did it. Some people would have been unavailable. Others might have refused to come. So a handful of people would have been drafted in to make up the numbers, like Andrew and me.'

'But it was a proper production company,' Sue pointed out. 'They advertised. They must have got hundreds of replies.'

'And probably threw most of them in the bin. Or picked a couple, if they could find some kind of tenuous connection, like working for the same company. But the only person she had to be sure would come out was Chris and he was in Canada.'

Sue nodded thoughtfully. 'She must have contacted him first, through an intermediary.'

'An old student friend, perhaps.'

'Or maybe Clive Monroe.'

'Oh, I don't think…'

'He *must* have known,' Sue insisted. 'He was there at the interviews. Well, the second round, anyway. I had to drag myself down to Cambridge for that.'

'He certainly knew Bella was involved with the production company,' the Australian conceded. 'She must have given him the job in the first place. But I doubt Clive would have had any idea of the real reason for us coming out here. She'd have kept him in the dark about that.'

Sue lay back on her blanket and stretched herself out. 'So Stephanie was right. Clive's an arse hole, not a bastard.'

'She fooled him just like she fooled the rest of us. Clive must have thought Bella was coming out here to supervise the documentary on the quiet.'

'Documentary!' Sue laughed. 'Actually, this would make a bloody good documentary. "Murder in Paradise". Shame we stopped filming, really.' She wriggled her toes and growled suddenly. 'Why couldn't the stupid bitch just have shot him at the start and have done with it? Or shot herself if she was so bloody miserable. Why did she have to rope the rest of us in?'

Steve shrugged. 'Killing him obviously wasn't enough. She had to make him suffer. I think that was the whole point, to create a climate of fear and paranoia. All these deaths. Bella just wanted to scare him out of his wits. And, you know, what better way than making him think there's a serial killer on the loose? Especially on an island like this, where there's no escape, no police to protect you.'

'No daddy to run to,' Sue agreed. 'Poor little rich boy. Yeah, she knew what she was doing all right. Clever bitch.' Sue scratched her nose and sighed quietly. 'Always so calm and rational. Just goes to show, doesn't it?'

Steve nodded. 'Sometimes it's the calmest, most rational people you can imagine.'

Francesca had not moved from the small patch of grass at the western edge of Cocoa Beach. She stared numbly out to sea. Andrew was padding across the sand towards her, but she did not look round. 'Frankie!' he called, sliding to a halt. 'I thought...'

'They're dead,' she whispered, still in a state of shock. She had come away from the bodies and sat down on the grass verge. 'She killed herself.'

Andrew gaped. 'What about...?'

'She shot him in the head. Then turned the gun on herself. She must have been in so much pain.' Francesca closed her eyes. 'I should have known. I *did* know, but I didn't... I thought coming here would be the best thing for her. It's funny. I thought *I* was the one who'd suggested it. But she must have arranged it all somehow. She always was so much cleverer than me.'

Andrew crouched down and touched Frankie lightly on the shoulder. She looked up at him then.

'We should get back to the others,' she said.

It was painful for all of them but some sort of inquest was unavoidable. Andrew and Frankie had returned to the camp site mid-afternoon and the four survivors had sat together for some time, trying to make sense of events.

'I don't think she ever intended to leave the island,' Steve declared, early on. Francesca was kneeling beside him, reapplying the make-shift bandage Andrew had wound around the Australian's leg. The bullet was still lodged in his right thigh, but it was embedded too deeply to risk extracting it without the proper equipment. 'Otherwise, she would never have been so careless with the evidence.'

Sue was once again sitting up in bed. The bandage around her head had come away slightly, but the woman seemed alert and in control. Most of the pain was still being masked by the medicine Stephanie had administered that morning. 'The big question we still haven't answered is why she poisoned herself like that. I mean, was that a mistake or what?'

'It wasn't a mistake,' Frankie said. 'She must have wanted to kill herself, even then.' The girl had finished retying Steve's bandage. She took one last look at the leg, then stood up and went over to sit next to Andrew. The A-frames were all close together now, in a small circle. 'Bella deliberately poisoned her own water, but then she must have had a change of heart and knocked the bottle over. You remember, Andy?'

The Mancunian nodded. Isabel had dropped her food bowl and it had upended the flask. The water had gone everywhere. At the time, they had thought it was an accident.

'But Chris was still alive then,' Sue pointed out. 'And Jeremy too. Why did she want to kill herself when she hadn't finished the job?'

Steve had the answer to that. 'Because of Jane Ruddock. Killing her was a mistake, we know that already. Isabel had been intending to poison Jeremy, but the bottles got mixed up.'

Sue scoffed. 'So, what, you think she felt *guilty?*'

'Why not? You know, I think she considered herself to be quite a moral person.'

The Englishwoman laughed. 'Moral! Yes, I suppose she must have done, the stupid cow. She did say to me she only killed people who deserved to die.'

'Her parents were devout Catholics,' Francesca interjected. 'She hated the religion, but she never escaped from that mindset.'

'But Jane had never done any harm to anyone,' Steve said. 'Killing her undermined the whole basis of her being here. It made Bella into just another mindless killer and the thought of that must have driven her mad.'

'She *was* just another mindless killer,' Sue stated, flatly. 'I can't blame her for killing Duncan. Lord knows, I'd have done it myself, if I'd had the guts. But Stephanie…'

'She obviously thought that was justified. And Jeremy too. She brought them here specifically to be murdered.'

'That's another thing she said,' Sue recalled abruptly, 'when she found me in the forest. She said everyone on the island was either a victim or a predator.'

'That's it,' Steve agreed, grasping at the idea. 'All of us here are victims. Andy and I lost our jobs because of boardroom politics. You were raped. Frankie lost out on her rightful inheritance. But everyone else was a predator. Duncan, Jeremy. Even Isabel in the end, which is probably why she took her own life.'

'But Jane wasn't a predator,' Frankie observed. 'Her husband left her for a younger woman. She was a victim.'

'And her death must have thrown Isabel off balance,' Steve concluded. 'It undermined her entire modus operandi.'

Francesca sighed. 'The guilt must have been unbearable,'

'And you reckon that's why she tried to poison herself?' Andrew asked.

Steve nodded. 'She could rationalise the other deaths, but not Jane's. So she planted the poison in Chris' rucksack as a parting shot, just for the hell of it, then drank the water and... faded away.'

'She did seem lost,' Frankie recalled. 'Distant from me. At the time, I thought it was just the illness. If I'd known...'

'You couldn't have done anything,' Steve reassured her.

'I could have tried!'

'So why did she change her mind?' Sue asked. 'Why knock over the water bottle? If she was Little Miss Penitent all of a sudden, why not carry it through to the end?'

'Because of Chris,' Francesca said, with sudden understanding. 'He came back from foraging with Jem, that afternoon. He was rummaging around in his rucksack.'

'Perhaps she was worried he might find the poison,' Andrew suggested.

Sue shook her head. 'If she hated him that much, just the sight of him would have been enough.'

'But there was more to it than that,' Frankie explained. 'Chris had brought her some fruit to eat, but when he came over with it, Bella deliberately turned away from him. She wouldn't eat it. He was quite upset. He really liked her. So when he went away, I…I told Isabel he fancied her.'

'Bloody hell!' Sue exclaimed. 'No wonder she changed her mind! She must have thought, "No, let's finish the bastard off."'

Francesca shivered. 'That's what she said before she killed him. "If I let him go then it will all have been for nothing."'.

'So if that idiot hadn't come back just at that moment, she'd probably have topped herself and we'd all have lived happily ever after!' Sue flopped back down onto her bed. 'Jesus!'

'It's all my fault,' Frankie realised. 'If I hadn't said anything to her…'

'Don't think like that,' Steve said. 'You're not responsible for anything Isabel did.'

'She'd probably have changed her mind anyway,' Sue agreed.

'She knew what she was doing and she took full responsibility for it.'

Francesca nodded sadly; but it did not make her feel any less guilty.

A brief silence descended. It had been a long day and none of the islanders had eaten much, though Andrew had grabbed a few bits of fruit on the way back from Cocoa Beach.

'So what happens now?' he asked.

'We get off this island,' Sue responded firmly.

Frankie shook her head. 'We have to bury the dead.'

'You know, that may not be possible,' Steve said. 'I'm in no fit state to dig a grave, let alone carry a body, and neither is young Sue here.'

'I'm all right,' the other woman muttered.

'They deserve a decent burial,' Francesca insisted. They all did, she thought. Isabel, Chris and Stephanie.

So many dead, and all because of a single mistake.

It might never have happened. Chris might have got into his car that day a minute later. Bella's sister might have decided to cross the road a little further along. There might have been a traffic jam which would have delayed them both. And if it had, then Frankie would never have come to this island and Isabel and the others would still be alive.

But it was pointless thinking that way.

She lifted a hand to her neck and caressed the silver chain Isabel had given her. The necklace had originally belonged to Susanna, Bella's sister. She had bequeathed it to Isabel and now Bella had passed it on to Francesca

'So come on Steve,' Sue was saying. 'You're the fountain of all knowledge. How do we summon a rescue party?'

The Australian was about to answer, but Frankie cut across him. 'I have a way,' she said.

Steve glanced at her in surprise. '*You* have?'

'I think so.' She showed him the necklace. Steve raised an eyebrow, not quite understanding. She grinned back at him.

Isabel Grant had planned for everything.

The following day, Andrew and Francesca swam out to the Rocks from Cocoa Beach. Frankie had never been there before and it was a few years since she had last swum such a distance. Andrew had come out to the island several times but even he hadn't visited the far side. The couple kept together as they swam, aiming wide to avoid the cross currents which smashed against the boulders. There was a small pebble beach on the far side, which Jeremy had discovered the day before he had died. Frankie wriggled awkwardly onto the jagged stones, with Andrew not far behind. She stood up and took a moment to regain her composure.

'What I don't understand is why she brought *you* here,' Andrew said, a few minutes later. He wiped a drop of water from his nose. Francesca was adjusting the straps of her swimming costume. 'I mean, she knew it were going to be awful. You were her best mate. Why would she put you through that?'

Frankie sighed, twisting some of the water out of her hair. 'There are lots of reasons, Andy. Her sister was on that machine for nearly a year. We hadn't known each other long, but I was the one who persuaded her to let go, to give the authorisation to switch it off. I suppose she never really forgave me for that.'

Andrew stretched his arms above his head and gazed out across the narrow beach. 'What do you think we're looking for?'

Francesca was not certain. 'A box, I suppose. I don't know how well hidden it'll be.'

They made their way up towards the centre of the island.

The container was slotted beneath an overhang only a few metres westward from the beach. It was covered in leaves and bramble but it was not difficult to find. Andrew spotted it first.

Frankie squatted down in front of the box. It was large, plastic and bulky. She pulled it forward.

'It won't be easy getting that back to the mainland,' Andrew observed.

There was a small padlock on the front, connecting the top of the container to the base. Francesca removed the silver chain from around her neck. On the end of it was a miniature key.

'I never noticed that before.'

'She usually wore it under her clothes.' Frankie slotted the key into the padlock and twisted it around. She removed the lock and lifted the lid.

The box was only half full; several items had already been removed. On one side, there was a muddy trowel and a box of ammunition. At the back, a plastic container was half filled with kerosene. The bulk of the space, however, was taken up by a small radio transmitter. It was similar in shape to the one at the Grotto. Francesca leaned forward and lifted it out of the box. A microphone was attached via a short lead and a frequency had been marked on the display.

'Do you think she used it while we were here?' Andrew asked.

Frankie was not sure. Certainly, Isabel could not have swum out to the island more than a couple of times. Her absence would have been noticed. The only time she had been left alone, as far as Francesca could recall, was during the girl's convalescence. Everyone else had been busy digging latrines or constructing shelters on the beach. Bella might have swum out here then, carrying Jane Ruddock's water bottle with her to fill up with kerosene. It might have been around that time that she picked up the revolver as well, hiding it somewhere close to the camp site so that it could be retrieved at a later date.

Andrew rummaged through the bottom of the box and found a thin Manila envelope, the front of which was adorned with some elaborate pre-printed calligraphy. 'Here, look at this,' he said, pulling it out and showing it to Frankie. 'She had quite a bit of money, didn't she?'

Francesca nodded. 'About eight hundred thousand, from her mother. It would have been split with Susanna if her sister hadn't died.'

'How much do you reckon is left?'

'I've no idea. Andrew, I don't think...'

He had already opened the envelope. '"*I, Isabel Margaret Grant*",' he read, '"*being of sound mind, hereby leave all my worldly possessions to Francesca Mary Stevens.*"' Andrew looked up. 'A couple of signatures and that's it.' He grinned. 'Hey, I didn't know your middle name was Mary.'

Frankie smiled shakily, a small tear running down her cheek.

'What's the matter?'

She took the letter and scanned it sadly. 'I think – I think this is her way of saying...she's forgiven me.'

On the morning of the twenty-third day, the islanders gathered their possessions and sat out on Candy Beach for the last time.

They had radioed St. Moreau and contacted the small office that Isabel had established on the island. A local woman had been paid a fee to keep a listening watch and she had arranged everything for them.

Steve had enquired after Clive Monroe but the woman did not know much. He had flown back to England, apparently. The company had recalled him to Cambridge, she said, no doubt on some serious sounding pretext. Isabel would have arranged all that in advance.

There was no time to bury the dead. The bodies would have to remain where they were for the present, though doubtless they would be flown home when circumstances allowed.

Steve had sat for some time with Stephanie McMahon, over at the Grotto. It was the first time the others had seen him display any real emotion. He had insisted she be dressed and covered over before they left.

No-one knew who had jurisdiction over the island, legally speaking, but it scarcely seemed to matter. Someone would take charge and there would be an investigation. The islanders would arrive back at St. Moreau together, but it would probably be a few weeks before any of them were allowed home.

Andrew held Francesca's hand. The girl would need a lot of kindness and support in the months to come. Of all those who had survived, she had probably suffered the most. But Andrew was in love with her, and she with him, and that would see them through.

They faced the horizon together.

Murder At Flaxton Isle
by
Greg Wilson

A remote Scottish island plays host to a deadly reunion..

It should be a lot of fun, meeting up for a long weekend in a rented lighthouse on a chunk of rock miles from anywhere. There will be drinks and games and all sorts of other amusements. It is ten years since the last get-together and twenty years since Nadia and her friends graduated from university. But not everything goes according to plan. One of the group has a more sinister agenda and, as events begin to spiral out of control, it becomes clear that not everyone will get off the island alive...

The Gunpowder Treason
by
Michael Dax

"A dangerous disease requires a desperate remedy..."

Robert Catesby is a man in despair. His father is dead and his wife is burning in the fires of Hell – his punishment from God for marrying a Protestant. A new king presents a new hope but the persecution of Catholics in England continues unabated and Catesby can tolerate it no longer. King James bears responsibility but the whole government must be eradicated if anything is to really change. And Catesby has a plan...

The Gunpowder Treason is a fast-paced historical thriller. Every character is based on a real person and almost every scene is derived from eye-witness accounts. This is the story of the Gunpowder Plot, as told by the people who were there...

The Scandal At Bletchley
by
Jack Treby

"I've been a scoundrel, a thief, a blackmailer and a whore, but never a murderer. Until now..."

The year is 1929. As the world teeters on the brink of a global recession, Bletchley Park plays host to a rather special event. MI5 is celebrating its twentieth anniversary and a select band of former and current employees are gathering for a weekend of music, dance and heavy drinking. Among them is Sir Hilary Manningham-Butler, a middle aged woman whose entire adult life has been spent masquerading as a man. She doesn't know why she has been invited – it is many years since she left the secret service – but it is clear she is not the only one with things to hide. And when one of the other guests threatens to expose her secret, the consequences could prove disastrous for everyone.

For more information, visit the website:
http://www.jacktreby.com

Printed in Great Britain
by Amazon

82199497R00132